AGENT'S MOUNTAIN RESCUE

Jennifer D. Bokal

HARLEQUIN
ROMANTIC SUSPENSE

HARLEQUIN®
ROMANTIC SUSPENSE™

Recycling programs
for this product may
not exist in your area.

ISBN-13: 978-1-335-62679-0

Agent's Mountain Rescue

Copyright © 2020 by Jennifer D. Bokal

This edition published by arrangement with Harlequin Books S.A.

For questions and comments about the quality of this book,
please contact us at CustomerService@Harlequin.com.

Harlequin Enterprises ULC
22 Adelaide St. West, 40th Floor
Toronto, Ontario M5H 4E3, Canada
www.Harlequin.com

Printed in U.S.A.

"We," said Holly. She sat up, grimacing with the effort. "We have to save her."

Up until that moment, Liam had felt alone—as if he were treading water in the middle of the ocean. Yet, to hear that Holly wanted—no, needed—to help his daughter was akin to being given a life raft. "I can't ask you to put yourself at risk, not after everything you've suffered."

"This is as personal for me as it is for you," Holly said. "Sophie may very well be your daughter, but I love her, too. Don't put me on the sidelines."

Liam didn't want to waste any more time while his daughter was in the hands of a killer. He needed to know what Holly knew, and arguing wasn't going to help him gather any information. After getting to his feet, he held out a hand to Holly. "Come with me. I can patch you up while you talk."

She wound her fingers through his, and he pulled her to standing. The color drained from her cheeks, leaving her creamy skin gray. She listed to the side. Liam wrapped an arm around her waist to hold her steady.

"Just breathe," said Liam.

* * *

Be sure to pick up other thrilling stories in the Wyoming Nights miniseries!

* * *

If you're on Twitter, tell us what you think of Harlequin Romantic Suspense! #harlequinromsuspense

Dear Reader,

Every once in a while, I write a hero who I absolutely fall in love with. Well, in *Agent's Mountain Rescue*, Liam Alexander is one of those heroes! He's tough, cool, brave, confident, handsome—all while learning how to be a good single parent.

I mean, what's not to love?

I had to give him an equally competent heroine—someone smart, caring and above all fearless. Enter Holly Jacobs, a woman strong enough to care for, and smart enough to understand, a man like Liam.

There was more for me to love about this book—and that came in the form of serial killer Darcy Owens. For me, as a writer, Darcy is a complicated character. This four-book series gave me the opportunity to explore the darker side of human nature and whether or not redemption is truly possible.

All of this is set in a place I've grown to love—the fictitious town of Pleasant Pines, Wyoming. I invite you, dear reader, to come to a place where nothing is as it seems. But where love conquers all.

Regards,

Jennifer D. Bokal

Jennifer D. Bokal penned her first book at age eight. An early lover of the written word, she decided to follow her passion and become a full-time writer. From then on, she didn't look back. She earned a master of arts in creative writing from Wilkes University and became a member of Romance Writers of America and International Thriller Writers.

She has authored several short stories, novellas and poems. Winner of the Sexy Scribbler in 2015, Jennifer is also the author of the ancient-world historical series the Champions of Rome and the Harlequin Romantic Suspense series Rocky Mountain Justice.

Happily married to her own alpha male for more than twenty years, she enjoys writing stories that explore the wonders of love. Jen and her manly husband live in upstate New York with their three beautiful daughters, two very spoiled dogs and a kitten that aspires to one day become a Chihuahua.

Books by Jennifer D. Bokal

Harlequin Romantic Suspense

Wyoming Nights
Agent's Mountain Rescue

Under the Agent's Protection

Rocky Mountain Justice
Her Rocky Mountain Hero
Her Rocky Mountain Defender
Rocky Mountain Valor

Visit the Author Profile page at Harlequin.com for more titles.

To John: For me, there's only you.

Prologue

The dark space was silent. Darcy Owens sat on the floor of the bunker, her back pressed to the earthen wall. Despite a fire smoldering in the Franklin stove, the room was damp, and gooseflesh covered her arms. Using the toe of her shoe, she pulled the heavy cast-iron door open. A wave of heat washed over her and she began to sweat.

On a cluttered shelf, a mahogany clock ticked off the seconds. The scrollwork of the timepiece's enamel-and-brass faceplate was at odds with the bleak surroundings. A narrow bed. A rickety table. Mismatched plates and a single pot on the stove for cooking. A barrel of rainwater for cleaning and drinking. An ax, the blade dulled from use, leaned against the corner.

Embers glowed white-hot and Darcy shifted to ease her discomfort. Her shoulder ached, a reminder that she'd been shot escaping custody. Time didn't seem real underground. It was always damp and cold; as if she'd been trapped in the darkest night of winter. How long had she been here? Less than a month, if she had to guess. Because of Rocky Mountain Justice, Darcy's identity had been discovered. Now, the entire world knew who she was. What she was.

With a smile, she wondered what was being said about her in the media. No doubt, they were amazed that she—a lone woman—had wreaked so much havoc.

Unless they all assumed that she was dead. That meant the search had ended. A tremor ran up her spine and she shivered.

"You awake?" a gruff voice asked from the darkness.

Darcy turned her gaze to the single bed and the hulking form lying upon the mattress. It was Billy...but then again, who else would it be? She said nothing, just stared into the gloom.

The day of her escape, Billy had found Darcy in the middle of the woods. She was near death from the gunshot wound and had been running for her life. In that moment, he had saved her. More than that, he'd kept her whereabouts a secret from the police. He said he didn't take to government involvement in the lives of free men. Moreover, he'd been living off the grid for years and had no intention of helping the authorities. At the time,

Darcy viewed him as a blessing. Now, she knew that being found by Billy was a punishment for all her sins.

Wasn't that what she had been taught? That eventually everyone had to make amends for their mistakes? But Darcy never imagined that living underground with a dangerous brute would be her price.

He hadn't touched her, not yet at least. But she'd noticed the side-eyed glances. When he looked at her, Darcy's skin crawled.

"Get me some water," Billy said. His large frame filled the entire bed.

She ignored the order, turning her eyes back to the fire.

"I told you to get me some water," he said, his tone threatening.

She slowly stood. Her vision dimmed. Dipping a cup into the barrel of rainwater, Darcy filled it to the rim.

She walked over to the bed. "Here," she said, handing the cup to Billy.

He swallowed down the water in one gulp, his eyes never leaving hers. "You better listen to me when I tell you to do something," he said, before wiping a threadbare sleeve across his mouth. "You've got nowhere to go and nobody to help you—'cept me, that is."

He slipped a hand up her thigh and bile rose in the back of Darcy's throat. Billy continued, "And since I've been so nice to help you, I reckon you can help me with something now, too."

"Do it." The words were just a whisper, so quiet that Darcy wasn't even sure what she had heard.

"Do what?" she asked. Her voice broke, sounding like the creaky hinge of an unused door.

"You're feeling better, ain't you? I'm the one who saved you, Darcy. Without me, you'd be dead," Billy said.

"Do it," the voice said again. Then it came to her. The Darkness had returned. She went cold and took a step back. Billy reached for her arm and pulled her to him. Pitching forward, Darcy landed on his large chest.

Her heart raced as the stench of his fetid breath filled her nostrils. Darcy became smaller and smaller, hiding in the corner of her mind. The Darkness urged her to move hard, move fast. Somehow, she obeyed.

There was a length of rope hanging over the headboard of the bed. Wrapping the ends of the rope in her fists, Darcy looped the rope around Billy's throat and pulled tight. His eyes went wide. He thrashed, rising to his feet. He pulled Darcy with him as he rose. Bracing her feet on the floor, she pulled the rope taut. Swinging his arms out wildly, Billy's fist caught Darcy in the temple. She stumbled back.

Billy tugged on the restraint, pulling the rope from her hands. She sprawled on the ground, her palms scraped and raw.

"I wish you wouldn't have done that. Not after all the goodness I showed you," Billy said. He stood, looming over Darcy.

She scooted back, scampering to the farthest point in the room—near the stove.

Billy took one step, and then another. Then he was on her. He pressed her down. His rough beard scratched the tender flesh of her face, her neck, her chest. He bit her hard enough that Darcy knew she'd have a bruise.

Do it.

Darcy didn't think, just acted. Reaching into the fire, she scooped up a handful of hot ash. Ignoring the pain in her palm, she pressed her hand onto his face. The acrid stench of burnt hair filled the underground bunker. Billy screamed and rolled on the ground. Darcy looked around wildly for anything that could work as a weapon…and her gaze fell on the ax in the corner.

"Now."

This time, she didn't hesitate. After bringing up the handle, she let the blade fall.

The clock on the shelf continued to quietly *tick, tick, tick.*

Then it was only Darcy and the Darkness.

Chapter 1

Liam Alexander pressed his foot down on the accelerator. The large engine roared and his car shot forward. Despite the frost-covered ground, he wiped a bead of sweat from his brow. His pulse raced as he glanced at the dashboard clock. His new boss expected him for an initial briefing in exactly ten minutes.

There was no way in hell that he was going to make it on time.

Deadlines. Office hours. Meetings.

Liam hated them all. They made him feel like he was locked in a cage. It was one of the reasons he had spent his entire life working as a tracker and guide. In the woods, there was no time clock to punch. He had enjoyed a life that took him to all parts of the globe. Then his priorities had changed.

Priorities. With the single thought, his gaze was drawn to the rearview mirror and the child buckled into the car seat. "How's it going, baby girl?" he asked his daughter, Sophie. "Are you ready for your first day of school?"

She held a sippy cup by a hooked handle and smiled. Apple juice slowly leaked onto her jacket. What would the new teachers think of Liam if Sophie arrived for her first day of school damp and sticky? The last thing he wanted people to think was that he was the bungling single dad—even if that was Liam's own worst fear. Wincing, he looked back at the road.

With Erin, Sophie's mother, on a twelve-month deployment in the Persian Gulf, Liam's daughter had to switch homes and parents. Liam's last gig—working as part of a search and rescue team for the Department of the Interior—took him to all parts of Western California. Death Valley. The rocky coastline. The endless miles of desert across the southern border. The Sierra Nevada mountain range. His job, to find hikers and climbers who'd gone missing, didn't come with regular hours and made it impossible to spend more than a few hours a week with his daughter.

Now, as a full-time dad, he needed a job that kept him in one place, along with the possibility of being home most night's for dinner. What he got was a job offer from Rocky Mountain Justice. While hardly perfect, it was good enough for him—for now.

All of the changes had been hard on Sophie. New

parent. New town. And now a new school. He glanced in the rearview mirror and watched Sophie stare out the window.

Not that he blamed her. Pleasant Pines, Wyoming—so near to where his family had lived for generations—was the last place he expected to end up.

His throat tightened and he coughed. Looking back at the road, he spoke, continuing on the topic of the school. "The name of your school is Saplings."

"S-sapling?" she said, trying out the new word.

"It's a baby tree," he said. "Pretty clever if you think about it. Our new town is called Pleasant Pines. A pine is a tree. The school is Saplings. If I'm a daddy pine tree, then you are a…"

"Sapling," Sophie said.

"A very smart sapling, too," Liam said. The GPS alerted him of a new set of directions, and he eased off the gas as he rounded a corner.

"I don't want a new school," Sophie said, her small voice holding a steely edge. "I want my *old* school. And house. And Mommy."

Ouch.

"You'll have the best time," Liam said, trying to cajole his daughter. "There will be a new teacher and new friends."

"Friends?" she asked. "Promise?"

"I promise." A white-and-black-checked flag appeared on the GPS. Their destination. "In fact, here we are."

After pulling into an empty space, Liam turned off the ignition. He reached for Sophie's small backpack that sat in the passenger seat and triple-checked its contents. Cup. Snack. Change of clothes. Blanket. Four stuffed animals—because she said they were all her favorite. Sophie was three years old—did she still use a pacifier? With a smile, he remembered those first months after her birth, when the pacifier was as much a lifesaver for Liam and Erin as it had been for the baby.

Then it happened. A shadow of memory, as real as a glimpse of a reflection in his rearview mirror. For a single second, Liam seemed to see Charlie, standing right in front of the car.

Liam shook his head to clear it and looked again. His cousin wasn't there. No wonder the memories were stronger here. After all, he was back in Wyoming.

"Daddy," Sophie said, protesting from her car seat.

"I'm here, baby girl." He untangled Sophie from her five-point harness, then lifted the child from the car. She reached for the single dog tag he always wore and ran the tag up and down the leather cord.

The dog tag used to belong to his cousin, Charlie. Liam always wore it—a reminder never to lose his focus, or his drive—just like his cousin. Charlie's doctrine had stayed with Liam and had made him one hell of a tracker. Today, what he needed was something a little more practical—like advice on how to be a good dad.

After closing the car door, he carried her toward the building. The early morning air was crisp, yet there was an undercurrent of warmth in the breeze, the promise that spring really had arrived. As he walked, his daughter settled into his arms, and Liam found it impossible not to recall the moments after her birth, when a nurse had held out the squalling, pink-faced newborn.

"You want to hold her, Dad?" she asked, sliding Sophie into Liam's arms.

In that moment, he'd felt two distinct emotions. A fierce and bone-deep need to protect his child. And the sickening notion that he was wholly unprepared to be a father.

Erin, slowly recovering from labor and delivery, had held out her arms. "Can I see her?"

Liam had reluctantly let his daughter go. Now he had to do the same thing all over again.

"Are you ready?" he asked.

She nodded slowly. "I guess."

"I know new things can be scary sometimes, but you *are* a brave girl."

Placing her small hands on either side of Liam's face, Sophie stared directly into her father's eyes. "I love you, Daddy."

Liam's chest ached and his throat tightened. He understood Sophie's fear of stepping into the unknown more than he could ever express to her. "I love you, honey. We can wait for a minute. Tell me when you want to go inside."

With a single nod, Sophie said, "Ready now, Daddy."

Shifting the child to his hip, Liam approached the school. Set near Pleasant Pines's city limits, the preschool looked like a perfect child's playhouse. The building was trimmed in a vibrant purple. A bright yellow sun had been painted on the glass front doors, along with the words *Welcome to Saplings*.

Hopefully, everything would go well, Sophie would

like the new class and teacher, and she'd let Liam ease out slowly. And, just maybe, he could still make it to the RMJ offices without being late. Or too late, at least.

Pushing open the door, Liam stepped into the school. He was greeted by an array of smells. Sweet juice. Lemon disinfectant. And the spicy scent of baking cinnamon.

Directly in front of him, a greeter sat behind a desk.

"Can I help you?" the dark-haired woman asked. She wore khaki pants and a long-sleeved royal blue T-shirt. A Saplings logo had been embroidered on the front of the shirt, as well as her name. Tonya.

Using his free hand, Liam unzipped the backpack and fished through the contents. "I registered my daughter for school online. Sophie Alexander." Finding the printout of the confirmation, Liam handed over the paper.

Taking the offered sheet, Tonya scanned the form. With a smile, she continued, "It looks like everything is in order. If you'd take a seat, I'll let the director, Dr. Holly, know that you're here."

"Holly Jacobs, PhD," he said, remembering what he'd seen on the school's site about the director and owner. "The woman who wrote that book."

Tonya nodded. "You can't believe how excited everyone was about Holly's book. The local paper did a cover story on 'Dr. Holly' when she came back, too." She put finger quotes around the director's name. "You know, local girl turned famous author who came home and all that. It was a big deal when Saplings opened." Tonya beamed. "Have you read the book?"

"No chance yet," he said, glancing at his watch. "I've been busy with the move and all."

In his mind's eye, he had about a million questions he could ask her. How to be a better father, for one. How to make sure he never dropped the ball for his daughter. And maybe he would ask—one day, at least. But not now, since he was running tight on time.

"If you could have a seat," said Tonya, indicating a row of folding chairs next to the wall.

Liam checked his watch. Damn. He'd never make it to work on time. After removing the phone from his pocket, he typed out a quick text to his new boss, Marcus Jones.

Morning's crazy. Be there soon.

He didn't bother to add, I hope.

In all honesty, Liam didn't mind a few more minutes with Sophie. Before Erin's deployment, spending time with his daughter meant he saw her twice a week for dinner—if he was in town. Sophie also stayed overnight at his place twice a month—again, if he was available.

It had given them time together, but Liam's job had kept him from being a full-time dad. Erin was a great mom, but he'd always regretted not being around more.

All of that was in the past.

Now it was the two of them against the world. Enrolling Sophie at Saplings was his first official decision as a parent.

Liam had to trust that he'd made the right one.

He wanted her in the best school possible and Saplings had sterling recommendations. The fact that they had room for Sophie in the program had been a relief.

"I'll let the director know that you're here. It'll just be a minute," Tonya said.

Liam looked at his daughter. For Sophie's sake, he'd get with the program. With a long exhale, he dropped into a wobbly metal chair. Out of all the challenges that he had faced in his life, Liam knew that single parenthood promised to be the most difficult.

"Good morning, my happy saplings. Today is blue day." Dr. Holly Jacobs smiled at the dozen children in the classroom. Like all of the other teachers and staff in the building, Holly wore a blue Saplings shirt and khaki pants. For her, the uniform created a cohesiveness among the team.

Not only was she the director of the school, but Holly also taught the class of three-year-olds. She loved that teaching allowed her to spend time with the kids. More than that, it saved her from having to come up with the money for another salary. And really, it's not that she minded doing triple duty as business owner, administrator and teacher. Saplings was Holly's passion project, and she never would have guessed how much passion really cost.

Or the number of debts she'd incur while trying to live her dream.

"I need everyone to find a carpet square," she continued to her class. "Then meet me at the weather board."

There was a flurry of activity as the children each found a square of bound carpeting and a place on the floor. The door opened, and Holly's assistant, Tonya, stepped into the room. Her dark eyebrows were drawn together, and her lips were pressed into a thin line.

One look at her assistant and Holly's morning coffee roiled in her stomach. What had gone wrong this time? she wondered. Another leak in the roof? A hotwater heater that needed to be replaced? *Please, don't let it be an outbreak of chicken pox.*

"Give me one minute, children," Holly said as she stepped toward Tonya. "What is it?" she asked, her voice a whisper.

"The new family is here." Tonya held out the enrollment form. "It's a father with his daughter. She's a three-year-old, so she'd be in your class."

Holly was always happy to have a new student. She scanned the paper and found the father's name. "Can you ask them to wait in my office? I'll be with them in just a minute."

"Well…" said Tonya. "He keeps checking his watch. You might not want to keep him waiting too long."

Holly looked at the class and back to the form. She couldn't afford to lose a student, not with all the repairs that the building still needed.

"Don't worry," said Tonya. "I can cover the class. He and his daughter are in the reception area. You go and meet the dad."

Was it Holly's imagination, or had Tonya put a special emphasis on the word *dad*.

"What is it that you aren't telling me?" Holly asked.

"Oh, you'll see soon enough."

Striding down the short hallway, Holly read the sheet. Name: Sophie Alexander. Age: three. Father: Liam Alexander. Legal guardian: Liam Alexander.

Emergency contact: again, he listed his cell number, not another person who could be contacted, like most other parents. Occupation: Private Security. The home address he'd listed was in a nice neighborhood on the south side of town. Time at residence: one week.

Rounding the corner to the front entrance, Holly looked up and stopped short.

Early morning sunshine streamed in through the glass doors. The beams of light captured a man in shadow. Even without the benefit of seeing his face, Holly could tell that he was large and muscular. He moved, stepping out of the light.

Brown hair skimmed the collar of his shirt. His shoulders were broad, and his arms were powerful. He wore cargo pants in olive drab and a black T-shirt that clung to his well-muscled arms. Despite his contemporary clothes, it wasn't hard for Holly to imagine him as a gunslinger from a long-forgotten age.

A little girl stood at his side and held on to her father's leg. She wore a pink dress with gray stripes and a cartoon of a cat wearing a tiara.

"You must be Liam Alexander," Holly said, trying to ignore her rapid pulse and the fluttering butterflies that had suddenly materialized in her stomach.

"Nice to meet you." Liam gave her a pleasant smile. Good Lord, did the man really have a dimple? Holly swallowed.

Liam's gaze flicked to the watch on his wrist before returning to her face.

Tonya had been right, Liam was running late. Yet, to what? Work? His intake form had several blank spaces, including the one where he listed his employer and their phone number.

She couldn't help but wonder why. Was there a secret he was keeping?

Kneeling before the little girl, Holly said, "I'm Dr. Holly. I'm going to be your new teacher. Your name is Sophie, right?"

The girl nodded. She had brown hair and dark eyes like her father, and seemed sweet and quiet.

"So, what does this interview process involve?" Liam asked.

"I usually give a tour of the facility and go over a typical school day. In the interest of time, let me show you Sophie's class," she said, leading the way down the hall. "I can point out the need-to-know areas on the way. Tonya, our greeter, is in charge of after-hours care." Holly recalled the empty spaces on the form. Did he know anyone at all in Pleasant Pines? "Tonya's also helped some families with overnight care—if that's ever a need. Oh, and I need to ask about the emergency contact."

"What about it?"

"You don't have anyone listed," said Holly. "We need someone to call in case of an emergency and we can't get a hold of you. For the sake of the form, can I list a relative? Or maybe a neighbor?"

"We just moved here from San Diego. I don't know anyone in town, and family is too far away to be quick help."

"I see," said Holly. Yet, she thought that there was likely more to Liam Alexander's story than he had shared.

Opening the door to the classroom, Holly stepped inside. "What do you think, Sophie? Will you like being a part of this class?"

A mural of a forest filled with smiling pine trees took up one wall. A book nook was tucked into one corner, and a puzzle table sat in the corner opposite. Between the two were several round tables, where children gathered during snack time and when she taught a lesson.

Another student, Ava, approached Sophie. "Hi. What's your name?"

"I'm Sophie. What's your name?"

"Ava." Holding out her hand, Ava asked, "You want to be friends?"

Sophie looked from Ava to her father and back to the other child. Letting go of her father's hand, she said, "Okay."

Holly couldn't help but smile.

Turning to Liam, Holly said, "I'm sure you saw this on the website, but we have a strict pickup time for late care. Six o'clock sharp."

"Six o'clock," he repeated. "Got it." Dropping to his knee, Liam pulled Sophie into a hug. He whispered, "Baby girl, Daddy loves you and I'll see you at the end of the day. Be good for Dr. Holly, okay?"

"Bye-bye, Daddy," she said, returning the hug.

Liam stood and turned to go, but not before taking one last look at the class. Holly's throat tightened, and her eyes burned with his final glance. For a single second, the man's terse exterior slipped away, leaving a different person in his place.

The question was—what kind of man was he, really?

* * *

Liam broke more than one speed limit as he raced to the headquarters of Rocky Mountain Justice. The drive was less than five minutes, yet it gave him time to think. The nervousness he'd felt since dropping his daughter off at school was finally gone. Sophie had made a friend and seemed settled and happy when he left. Then his mind wandered to Sophie's beautiful teacher, Holly Jacobs.

He thought of her leading them down the hall, and the image of her curves made his breath catch. Reddish-golden hair fell around her shoulders. Her lips were full. Her eyes were the color of the Pacific Ocean.

In reality, it didn't matter how attractive he found her. He couldn't think about hitting on Sophie's teacher—that was just asking for trouble.

Shaking his head, Liam skidded to a stop in front of a Victorian-era mansion. He checked the address he'd been given. He was at the right place. The house looked like any other well-kept home on a street of similar residences. It was at odds with what he knew about Rocky Mountain Justice. They described their outfit as private security, but he knew better. They were mercenaries… perhaps with a bit of a conscience. A group of highly professional, well-trained operatives.

As he approached the front stoop, Liam noticed a small camera, just the size of a dime, set into the molding around the door. Before he could touch the knocker, a disembodied voice said two words. "It's unlocked."

The latch gave a soft click and Liam turned the handle. He entered the foyer, which had been transformed into a holding cell, complete with a reinforced steel door. The door slid open.

A tall man with a shaved head, dark brows and dark eyes stood on the threshold. Liam had never met Marcus Jones, but recognized him from the interviews they'd conducted via Skype. Marcus wore a black button-up shirt, open at the neck and jeans. "Welcome," the other man said as he checked his watch. A not so subtle way to let Liam know that he'd been late.

Liam said, "It was a rough morning."

"I actually wanted you here two weeks ago."

"You have me now." Liam wasn't willing to give any excuses. Sure, when he worked for the government, he could be deployed anywhere throughout California in a matter of hours—if not minutes. But that was when Erin was the custodial parent.

Marcus seemed mollified by Liam's words and explained that the old house had been modified for security and to serve as a tactical hive. Liam's new boss approached the closest door and entered a five-digit code. From there, his face was scanned. The lock clicked, and he pushed the door open. It led to a standard conference room, where a man waited at a large wooden table.

The back wall was covered with local maps. Areas had been outlined with a red marker. There were also aerial photos, connected to the map with pushpins and strings.

Several pictures of a woman filled one wall. She sported long blond hair in most of them, but in a few of the photos she was a brunette. Those pictures were surrounded by dozens of other images of men. Were these all the victims of the notorious serial killer?

"Is this her?" said Liam, gesturing to a picture of the woman. "Darcy Owens? The person who you hired me to find."

"It is," said Jones. "How much have you been told about her?"

Liam shrugged. "I've read the case file. Her first victims—" he gestured to the photos on the wall "—were found in Las Vegas, linked because she left a ripped two-dollar bill with each. She seemed to go dormant until she showed up in Pleasant Pines and began killing again. After her identity was discovered, she escaped into the woods, with a gunshot wound in the shoulder. And she hasn't been found yet."

"You've obviously done your homework," said Marcus.

Liam shrugged. "I spent four years in the Marines. The Corps taught me to always show up prepared. I'm here to do a job. I figured I should be up to speed."

Marcus gestured to the conference table. "Have a seat and let me introduce you to Wyatt Thornton."

Liam dropped into an empty chair at the head of the table.

Wyatt said, "I'm new to Rocky Mountain Justice, too. I retired from the behavioral science unit with the FBI and came back to work to find Darcy Owens."

Liam took one look at the guy—pressed button-up shirt and khaki pants, complete with a razor-sharp crease—and smothered a groan.

Lifting his chin, he said, "Hey. Good to meet you."

Wyatt Thornton's eyes narrowed with a quick look

of dislike, which was gone as quickly as it had come. "Same."

Work as a tracker tended to make Liam a cog in a greater machine. When a person went missing, a battalion of personnel was called in for the search. Pilots. Law enforcement. Medical personnel.

When it came down to it, though, Liam worked best alone. Always a step or two ahead of the rest, he followed the signs left behind by the people he was trying to rescue—even if, too often, a different outcome was the end result of his search.

It was more than the solitude that he sought. Really, he hated egos. His own notwithstanding.

People with too much confidence made mistakes. He'd learned that firsthand. And his first impression of Marcus Jones and Wyatt Thornton was that these two men had confidence to spare.

Still, Liam refused to think of joining RMJ as a mistake. He'd uprooted his daughter's life to be here and he was determined to make this job work.

Without another word, Wyatt began the briefing. "Darcy Owens has been an active serial killer for over five years. We have verified a dozen victims but suspect there may be more. Until now, there haven't been many documented female serial killers. From my evaluation, she's one of the most devious people this agency has ever encountered—manipulative enough to convince a man to take his own life."

True, knowing all about a person was a key to finding them. Every good tracker took in as much information about a subject as possible. The details, large and small, could help predict how they would act in any given environment. But there was more to tracking than knowing about the target, and Liam itched to get started.

Because once he got into the woods, it was only him and the killer.

Chapter 2

Liam was lost in his thoughts, the map on the wall having captured his attention. He could clearly imagine the terrain. He'd conducted search and rescue operations in every imaginable climate, yet the woods and the mountains were his favorite. It was where he felt most at ease.

If the query was still in the woods, Liam would find them—even if they didn't want to be found.

Marcus cleared his throat, drawing Liam back into the conference room. "Since you're new to the team here," he said, "I'd like your thoughts."

Taking a deep breath, Liam said, "As far as I can tell, this is simply a mathematical problem."

"How so?" Marcus asked.

"In mountainous terrain, a healthy, well-trained and well-equipped mountaineer can travel seven to eight miles in a day. But we know that the killer was injured and had no survival skills." He stood and moved to the wall, placing a finger on the pushpin that represented the last known location of Darcy Owens. Turning to the two men, Liam asked the one question that had bothered him since being contacted. "Why is Rocky Mountain Justice looking for a serial killer, anyway?"

"The district attorney's office is in charge of the case and she hired RMJ," said Marcus.

"Why wouldn't the DA work with the FBI?" Liam asked. "Or the state police? An at-large serial killer seems like a pretty big priority for law enforcement to ignore."

"They're still following up on any lead that comes in," said Wyatt. "But after all this time, they assume that Darcy's dead or, somehow, she left the area."

"You don't think the same thing?" Liam asked.

Marcus answered the question. "We're conducting an independent investigation. We don't have as many rules, so we can follow up on leads immediately."

"If she's still alive," said Liam. "She must have had help."

"There's nothing in Darcy's case file to indicate that she had an accomplice. So, I'm not sure why you'd assume she had help," said Wyatt.

"All I do know is that with a wound like the one you described, she couldn't survive without medical care, food and shelter."

Wyatt leaned forward. Maybe Liam had been wrong, and the strait-laced former FBI Agent wasn't so bad after all. "What else do you know?"

"I know that the terrain won't allow for the passage

of an automobile, even an all-terrain vehicle. It also means whoever helped her was on foot, or possibly horseback, but not likely." Between finger and thumb, he measured out a distance that represented approximately three miles on the map. After grabbing a stray pen from the table, Liam slowly traced a circle. "Your killer is somewhere in this area," said Liam.

"That region's already been searched," said Marcus. "Even though it's heavily wooded, nothing's been found."

"Did they use FLIR?" Liam asked. Forward-looking infrared was commonly used on aircraft by military and law enforcement to find missing people. The technology had been perfected to find the heat signatures left by contacts.

Marcus slid a manila file across the table. "A grid search was conducted more than once. It came back clean."

Flipping open the file, Liam scanned the pictures. The photos were only of colors and shapes. Blue. Green. Red and yellow for something alive. Wolves. Bears. Even animals as small as squirrels had been found. No humans—nothing even close.

"The way I figure it," said Liam, handing the folder back to Marcus, "Darcy has to be someplace close, because whoever helped had to carry her on foot. Even someone familiar with the area couldn't make it more than three miles carrying a body—roughly one hundred and forty pounds of dead weight. That means one thing—if Darcy Owens is alive, then she's around here, somewhere." He pointed again to the map.

Wyatt was the first to speak, his words dripping with

sarcasm. "You really think that we'll find a serial killer that easily."

"I've done this before," said Liam. "Besides, didn't you bring me on board to find this person? If you don't want to listen to my advice, why am I here?"

Marcus said, "We can try and search the area again. It certainly couldn't hurt to have a fresh set of eyes looking at the terrain. I'll assign two operatives to go with you."

"If Darcy Owens is out there," said Liam, "she's as good as found."

The door to Holly's class opened. She looked up. For some insane reason, she hoped that Liam Alexander had returned. Sure, he'd been distracted and tense. At the same time, Holly felt as if she'd glimpsed something more to the man than his rough manners suggested.

Instead, Thomas Irwin, manager of Pleasant Pines Savings and Loan, stood on the threshold. His children were students at Saplings, but he rarely took time to speak with Holly.

Swallowing down a kernel of disappointment, Holly said, "Hi, Thomas, what can I do for you today?"

"Do you have a minute?" he asked. "Can we talk in the hallway?"

Holly glanced around her room. It was free time and all the children were engaged in activities. The assistant teacher sat on the floor, helping a group of students build a tower with blocks. "Sure," she said, and followed him to the corridor.

Thomas wore a gray pinstripe suit, white shirt and yellow tie. His dark hair was slicked back from his forehead. Brushing a piece of lint from his pants, he said, "I hate to bother you with this at school, Holly. There's a problem with the loan."

Her insides turned icy. "Which one? The main mortgage or the business equity loan?"

"It's the financials in general, I guess."

"I know I've gotten a little behind on the payments and I appreciate your understanding—"

Thomas lifted a hand, stopping Holly. "That's just it—I can't be understanding. Not anymore." His gaze dropped to the floor.

Holly's hands began to tremble. She tucked them under her arms. "I can see that this is difficult for you— Say what needs to be said."

"The bank is calling in the loan. By the end of this week, they'll own the day-care center."

"Isn't there anything I can do?"

"Not unless you can come up with the twenty thousand dollars ASAP," said Thomas.

The sum knocked all the air from Holly's lungs. She staggered backward. "Can I refinance again? You know I needed that second loan because we had to replace the roof. Besides, what would the bank do with a day-care center?"

Thomas exhaled. "That's the other thing. The bank received an offer to buy the day-care center from Alphabet Soup. It's a chain of schools run out of the Dallas area."

Holly began to sweat. Her ears buzzed. "Dallas? As in Texas?"

Thomas continued to talk. "They have schools all over the country with a standardized curriculum. They're looking to take over Saplings, I suppose. And this is good news for you, too. The sale will pay off everything you owe the bank."

"You can't do this," said Holly. "What about the children? Or the town? Everyone relies on Saplings to provide a warm and nurturing environment."

"Pleasant Pines will still have a day-care center," said Thomas. "There will be no disruption in the children's education." He hesitated. "You just won't be running it anymore."

A fire of indignation began to burn in Holly's middle. All her plans for Saplings were going up in flames. Shoot, her life had just been scorched, leaving nothing beyond dust and ash blowing in the wind.

"No," said Holly. "You can't do this."

"Holly, your dad was my track coach and my favorite teacher. And I remember when you were little, and you'd come to all our meets. Trust me, if there was any other way for you to get out of this mess, I'd find it."

"Is that supposed to make me feel better?" Holly asked.

"Face it. This school has left you in debt since the beginning." Thomas's cheeks reddened, the blush traveling all the way up to his forehead.

True, Holly had been struggling with cash flow since she'd opened the school. "What if I could get you the money?"

"All of it? All twenty thousand?"

Holly's shoulders slumped as a plan began to form. Hadn't her agent said he could sell whatever book she would write next? Even though that was several years ago, the offer had been more than what she needed now.

"I need to make some calls," said Holly. More than

contacting her agent, she'd need to think of a new book idea to pitch. That'd take some time, a luxury she didn't have. "Give me some time to see what kind of money I can find." Holly bit her bottom lip and tried to think of how long it might take to pull together that kind of cash. "A month?"

Thomas shook his head. "I can't do that. The people from Texas want to close the deal by the end of the week. If you want to keep Saplings, I'd need assurances from you soon."

Rolling back her shoulders, Holly said, "What about this evening?"

"Can you stop by the bank before it closes this afternoon at four?"

"You know I can't do that. The school is open until six."

Thomas sighed. "Look. I'll make you a deal. Meet me tonight at six at Sally's on Main. My wife and I always take the kids out for dinner on Monday. You can let me know what you've come up with and I'll work with you if I can."

"Thank you," said Holly, as relief washed over her. "I'll see you later."

"Don't be late," Thomas admonished as he exited.

Holly was never late, but this was definitely one meeting she wouldn't miss.

With her head swimming, Holly returned to her room and surveyed her class. A dozen bright and happy children were making flowers from tissue paper, muffin liners and pipe cleaners.

Her throat burned with frustration. She couldn't believe that her entire life would be decided in a matter of hours. Until then, she had a job to do and children who needed her attention. One of those children, Sophie Alexander, sat at the table and was creating a pipe-cleaner stem for a blue paper flower.

Kneeling at the child's side, Holly said, "That's very pretty."

Sophie, intent on her work, didn't look up. "It's for my daddy."

Her father, Liam Alexander. Holly felt a tightening in her middle...and it wasn't wholly unpleasant.

"I'm sure that your daddy will love the flowers." Holly was curious about the mother, who wasn't listed on the school's enrollment form, even as an emergency contact. "Would you like to make a bouquet for anyone else?"

"My mommy," said the little girl. "But she's far away. That's why I live with Daddy."

Holly picked up a muffin liner and marker. Tracing the paper pleats, she asked, "Where'd your mommy go?"

"She works on a big ship and her job is to keep us all safe."

Understanding crept through Holly. "Is your mommy in the navy?"

Sophie looked up from her artwork. "Yes."

From the beginning, she had assumed that Liam was a single father. While he might not have a partner in his life at the moment, he could be far from available. She knew she shouldn't be interested in his personal life, never mind his love life, yet she was.

So when Holly asked, "Did you live with your mommy and daddy before your mommy left?" she knew full well that she wasn't asking from an educational standpoint.

"No," said Sophie. "I used to live with Mommy. I miss her, but I talk to her on the computer. Daddy helps me call."

"It's nice to keep in touch."

Sophie nodded. "It is, but I miss her."

Holly stroked the child's downy head. She could well imagine the little girl's sadness and understood her loneliness. "I bet," she said.

"Sometimes I miss my mommy so much I want to cry." She looked at Holly. "But Daddy says even though she's far away, Mommy loves me and misses me, too. Do you think so, Dr. Holly?"

Emotion lodged in her throat. "Yes," she said. "I do."

Sophie turned back to her project. "Then I'm gonna make more flowers for Mommy and give them to her when she comes home."

It had been a long time since Holly had been forced to confront her longing for children. She'd spent a lot of time compartmentalizing her feelings, doing the opposite of what a good psychologist ought to do, she supposed. But it was easier than dealing with questions from well-meaning people about her lack of relationships or family. Questions she'd heard so much, in fact, that she had a ready answer—*my career is important. It wouldn't be fair to my family for me to be so focused. Blah, blah, blah.* The truth was much more complicated. A car accident in high school had changed Holly's life. It was a stupid mistake; the driver had been going too fast and nobody in the car had enough sense to tell him to slow down. The crash left her in the hospital for months, forcing her to miss the end of her sophomore year. It also crushed her pelvis and ruptured several organs. The incident didn't leave her sterile, but the doctors discouraged her from ever bearing a child, as it could be dangerous to both Holly and the baby.

It was a warning she heeded.

It was also why, even now, Holly avoided any long-term relationships. And, if she was honest with herself, it was the exact reason that Holly had always wanted to work with children, and why she'd opened her school after returning to Pleasant Pines.

"Sophie Alexander, you are one smart cookie," said Holly, giving the little girl's nose a tweak.

"Cookies? I love cookies."

"I'm glad you're in my class, Sophie," said Holly as she stood.

"Me, too," said Sophie, with a wide smile.

Holly patted the child's head, then turned, ready to engage with another student who also sat at the table.

"Dr. Holly?" Sophie called.

Looking back at Sophie, she said, "Yes?"

"You don't have to be worried about my daddy. He's just not used to taking care of me."

For Sophie's sake, Holly hoped that the child was right.

Sweat covered Darcy's brow. The wooden planks of the bunker floor were slick with blood. A trapdoor, set into the ceiling, was flung wide open, letting in light and fresh air. She hefted up the ax once more and brought it down. *Thwack*.

Free of the shoulder, Billy's arm flopped to the side.

Darcy could never hope to carry the whole body out of the pit. That meant she had to dispose of the corpse bit by bit. It was gruesome work.

She might have succeeded in killing Billy, but she was still far from civilization. After hefting the arm from the floor, she climbed the rickety ladder. The sun burned her eyes, but she didn't care. At least she was out of the hole. A rusting wheelbarrow she'd found under a tree, was now overflowing with the pieces of Billy's butchered body. She dropped Billy's arm on top of the pile and then, holding tight to the handles, began to walk, pulling the heavy wheelbarrow behind her.

Darcy felt no pride for having taken Billy's life. Killing the man had been about survival, plain and simple. How far had she come? Darcy figured it to be less than a quarter of a mile—yet, it was far enough. She tipped the wheelbarrow, and the contents tumbled to the ground. The head was the last to roll out. In death, Billy's eyes were open, his expression one of shock. Using the toe of her shoe, Darcy flipped his face to the other side.

Turning back to the bunker, memories flashed through her mind. The faces of her victims. The life seeping from their bodies...and that power transferring to her. Her flesh tingled with excitement. But then, another memory came, sending a chill down her spine. The stench of her father's breath, hot on her neck as she lay there, powerless and alone. With her eyes closed tight, she'd taken refuge with the Darkness.

Could she ever break free from her past?

Maybe. If she wanted to stop killing.

The question was...did she?

Darcy returned to the blood-soaked bunker. Surveying the small space, she spotted a metal and plastic object under the bed. Bending low, she reached out to grab it…and froze, her eyes wide. It was a flip phone.

Darcy scrambled across the floor. Gripping the phone, she lifted the faceplate. The screen illuminated and showed a strong signal, even underground. There was only one person she could contact. But should she dare?

She stared at the keypad. Her thumb hovered over the first digit. Quickly, before she could overthink it, she dialed a number that long ago she had sworn never to never use.

He answered on the third ring. "Hello?"

"I need some help," she said.

"Who's this?"

"You know who it is."

He paused. "You're all over the news," he said. "And presumed dead."

"I'd like to keep it that way. Unless you really do want me to die—"

"Don't be stupid," he interrupted.

Despite the fact that she was in no position to make demands, her temper spiked. It left Darcy hot and shaking. "You *owe* me."

He sighed. "Fine. What do you need?"

"A new identity. Maybe a job if you can swing it."

"I can help you with both. Give me some time. Call back in one hour and I'll give you the details." He continued, "I can't keep helping—not after everything you've done. In fact, I'm just lucky that nobody has connected the two of us."

Darcy rolled her eyes. "You don't need to tell me. I already know."

"Good," he said. "And Darcy?"

"Yes?"

"After today, don't ever call me again."

Carefully, she placed the phone on the cluttered shelf. The wound on her shoulder ached and burned, but that no longer bothered her. Because Darcy Owens had been presented with a second chance—and it was a chance that she refused to waste.

Chapter 3

Following the briefing at Rocky Mountain Justice's headquarters, Liam was introduced to two other operatives, Luis Martinez and Julia McCloud. Luis was a former cop from Denver with a dark crewcut and an easy smile. He'd joined RMJ about a year ago, after helping the agency close another operation. Liam liked the man immediately. Julia was a former Army Ranger and had attended a session he'd taught years before at the mountain survival school, located at Fort Drum.

Liam didn't recall the blonde soldier, but then again, during his time with the Department of Interior, he'd taught hundreds if not thousands of people from all branches the military and it was impossible to remember them all. Despite the fact that Liam preferred to work alone, Julia and Martinez seemed like decent partners.

Sitting in the passenger seat of a black SUV, Liam stared out the window. He recalled the last time he was in Wyoming and his throat tightened at the memory. He pushed all the recollections away and returned his attention to his new colleagues.

Martinez drove, while discussing the finer points of the case. "When Darcy Owens first turned up as a suspect in these serial murders, it was in Las Vegas," Martinez said. "Wyatt was the behavioral scientist assigned to the team investigating the case."

Julia, in the back seat, continued the story. "Things sort of went sideways when the wrong man was arrested and Wyatt's career was ruined."

"The guy seems pretty uptight," said Liam. "Maybe he was hard to work with and that's why his career went south."

"Wyatt's a good guy, but if it seems like he's intense about finding Darcy, you'd be right. As it turns out, she became fixated on Wyatt and followed him to Wyoming, where she started killing again. Basically, she was targeting him, using the murders to lure him out. When she tried to kill the woman he loved, he was forced to choose between saving her life or letting Darcy escape." He met Liam's gaze. "What would *you* have done?"

Well, he deserved that for sure. Perhaps Liam *had* been too quick to judge Wyatt. Maybe next time, he'd give him another chance.

Learn from the past, damn it. This has to work out.

Chastened, Liam cleared his throat. "Since we're hunting for Darcy, I can guess what Wyatt chose," said Liam. "I can also imagine that's why Rocky Mountain

Justice is involved. The organization is cleaning up a mess it helped to make."

"It's a bit of a harsh assessment, but you're right," said Julia.

"I guess it helps me understand Wyatt a little better," said Liam. "By the way, how's his girlfriend?"

"Thankfully, she survived the attack and is doing great," said Julia. "She was a PR exec in Chicago before moving to Wyoming. Now, she's working for the town of Pleasant Pines—promoting the area for tourism and such. Her latest crusade is to find a new sheriff."

Liam remembered a heartbreaking detail about the last sheriff from the case file. "That's right. Sheriff Haak was a victim of Darcy's, too, right?"

"Yeah. He was shot while trying to save Everly's life. She feels that she owes it to him to find a good replacement," said Martinez.

Staring out the window, Liam watched several large birds circling, their rotations becoming tighter. *Vultures.*

A sign that they had located their prey?

Bracing his hand on the dashboard, Liam said, "Stop."

Martinez dropped his foot on the brake.

"See that," said Liam, pointing through the windshield. "They're scavengers and hunting carrion. From the looks of that flock, there's something there we should check out."

Julia said, "I'd say it's several miles through the woods without any trails."

"There's a cutout about half a mile up the road. From there, we'll have to make our own trail," said Martinez.

"Then let's get after it."

Already Liam's palms tingled, itching with the need to be in the woods. As a very small boy, Liam spent his summers in the forests of Wyoming—not far from where he was now. It was those early days, running through the woods, camping with his grandfather, learning how to track animals and follow trails, that had led Liam to a life of a tracker.

Maybe he shouldn't be surprised that he was back in the state where his mother's family had lived for generations. After all, wasn't there some saying about all roads leading home?

After reaching the end of the road, Martinez killed the engine and used a switch to remotely open the rear liftgate. "Your gear is in the back," he said.

Liam rounded to the back of the vehicle, where Julia waited. She held a black backpack by one strap. "You have two days of rations and water in here. Walkie-talkie. Satellite phone. Set of keys to the SUV. First-aid kit. Rope in a rappelling sack. We all have the same equipment."

He took the backpack, then slipped his arms through the straps.

"This is…" said Julia as she held out a semiautomatic pistol "…your sidearm. It's a Glock. The magazine holds fifteen rounds and there's one in the chamber. Yours for as long as you're with RMJ."

He gave the firearm a quick once-over. "It'll do just fine," he said. Since he hadn't worn a holster, Liam was forced to tuck the gun into the waistband of his pants at the small of his back.

All the same, Liam *had* thought to bring his own machete. It was in a scabbard with a thigh strap. Unsheathing his blade, he watched as the edge glinted in the light. He gauged the heft and balance. He often needed it when working in the woods, to cut through thick branches. It looked as though he'd been right to bring it today.

"Let's go," he said, taking a step off the road.

Overhead, the frenzied call of birds filled the morning. He inhaled sharply. The tang of pine scented the air. There was also the deep, dark aroma of earth and rotting vegetation. And a deeper, darker smell lurking beneath.

Death.

Refocusing, he turned his gaze to the sky. The air was thick with birds.

"There's something up ahead," he said. "Birds don't get excited like that for nothing."

"What do you think it is?" Julia asked.

"There's only one way to find out," he said. "Come on."

The farther they ventured into the forest, the thicker the woods became. Using his machete, he hacked through brambles that clung to the trunks of trees, creating a wall of green. Sweeping his arm back and forth, it was as if the blade was an extension of his body. Sweat dampened his back and dotted his upper lip. The branches became thicker, denser.

Liam wondered if he'd gotten it all wrong. There was no way that anyone—even a professional tracker, like him—could have gotten through these woods.

He lifted the machete, then brought it down, cleaving a limb in two. His shoulder burned from the exertion, but the woods thinned out and Liam stepped into the clearing. His breathing came in gasps and sweat covered his back, chest and arms. A stiff breeze ushered in a bank of clouds, blotting out the sun and turning the sky gray.

Dozens of birds carpeted the ground. Beneath the swarm of wings and feathers was a heap of blood and gristle. It was a body, certainly. Was it even human? Had they come all this way for nothing?

As the trio from RMJ approached, the birds screamed in protest and took flight.

Julia stopped short. "Oh, my God," she gasped.

Liam immediately found what Julia had seen. A head, without a body. Because of the damage done by the birds it was impossible to identify the victim. Yet, parts of a beard clung to the skull, so there was no way it could have belonged to Darcy Owens.

Then he took in the whole scene. There was more carnage than just a head littering the clearing. And Liam wondered just who in the hell had killed the poor bastard.

And, more important, where was the killer?

Holly already knew she wasn't going to spend much time in the classroom today. Yet, keeping Saplings in business was as important as any lesson she might teach, and that meant doing everything in her power to get the money for that payment to the bank. Taking her cell phone to an empty classroom, Holly pulled up her contact list and placed a call. It was answered after the third ring.

"Hello?" said a male voice.

"Franklin," she said. "It's Holly Jacobs. It's, ah, been a while."

"It certainly has," said her former literary agent, Franklin Nelson. "The last time we spoke, you were turning down my offer to write a second book. How have you been?"

"Uh…" she said. "Good. Pretty good."

"What have you done with yourself for the past six years?"

"I moved back home to Wyoming. I took all the money I earned from the book and opened a day-care center. I get to help people every day," she said.

"You helped millions of people with your book, you know that."

"But not personally," she said. She started to sweat, defensive of her decision to come home and help her community.

"It's hard to help a million people without using some kind of mass media," said Franklin. "I'd love to catch up with you more, but to be honest, I'm busy with a deadline. Is there anything I can help you with?"

She did need Franklin's help, but was she really willing to travel the same path twice?

Her runaway bestseller had only meant to be a doctoral thesis. The book on childhood trauma struck a chord in the market and Holly became an overnight sensation. Bestseller lists. Talk shows. Parties. Conventions and conferences. She was living every author's dream of success. There had even been speculation about a TV talk show.

Then the book fell off the bestseller lists and almost overnight, Holly felt as if she were forgotten. It had broken her heart and shattered her soul. Was she really ready to try again?

"Holly," Franklin said, bringing her back to the present. "Is there anything I can help you with? I mean, you called for a reason."

Drawing in a deep breath, Holly asked, "Does the offer still stand? Is there still interest in another book?"

"Wow. Of all the things I thought I'd hear today, that was not on the list. I just have to wonder, why the change of mind?"

There was no sense in lying—or even hiding the truth. "I need money."

"How much?"

"Twenty thousand dollars."

Whistling through his teeth, Franklin said, "You haven't written a book in years and I can't justify asking for an advance that large, especially not without a viable proposal that I can submit."

Holly rubbed her forehead. She shouldn't be surprised by the answer. "What can you do?"

"When can you get me pages to read? Once I see, what your thesis is, I can possibly shop the project around."

Possibly. No guarantees at all. Well, what the hell did she expect?

"That's just it," said Holly. "I don't have anything— not now. Not yet." She quickly changed tactics.

"It sounds like you want something other than to reenter the publishing industry. Why don't you tell me what's really wrong?"

"Unless I get twenty thousand dollars by the end of the week, the bank will take my school." In speaking the words, Holly understood how truly dire her situation had gotten. Her eyes stung and her throat began to close.

There was silence for a moment. "I can't help you right now. Not without a book—or at least a few chapters."

"Thanks, Franklin," she said. "It was worth a try, right?"

"And, Holly, if you ever put together a proposal for that second book, let me know."

"Of course," she said, even though they both knew it was a lie.

As she disconnected the call, the coldness of her reality set in. If she couldn't convince the bank to give her an extension on her loans, she was going to be out of more than the school. Holly would be out of a job.

Chapter 4

Liam stepped into the clearing and knelt next to the skull. Even he found the scene repulsive—and he'd found dozens of bodies in all phases of decomposition. Swallowing down his revulsion, he asked, "There's no way to ID him. Nothing…" He turned away and coughed, then turned back to the ruined head. "Nothing left. Did anyone live out here? Or have a vacation cabin?"

Julia hung back, a hand still covering her mouth. With a shake of her head, she said, "Not a clue. I'm calling this in. We can get a CSI team here by helicopter within a half hour." She swung her backpack off her shoulder, unzipped the top pocket, then withdrew a satellite phone.

Liam stood; a plan had already been formed as he

listened to Luis and Julia. "This is a fresh body. Who-ever killed this guy might still be close by."

Glancing over her shoulder, Julia said, "You're right. They could be watching us right now." She wore a side-arm on her hip and instinctively rested her palm on her holster.

Liam said, "Make the call, Julia. Then we have, what'd you say, thirty minutes? That's about the time we need to try and find the person who did this."

Julia made the call. As she stowed the satellite phone, she said, "The choppers' on the way. ETA half an hour."

Liam dropped to his knee once more and examined the skull. "Do we suspect this is a victim of Darcy Owens?" he asked.

"I'm not so sure," said Martinez. He kneeled next to Liam. "Her standard MO was to poison her victims, not hack them to pieces."

"Maybe the carving up was done postmortem," sug-gested Julia. "Maybe he was poisoned and then cut up for transport."

"No such luck," said Martinez. He pointed to what was left of the throat. "See that—it's bruising. This per-son was strangled before they were struck."

Liam grunted.

"You have a problem with our profile?" Martinez asked.

"Look, I respect what you do. But it doesn't take a lot to put two and two together here," said Liam. "You hired me to do what I do best, to help you track and find a serial killer who went missing in these woods. And here, we have the victim of an obvious homicide. Un-less you think this guy cut himself into twenty pieces?"

Julia rolled her eyes at Martinez.

Martinez shrugged and asked, "Okay, let's say you're right. Do you think he was killed here?"

Liam shook his head. Martinez continued, "There's not enough blood to make me think he was killed here, either. Which means that the body was dumped in the glade."

Liam said, "Whoever dumped this body had to be on foot. There are no roads in or out and the undergrowth is too dense for an all-terrain vehicle. Which means if there's a trail," Liam said as he scanned the surrounding woods, "then I can find it."

Without the sun casting the woods in light and shadow it was easy to find. A gap in the foliage, where several branches had been bent. He moved closer to investigate. There was a single groove carved out of the soil.

Martinez came up from behind. "What is it?"

"It looks like a tire track from something small. A bicycle, maybe, but it'd be a hell of a way to transport a body. Still, it could be done."

"Or maybe it's from a wheelbarrow," suggested Julia.

Liam stood and dusted his hands on the back of his pants. "Yeah. It makes more sense to carry a body in a wheelbarrow. Still, the person would have to be close— you can't maneuver a wheelbarrow up and around mountains."

"Which means what?" Martinez asked.

Liam's eyes followed the path left by the single wheel. It ran straight through the woods. *It couldn't be this easy, could it?*

Holding back a low-hanging branch, Liam said, "This way."

As far as tracks went, these were fairly simple, Liam thought. The wheel had cut a neat furrow in the newly thawed ground. The path ran along the spine of a ridge, and as it wound down the other side, Liam stopped. He dropped to his knee and motioned to Julia and Martinez to get low and stay quiet.

"What is it?" Martinez asked, his voice a whisper.

"Look there. Do you see it? A trapdoor set into the ground. It's just beyond the copse of trees."

"It must be some kind of underground shelter," said Julia, shading her eyes from the sun.

"Your guess is as good as mine," said Liam. "But you're probably right."

Julia said, "If Darcy's been hiding out in a bunker in the woods for the past two weeks, it would explain why she was never picked up on any infrared searches. They could have flown directly overhead and never caught a glimpse of her. Dirt makes a hell of an insulator."

Martinez nodded. "It makes perfect sense. What do we do now?"

Julia said, "There might be a back door to that bunker, and she could escape if we try a frontal assault. More than that, we don't know what's waiting for us down there. Could be nothing or it could be deadly."

"You have a point," said Liam. After all, searching the woods had been his idea. That meant he was responsible for the safety of his coworkers.

If things went south, it was all on him.

It was yet another reason he preferred to work alone.

The double doors were metal and flung wide open.

They rested at an angle, supported by the hinges, and weren't flush with the ground. It reminded Liam of a root cellar he'd seen once, at an old cabin used by early settlers in Wyoming. But there was no homestead nearby—no reason for there to be a door leading into the bowels of the earth. An inexplicable shiver ran up his spine. Quieting his mind, Liam focused. Then he sensed it, felt the evil that had been here.

Martinez withdrew a pair of binoculars from his backpack and focused on the door. "There's a ladder," he said. "I can see the top rungs over the lip of the entrance."

"Anything else?" asked Julia.

"Nothing," said Martinez. "You want to take a look?"

"Sure thing." Julia held out her palm and Martinez passed over the binoculars. It happened without warning. The sun, hidden behind a bank of clouds, broke through. The light glinted off the lens, sending a burst of light straight at the trapdoor.

"Damn," cursed Liam. "So much for staying concealed."

Darcy had washed in the rain barrel, cleansing her skin of grime, blood and the sickly-sweet stench of illness. As she slipped her shirt over her head, she saw it. A single flicker of light, like the flash of a camera, high on the wall.

The light meant only one thing—someone was outside. For a minute, she actually considered surrendering.

No. She'd never give up…or give in. Especially since she'd gotten this second chance and had her whole life yet to live. That meant she had only one choice—run.

She climbed the rungs of the ladder and quickly peeked into the woods, then dropped back out of sight. Three figures, faceless in the noon-hour sun, were advancing on the bunker. They all carried handguns, the barrels glinting in the light. If she hesitated, Darcy would be surrounded, with no chance of escape. Hefting the ax from the corner, she moved to the ladder's base and held her breath. With one hand, she climbed higher. Higher. Higher.

There was the faint crunching of boots on undergrowth. The people were close. She counted—*one, two... Go.* Launching herself upward, Darcy landed on the ground and swung the ax in a wide arc.

A tall man with a dark crewcut jumped back as the blade passed only inches from his chest. Heart racing, pulse pounding, Darcy kicked out, aiming for the man's knee. Her foot connected with flesh and bone and sinew. He cried out in pain and surprise as he crumpled to the ground. She turned and sprinted deeper into the woods.

Trees rushed past her as she ran one way and then another. Behind her, she heard the sound of running feet.

There was a sharp pop, followed by a boom. The tree next to her exploded as the bullet struck the trunk. She ducked. It wasn't enough. A splinter caught her in the cheek. She needed to lose her pursuers, but how? She threw the ax, watching the blade tumble end over end. It landed on the ground with a thump. Sprinting in the opposite direction, she hoped that her pursuers would follow the sound, giving her a moment to slip away.

"Where'd she go?" a man asked. From her hiding place behind a tree, the pursuers were nothing more than forms and figures. She longed to change her stance and see their faces, but didn't dare move.

"She left the ax," said a woman. "What should we do with it, Martinez?"

Damn. Maybe Darcy shouldn't have gotten rid of her single weapon. If they found her now, how would she ever be able to fight back?

"You have a tarp in your bag? Let's wrap it up. Eventually, it'll be turned over as evidence."

There was the sound of a bag unzipping and the crinkle of folded plastic. Darcy assumed it was the tarp. The woman continued. "Okay. I'm good."

"How's the knee?" asked another man.

"My knee hurts like hell, but I think it's just a bad bruise." His admission meant that he was the one with the crewcut. Crewcut added, "Clearly, Darcy had more survival training than we originally thought."

"That still doesn't tell us where she went," said the woman.

"Let's split up," said the other guy. Darcy was fast picking up the different intonation of the voices. "We can cover more ground. Stay in contact if you see or hear anything. Otherwise, maintain radio silence."

His words trailed off and Darcy imagined that his gaze had been drawn toward her. Again, she screwed her eyes shut and pressed her back into the tree's trunk. She held her breath and waited. There was nothing. Slowly, she peeled open her eyes and watched as the man disappeared behind a copse of trees.

Darcy remained crouched down until her legs went numb. After a while, she had no idea how much time had passed, but she knew that she needed to get out of the woods. Too bad she didn't know where to go, much less what to do next.

She heard a twig snapping in two, and Darcy's senses became keen and sharp. She dropped low and searched the woods. There, to her left, was movement. A person? Definitely. Scuttling along the base of trees, she moved from one trunk to the next.

Had she lost them?

Darcy drew in a deep breath. The man was close. He had his back to her. Certainly, he wouldn't be so vulnerable if he knew that she was nearby. The kill wouldn't be easy, yet she could already feel his hot blood washing over her hands. Her pulse grew, pounding in her skull. Darcy eased forward an inch, and then two.

Was that what she wanted? To kill again? Hadn't she sworn off taking another life?

She paused and yet the urge to kill pushed her forward.

"Do it," said the Darkness.

"No," she whispered. "I won't. Not anymore."

"Do it." The Darkness was seductive, a siren's song she could not ignore. *"Do it. He deserves to die."*

But, did he?

"No, he doesn't."

The Darkness was silent for a moment.

The man stepped away, his silhouette disappearing. Then he was gone. Darcy slumped down. She'd done it. She'd resisted the urge. As if a physical burden had been lifted, Darcy felt clean. For the first time in years, she was free.

A weak sun offered little light and no warmth. Folding her arms across her chest, Darcy shivered until her teeth began to rattle. She was ready to reenter the world and refashion her life. All she needed was to call the contact back. Damn. She didn't have the phone, which meant she had to return to the bunker—the place where all of Darcy's nightmares became real.

Chapter 5

Julia McCloud pulled the walkie-talkie from her pack. She knew that there was something the team had missed. Setting the channel, she pressed the talk button. "Martinez," she said. "Are you there?"

His voice followed a burst of static. "You got something?"

"If we don't look through that bunker, we're neglecting a big opportunity."

"Agreed," said Martinez. "You want me to meet you there?"

The thought of coming face-to-face with Darcy Owens—or who knows who else—made her a little sick, but they couldn't afford to cut the search for Darcy by two people. "No," she said. "I'll be in touch if I find anything interesting."

After stowing her walkie-talkie, Julia retraced her steps to the bunker. Her backpack now weighed down by the tarp-wrapped ax, she kept her sidearm drawn and her vigilance high. Within minutes, the open trapdoor came into view.

A metal ladder and wooden floor were visible from where she stood. Holding her Glock .23 out and ready, she stepped on the first rung. The temperature dropped and the coppery stench of blood rose up from the hole. It gave Julia the distinct feeling that she was climbing into a meat locker.

Her stomach threatened to revolt, and she turned her face to the sun. Taking one more breath of sweet, clean air, Julia lowered herself all the way down to the floor.

As she had noticed from the ground, the floor was made up of wooden planks. What she hadn't seen was a bloodstain, black in the gloom. Julia assumed that the victim from the clearing had been killed in this room. But what other clues were there?

A single shelf, affixed to the wall, was covered with debris—papers, tools, tins of food, a plate, a cup and a fork. Inexplicably, there was a fine clock, ticking slowly. A round, black wood-burning stove sat in the corner. An exhaust pipe snaked up the wall and disappeared into the earthen ceiling. Was it just bad luck that the heat signatures from the fire hadn't been picked up during an aerial search of the area? Or had the dense forest somehow helped conceal it?

There was little else in the room. A table. A bed.

Had this bunker belonged to the dead man? It made sense, yet who had the man been in life? She side-stepped the bloodstain and approached the stove, where a pile of ashes remained.

Her gaze stopped. Now there was a clue that might mean something. She'd found a flip phone—an older model, sure—but if it belonged to Darcy, it was certainly important. She set her gun on the shelf, and her backpack on the floor next to the ladder, the ax handle sticking out. After picking up the phone, she lifted the faceplate. The screen was an incandescent green. Seven numbers appeared on the display.

Slipping her personal phone from her pants pocket, she turned on the flash before snapping several pictures.

The air had changed, becoming heavy and oppressive—like the sky minutes before the violent explosion of a thunderstorm.

Shifting her weight to the balls of her feet, Julia pivoted slowly. Framed with white light, Darcy Owens stood at the top of the ladder. Julia's mouth went dry; her heart began to race. She inhaled slowly, focusing all her attention on her adversary. It had been a little more than two weeks since Julia had last seen Darcy, yet looking at the other woman's appearance, a decade could have passed. She held no weapon, but that didn't matter—her kill count proved what a cunning adversary she was. And Julia knew she couldn't take her eyes off her for a second.

Her blond hair hung limply around her shoulders. Her skin was waxy. Sweat stained the front of her loose shirt. She'd lost ten pounds—maybe fifteen.

"You shouldn't be here," Darcy said, her words a whisper. Not bothering to turn around, she kept her gaze locked with Julia's as she descended the ladder.

Holding her eyes steady, Julia dropped her hand to her holster and found nothing but air. Her stomach dropped to her feet. Where was her gun? Then she remembered, and she flicked a quick glance at the shelf. The steel barrel of her Glock glinted in the weak light. Julia muttered a curse as she slowly lifted her hands, palms out, and feigned surrender. Yet, Julia could never let her guard down—if she did, then she'd never make it out of this tomb alive.

"You don't look so good," Julia said, trying to draw the other woman into a conversation. "We can get you medical care. Why don't you tell me what happened to you?"

"Who is *we*?" Darcy asked, ignoring her question. Her eyes flicked to the ax handle, sticking out of Julia's backpack, then back to the agent.

"My…friends," said Julia, trying to think on her feet. But she knew Darcy wouldn't buy it.

She was right.

Darcy looked at her carefully, then nodded in recognition. "You look familiar. I saw you at the Pleasant Pines Inn, didn't I?"

"You did," said Julia. She'd helped investigate the apparent suicide of a cook at the inn, who'd initially been suspected of all the killings. In the end, it turned out he'd just been another of Darcy's victims. "If you come with me—"

Darcy interrupted, "I'm not giving up." She gripped the handle now.

Julia slid one foot forward, then the other, closing the distance to the gun by a fraction of an inch. "Tell me about the guy in the glade."

"Billy," said Darcy, with a snort.

"How'd you end up here?"

"He found me after I got away from Wyatt." Darcy paused and touched her shoulder—the same place where she'd been shot. "Billy found me in the woods and brought me here. He nursed me back to health."

"No offense," said Julia. "You don't look healthy."

Darcy didn't respond.

Julia decided to try again. "But you killed him, even though he saved your life."

"He was garbage," said Darcy. Her cheeks flamed red. A bead of sweat ran down the side of her face. "He had to die, and don't ask me to feel bad about it, because I don't."

"Let me help you. You need proper food and medical care. We'll figure out the rest."

One. Two. Three. Julia focused on the Glock and lunged forward. Her fingertips brushed the gun's grip at the same moment Darcy dragged the ax from the bag…but before she could squeeze the trigger, her palm filled with pain as the ax's blade struck her hand. The gun slipped away, clattering uselessly to the floor. Hot blood poured from gaping sockets where fingers used to be.

Darcy swung the ax around. The blade caught Julia in the gut. Her stomach erupted with blazing pain, and her knees no longer held her upright. She tumbled to the floor, a hand splayed across her wound.

As if she was underwater, Darcy Owens's face hovered above Julia's. "I wish you hadn't gone for your gun," she said, shaking her head sadly.

"I—I…" The pain was all-consuming. It was a blaze that engulfed her body, mind and soul. "I…" she stuttered. But there was really nothing to say.

Julia felt rough hands on her back and knew that Darcy had stripped away her backpack. She wondered how the hell she'd warn the others. Then her world went black.

The waiting room at the hospital in Cheyenne consisted of seven chairs, upholstered in maroon or teal cloth. A table, covered with a faux wood laminate, sat in the middle of the floor. Overhead, fluorescent lights glowed and hummed. Liam leaned against the wall and traced the outline of a linoleum tile with the toe of his boot. He checked his watch. It was quarter past three in the afternoon. What a hellish first day on the job. He knew that they were more than a little lucky that the helicopter, along with a CSI team, had been called to the scene. If it weren't for the chopper arriving only minutes after Liam and Martinez found Julia, she'd be dead.

To make matters worse, the SUV driven by Martinez had gone missing, turning up thirty miles away at a truck stop.

It meant only one thing: Darcy Owens was at large and could be almost anywhere in the world by now.

Martinez sat in a chair, holding his head with his hands. It was hard to not feel bad for the guy. Was it guilt because he'd given the okay for Julia to search the bunker alone? In reality, it might not have mattered what he said. Julia had made a choice and things hadn't worked out well. Certainly, Martinez knew he wasn't to blame.

Having been picked up by the helicopter, and then delivered to the trauma center, Liam and Martinez were stranded at the hospital in Cheyenne. While airborne, they'd contacted the rest of the team from RMJ. Someone was on the way from Pleasant Pines.

The door to the waiting room opened. Marcus Jones crossed the threshold. He was accompanied by a woman in her fifties, with streaks of gray lightening her dark hair.

Jones quickly introduced Liam to the woman. She was Katarina, RMJ's IT and communications expert.

"Any news on Julia?" Marcus asked.

"She's still in surgery," said Liam. "No word yet."

"What happened out there?"

Luis gave a succinct rundown of events, starting with finding the body and the trail to the bunker. The chase through the woods after Darcy. He ended with the fact that Julia had returned to the bunker and when she couldn't be raised on the walkie-talkie, the two men went to investigate.

"Liam found Julia first. She had a deep wound to her gut. He was patching her up, trying to slow the blood flow as best he could when I got there," said Martinez. His voice sounded hollow. Then again, he hadn't bothered to lift his head when he answered. Maybe his words were echoing off the floor.

For a moment, Liam felt a pang of envy—a quick punch to the chest. What would it be like to have a friend, a colleague, a partner, who touched his soul so deeply, that their pain brought about a personal anguish?

Like a forgotten dream, Holly Jacobs's face floated through his mind.

"Anything else?" Jones asked.

Like posing the question again would somehow change the answer. "We found her gun, but not her backpack," Liam said.

It was the missing backpack, and extra keys that were inside, that had enabled Darcy to steal the SUV.

"That's it?" Jones asked.

"Yeah," said Martinez, his tone sullen. "That's it."

Liam went back to tracing the tile. His toe stopped moving a split second before the flash of memory came back. "No," he said. "It's not it."

All eyes turned to Liam. He reached into a side pocket, low on his leg. "I found this." He held up the slim cell phone. "It was on the floor near Julia's gun. With everything it took getting her out of that bunker, well, it slipped my mind." Liam had messed up big-time. He stopped talking. "No excuses, just my apologies. I'll get in touch with the Feds and turn this over—"

"Don't you dare," said Jones, interrupting Liam. "Not yet at least."

Liam's surprise at the ignored protocol must've registered on his face, because Marcus continued, "We need to see what's on that phone first. Katarina, can you get past her password?"

"Not a problem," she said.

Rising to her feet, Katarina held out her hand. Liam handed her the phone and waited as she tapped on the screen.

"It looks like there are several text messages between Julia and Luis from yesterday."

Martinez lifted his head. "There was a game last night. We were watching and texting."

"One phone call," said Katarina. "She called her parents and talked for an hour."

"She always calls them on Sunday night," Martinez added.

"Nothing else," said Katarina, looking at Luis a little funny.

"Well, she had her phone out for a reason," said Jones. "Photos?"

She searched the app quickly. "Julia took several pictures of a flip phone."

Liam peered over Katarina's shoulder. The photos were stacked three across, with one row atop the next. "It's hard to tell because the background's so dark." He squinted at the pictures. "Actually, it looks like she took these in the bunker. She must have found something on this. Is there something on the phone's screen?"

Katarina tapped open the picture and expanded the aspect, then played with the filters to lighten the image. "I can do a better job clarifying the other images if I upload this to the system, but this should be clear enough to get the number from this one."

A photo was filled with a set of seven numbers, along with a time stamp. Three minutes and fifty-two seconds.

"You think this phone belonged to Darcy? You think she called this number and talked to someone for almost four minutes?" Marcus asked.

"There's only one way to find out." Liam removed his own phone. After turning on the speaker feature, he dialed the number.

It rang once, then someone answered. "White Wind Resort and Spa. This is Nathan. How may I help you?"

"Sorry," said Liam. "Wrong number." He ended the call and looked around the room.

Luis spoke next. "I'm obviously missing something. What is the White Wind Resort and Spa?"

"It's one of the most exclusive resorts in the state. Rooms that go for three grand a night. Steak dinners that cost more than my car payment," said Liam.

"How do you know all of that?" Martinez asked.

Liam gave a one-shoulder shrug. "My grandparents lived near the resort. I visited them a lot when I was a kid. I remember when the White Wind was being built." He didn't add that many of his relatives had been displaced when the families' property became prime real estate.

"We'll have to turn over the phone to the Feds and see what they can turn up." Marcus sighed.

"What do we do now?" In most search and rescue operations, the missing person wanted to be found. And, well, Liam had done his job and located Darcy Owens. It's just that the wily killer had gotten away.

"While we wait for news about Julia, I'll contact the FBI and turn over the pictures on the phone," said Jones. "Then, this evening when we get back to Pleasant Pines, we'll meet with the DA. Our role in the case will have to be reevaluated."

This evening? Sure, he understood the importance of the case, it's just that he had other priorities. "I have to take care of my daughter. She's three."

Jones stared at Liam and slowly blinked. "I didn't know you have a child."

"Well, you didn't ask." Liam felt his defensiveness

returning—it was a wall that separated him from the rest of the team.

"I guess I just assumed," said Jones. "Your work history put you all over the map." He paused.

"What do you want me to say?" asked Liam. "Things changed when Sophie's mom was deployed. That's why I accepted this job. And it was her first day at a new school today—I'm supposed to pick her up by six."

"If you are looking to be back in Pleasant Pines by six o'clock," said Katarina, "I hate to tell you, hon, but you are late."

"Late?" Liam repeated, as if the word held no meaning.

Her eyes held compassion and understanding as she swiveled her wrist to show him her smart watch. "Yep. To get back to Pleasant Pines by six o'clock, you needed to leave twenty minutes ago." She held out a set of keys. "Take my SUV back, if you want. I'll catch a ride with Marcus."

Closing his eyes, Liam cursed under his breath. More than getting back to Pleasant Pines, he couldn't pick up his daughter without her car seat. It meant stopping at RMJ's building and picking up his own car—making him even later than he was already. Then he looked at Marcus. "I've got to go. I promise, I'll help figure this out. I made a commitment to RMJ. But my kid comes first to me. Always."

Chapter 6

Holly Jacobs sat at the art table with Sophie Alexander, the final student who remained at the day-care center. Glancing at the wall clock, Holly sighed. Six twenty-five. She was beyond late for meeting up with Thomas Irwin at the diner. Her life was just unraveling.

Sure, she'd thought about calling Tonya and asking her to stay with Sophie. But her friend lived twenty minutes outside Pleasant Pines. By the time Holly realized that Liam Alexander was seriously delayed and she'd have to extend aftercare, Holly was so late that there was no point in asking Tonya to drive all the way back.

"Is my daddy gonna be here?" Sophie asked, looking worried. "I don't like being the only-ist person at school. Mommy always picked me up on time."

"I'm sure he's on his way," said Holly, trying to

smile. She'd already called his cell phone several times. Each had gone directly to voice mail. "I'm sure your daddy will be along any minute," said Holly, this time her smile was sincere. Still, her eye was drawn to the clock. Six twenty-six.

"Do you hafta get home?"

"Me? No, not at all. I was just wondering about the time."

"My mommy says not to lie, and Dr. Holly, I think you are lying."

Holly couldn't help but give a surprised laugh. "Here's something that I know is true. I'm happy that we can spend a little extra time together. What do you want to do? Puzzles? A game? I love to play Candy Land."

"Candy Land," said Sophie, her smile wide. "That's my favorite game, too."

For safety's sake, the front door of the day-care center was locked after business hours. The door buzzer began to ring before Holly had a chance to collect the board game. "I bet that's your daddy," said Holly as she crossed the room. "Let me check before we open the door."

Each class was also connected to the intercom system via a phone. Lifting the receiver, Holly said, "Yes? May I help you?"

"It's Liam Alexander. I'm here to pick up my daughter, Sophie."

Holly clenched the handset tighter. The nerve. *It's me, Liam Alexander. I'm here to pick up my daughter, Sophie.*

No *I'm sorry I'm late*?

After letting out a long, low breath, Holly said, "I'll

bring Sophie to the front door. You can sign her out there." She hung up the phone. Turning to Sophie, she said, "That's your daddy. I'll take you to him."

"I need my flowers. I want to give them to my daddy."

Ah, yes. The art project for the day. Sophie's lone bouquet sat on the counter and Holly handed it to the girl.

"Ready to go?" she asked.

With a smile, Sophie nodded. "I'm ready."

Holly had long since gathered all of Sophie's belongings, and her own, as well. Everything sat in a neat pile next to the door. After collecting all the bags, Holly took Sophie's hand and together they walked down the corridor, silent except for the sounds of their steps.

The closer they got to the entrance, the more Holly's anger grew. She didn't want to scream at Liam Alexander…well, actually she did. By being so late, he'd ruined her life, after all. Yet, she was resolute that she would remain calm in front of Sophie.

They approached the glass front door. The setting sun hung low on the horizon. The light brought out red highlights in Liam's dark hair that Holly hadn't noticed before. His shadow stretched out long and powerful, just like the man. Her breath caught in her chest and some of Holly's anger melted away—just not enough.

After entering the lock code, Holly pulled the door open. The evening air was cool, and Holly inhaled. Sophie ran to her father, paper flower bouquet in hand.

"Daddy." Sophie took a leap and landed in her father's arms. "I made these for you," she said, handing over the flowers.

"For me?" Liam's cheeks reddened. "I love these. What a great job you did, honey."

In that instant, Holly's heart melted.

When Sophie said, "I love you, Daddy," Holly's eyes began to water. She turned back to the door and re-armed the alarm.

"How was your day, baby girl?" Liam asked.

Holly stood next to father and daughter, partly charmed with the love between the two, partly seething that she had missed her meeting and Liam had yet to apologize—or even give a lame excuse.

She cleared her throat and held out Sophie's bag. "You have a lovely daughter, Mr. Alexander. I'm sure you recall I mentioned that the pickup time is six o'clock."

Sophie wiggled from her father's arms as Liam reached for the offered bag. "My day went sideways."

The child wandered over to a flower bed and started hopping from one paving stone to the next.

Stay professional. "Everyone's day goes awry, and I understand—trust me, I do. Keep in mind that you aren't the only one with responsibilities." She leaned in close, lowering her voice to keep from being overheard by Sophie. Liam's scent—sweat and earth—washed over Holly, leaving her slightly drunk on the smell of masculinity. Yet she continued, "More than being late, your daughter was worried."

He paused. "There was an accident at work. My co-worker was airlifted to the hospital in Cheyenne and I ended up in the helicopter with her."

Of all the things she thought he might say, that wasn't one of them. A look passed across his face. What was it? Hurt? Concern? In the end, Holly decided that Liam was weary. It was a chink in his armor. A window in the wall that surrounded him.

It also brought up a new and interesting question. What exactly did Liam Alexander do for a living? His form had said private security. But what exactly did that mean? "Where do you work again?"

He waved away her question. His face was once again unreadable—the armor repaired, and the wall made whole. "I'm here now, aren't I? I'm sure I'm not the only parent who runs late on occasion. What was I supposed to do?" Liam asked.

Oh, the things Holly wanted Liam Alexander to do. Apologize. Explain. Take a flying leap. The list went on and on. "I don't have time to argue with you. Tomorrow, be punctual." With that, she forced a smile on her face for Sophie and turned for her car. By the time Holly unlocked her door, her hand was trembling. She drove straight to the Sally's on Main, despite her racing heart and the need to press her foot hard onto the accelerator, she kept the car's speed to five miles an hour under the limit. As she pulled into a parking space three doors down, the time on her dashboard clock read 6:35 p.m. Maybe she could still catch Thomas.

After turning off the ignition, Holly grabbed her tote bag and the knot in her stomach loosened a little. She rushed up the street, then opened the door to Sally's. Breathless, she scanned the room. The town physician, Doc Lambert, sat at the counter and looked up as Holly entered. "How's my favorite patient?" he asked.

Holly was sure he said that to all his patients, yet the elderly doctor was her father's best friend and had been a part of Holly's life from the beginning. "Good, Doc. And you?"

He wiped his mouth with a paper napkin. "Just finished dinner or else I'd offer to buy you a burger. How's your mom and dad?"

"Both good," she said. "I talked to them last week. Call Dad. He'd love to hear from you." Holly paused. She longed to confess her troubles to her old doctor. Then again, it wasn't as though there was anything he could do to help.

"Are you sure you're okay?" Doc Lambert asked.

"I am," said Holly slowly. Then she spied Thomas Irwin sitting in a booth near the back, tapping his foot impatiently. "I'm meeting someone."

"I'll let you go. Good to see you," said Doc.

"You, too," said Holly, her chest suddenly tight.

The top two buttons of the banker's oxford shirt were undone, and his yellow tie was tucked into the pocket.

Approaching the table, Holly said, "I'm sorry I'm late. I had to wait for a parent to pick up their child." Noticing that he was alone, and not with his family, as he had promised, she asked, "Where's your wife and the kids?"

"My daughter has a T-ball game," he said. "They had to leave."

His tone was icy, and Holly wrapped her arms over her shoulders to quell a shiver.

"Well," said Holly. She'd been able to get a cash advance from her credit card, although with that money gone, she'd have nothing else left. "In the next few days, I can get you an extra two thousand dollars. I hope it's enough that I can refinance."

The bank manager shook his head. "I wish I could help you, but I can't."

"What? Why not?"

Standing, he said, "First, I don't have time for a meeting now. As I said, my daughter has a T-ball game. Unlike some people, I'm always prompt."

Heat crept from her chest to her cheeks. "If I can just set up another meeting—" Holly began.

The bank manager continued, as if Holly hadn't spoken at all. "Second, you might have some money, but I would need more. Or possibly some collateral."

Like a deflated balloon, all the air leaked from her lungs and Holly slumped. "I—I don't have more. Thomas, please."

"Well, then that's very much a problem." He drew in a deep breath.

"You can't do this to me. Please," she said, painfully aware that she was close to groveling. "I can come in first thing in the morning. Give me tonight to see what kind of collateral I can find."

"I know what you're doing, Holly. You're trying to take care of the town, that's admirable of you."

At least he was polite enough not to mention the car accident specifically. Then again, they both knew what had happened and he was right. All of Pleasant Pines had rallied around Holly after the wreck in high school. Nobody had blamed her at all for the crash, even though they could have. Years later, the town had celebrated her success, even after the fame from her bestseller had slipped away.

It was these debts of kindness that she felt needed to be repaid.

But what if she were free from her responsibility? She felt like a weight had been lifted from her shoulders.

Thomas continued, "Be honest with me—will a few hours make any difference? More than that, can you guarantee that you'd be able to attend another meeting? You know you have to be in school tomorrow."

They both knew the answers to each question.

"No," she said. "I guess not."

"I thought as much," said Thomas.

She took a deep, shuddering breath. "You have to guarantee me that all my employees will keep their jobs. Please, these are your neighbors."

"I promise that the staff will still have work." He sighed. "Holly, you don't owe this town anything."

"This is my home," she said, her voice a whisper. "I owe them everything."

"Remember, you have to take care of yourself," he said.

Thomas's words of encouragement, while well-meaning, left Holly feeling more like the little girl on the sidelines and less like a grown woman with a doctorate. She nodded, "Thanks."

"Now, I really do have to go." He paused. "If anything changes for you this week, let me know."

Thomas stepped away from the booth and she watched him walk out of the restaurant. Dropping into the recently vacated seat, Holly looked out the window. She stared at the sun, dipping below the horizon. It leeched all of the color from the town square, turning the world gray with swipes of pastel pink and purple.

Was that it? Was she really going to lose her school? Her throat was raw, as if she'd swallowed broken glass.

Well, she might not know exactly what path her life would take now, but she certainly knew who was to blame for the detour: Liam Alexander.

Holly couldn't sit at a booth in a busy restaurant any longer without placing an order. Her appetite was gone, and she wasn't sure when it would come back. Besides, she knew she needed to contact all her employees and let them know that, come next week, she would no longer own the school.

Stepping away from the booth, she placed a call to Tonya, knowing that it would be the hardest conversation. "Hey," she said as soon as the call was answered. "We have to talk."

"Those are ominous words," said Tonya. "What's the matter?"

She pushed open the front door and stepped into the twilight. Now that the sun had set, the temperature had dropped. Holly hadn't thought to grab her jacket from the car, and now she shivered with the cold. "As of next week, Saplings will have new owners." The words caught in her throat and came out as a croak.

"What? Are you kidding? This isn't funny."

"I wish it was a joke," said Holly, her eyes burning. "The bank is calling in the loan and selling the day-care center to a big chain of schools out of Dallas. Don't worry, though—they're keeping most everyone, so your job is safe."

"What do you mean by *most everyone*?"

"Everyone. Except me."

Tonya sucked in a breath. "Holly, I'm so sorry."

She didn't want her friend's sympathy—especially since Holly blamed herself. She continued walking to-

ward her car. A set of headlights cut through the gloom
and a silver sedan pulled into the space next to Holly's.
"I owe twenty thousand dollars to the bank."

Tonya continued, "You could talk to the bank, and
I don't know…renegotiate the loan."

"I tried that, but the manager won't work with me."
Holly paused, not wanting to admit that it was her fault.
Yet, she wouldn't lie—even if it was by skipping over
the truth. "I was more than half an hour late to a meeting."

"Can I ask you a question?" Tonya didn't wait for an
answer. "Why were you over thirty minutes late in the
first place? It's not like you."

"It wasn't my fault," Holly said, frustration boiling
into her tone. She arrived at her car and sat on the hood.
"I was with the new student."

"Sophie Alexander?"

"Her father was half an hour late. No apologies. No
call to give me a warning, much less asking if being
thirty minutes late was a problem. Nothing. What a
jerk."

Holly heard a slight cough coming from behind her.
She turned, casting a glance at the silver car. Yet, it
wasn't the auto that caught her attention. There, sitting
behind the steering wheel, was the topic of her conversation. Liam Alexander.

Holly's words stuck with Liam.
Your daughter was worried.
You aren't the only one with responsibilities.
She'd been right. So, when he asked his daughter
what she wanted for dinner—and she'd replied with

the expected answer of chicken nuggets—he knew just where to go.

Sally's on Main.

He pulled into a parking place near the restaurant and glanced out the window. There, standing next to her own car, was Holly Jacobs with a phone pressed to her ear.

From where he sat, it was impossible to miss her conversation—along with her long list of woes.

No new financing.

Twenty-thousand dollars owed.

School sold to another buyer.

Late because of the new student. Because of *him*.

What a jerk.

Yeah. Damn it, he was. And worse.

Holly glanced over her shoulder. Her eyes met his. "I've got to go," she said to the person on the other end of the call. She lowered the phone, her gaze still holding with his. Liam stepped from the car, unwilling to back down from the challenge.

"Daddy," Sophie called from her car seat. "Is that Dr. Holly?"

Holly glanced in the car's rear window. She smiled and waved. "Hi, Sophie."

With a clap, Sophie chanted. "Dr. Holly. Dr. Holly. Dr. Holly."

"We're stopping for some dinner," he said, feeling as though he owed Holly some explanation.

"Have you eaten at Sally's before?"

"Years ago," he said.

"The food's still really good. You have to try the pie."

She bent down to look in the window. With a wave at Sophie, she said, "I'll see you soon, kiddo."

I'll see you soon? If Saplings was closing, would Holly be so nonchalant about school? Perhaps Liam misheard Holly's conversation, or at least misunderstood what had happened.

"I'm sorry…for being late today."

Holly sighed and shrugged. "It happens more often than you'd think. Don't worry about it. Really."

Liam had said he was sorry. Holly had accepted and told him not to worry. He'd set a good example for his daughter. Was that it? He looked down at Sophie. She stared back, and her big brown eyes held a look. Then he knew. In his daughter's face, he'd seen expectation. She expected him to say more, to do more, to be more.

Or maybe, Liam needed to be more for himself.

The life he had lived—responsible only for his day, for himself—was over. He had to accept that. At RMJ, he was part of a team. At home, he was all Sophie had.

He sucked in a lungful of air. "I didn't mean to eavesdrop, but I overheard you on the phone."

Holly's gaze dropped to the ground and she worked her teeth over her bottom lip. Maybe he shouldn't have been so forthright. Then again, the damage was done, and he forged ahead.

He continued, "Anyway, I heard you talking to your friend and about what had happened with the bank's manager." His gut clenched. "You missing that meeting is on me."

She shrugged.

"Is it true? Is the school closing?"

"Saplings will be under new management—people

with a little more business acumen than me." Holly gave a mirthless laugh. "You won't have to worry about it affecting your daughter's care, though. I'm told the other company plans to take over right away. The transition should be seamless."

"I wasn't asking because of Sophie, although that's reassuring to hear. I'm worried about you." He inhaled. "What can I do to make it right?"

"Unless you have twenty thousand dollars you want to give me, then not much."

Liam shook his head. "I can't help you with any cash, but I wish I could."

"Truly, thanks. It takes a lot of courage to apologize." Bending down to Sophie's level, she said, "I bet you already knew that your daddy was super brave."

"I did," she said, nodding her head.

After unbuckling Sophie from the car seat, Liam balanced his daughter on his hip.

"Will I see you tomorrow when I drop off Sophie?"

Holly shook her head. "I'll be around, but busy with tying up some loose ends. So… I won't be in the class." She swallowed.

"Then I guess this is goodbye," said Liam.

"Yeah," said Holly. "I guess it is."

For some reason, he viewed Holly's loss personally. Was it because she was the only person he knew in Pleasant Pines, beyond his coworkers? Or was it something more, something he had yet to name? In the end, he decided that it didn't matter. "Have you eaten yet?"

"Dinner? No, I was here to meet with the banker…" Her words trailed off and Liam's jaw tightened. The meeting hadn't gone well.

"Why don't you join us?" he said. "I really can't make up for what happened, but I can buy you a meal."

Holly began to shake her head. Her lips parted, ready to refuse. Liam spoke again, before she could say anything. "I heard that the food's good," he said, repeating her earlier sentiments. "Especially the pie."

She laughed. The sound lodged in his chest.

"I don't know," she began.

"Dr. Holly, please," said Sophie. "You have to have dinner with us. Please. Please. Please."

Holly gave him a wry smile. "How can I refuse you both?"

Sure, Liam had invited Holly out to dinner just to be polite. Why did excitement, like an electric charge, course through his veins? Was it just because he'd now be spending more time with Holly?

Chapter 7

Holly walked through the front door of Sally's on Main with Liam and Sophie right behind her. The owner—Sally herself, a cheerful middle-aged woman—stood behind the counter and smiled as they entered. "There's my girl, Holly. Welcome," she said. "There's a booth in the back, unless you want to start waiting tables again."

Sally turned to a patron who sat at the counter. "Holly waited tables for me every summer. Started after her senior year of high school and stayed all the way through college. Best waitress ever."

"Thanks, Sal," said Holly, hoping that the offer for a job was only a joke—and not something she'd need to do in order to make ends meet.

The empty table was the same place where Holly had just received her life-altering news from Thomas.

She took a minute to mull over the idea that the space was somehow cursed. Yet being there with Liam and Sophie didn't seem so bad. After sliding into the seat, Holly handed Liam a menu from the metal stand at the end of the table.

"What do you think you're going to get for dinner?" asked Holly.

The child answered, "Chicken nuggets. Chicken nuggets. Chicken nuggets."

"Sounds to me like that's your favorite food," said Holly.

Liam grunted in agreement. "She'd eat them morning, noon and night if I let her."

"It's pretty typical for kids to have a strong preference for one food or another—oftentimes they're very brand loyal, too. It's good that you're offering her other choices. It'll help Sophie develop tastes for different foods."

"I'm glad to hear that I've done something right," he said.

A waitress stopped by the table. After delivering a coloring sheet and box of crayons to Sophie, she took everyone's order. Chicken nuggets and apple sauce for Sophie. A Reuben sandwich and side salad for Liam. As it turned out, Holly was hungrier than she originally thought. She ordered a burger and fries.

Yet Liam's words stayed with her. It seemed like he viewed himself as a bad parent. She could just let it go, but what if her reprimand at the school had played into his belief.

"Are you upset about what I said earlier when you picked up Sophie? Really, you aren't the only parent to show up late. People have issues at work all the time. It happens. Don't be so hard on yourself. It doesn't mean you don't love your child."

Liam picked up a packet of sugar and flipped it end over end. "I'm never happy when I screw up," he said. "Never. But it's more than today. It's just…" He shook his head.

Holly had gotten another glimpse of the man behind the wall. She sensed that he was about to retreat—possibly by saying something brusque. What was best? Wait for him to say something? Or charge ahead?

"I'm just used to working alone," he said. "Being alone."

"Sophie told me that she used to live with her mom, who is in the navy."

"Oh, Sophie told you that? Did she?" He tickled his daughter's side.

"Dad-dee…" she said through her giggles.

"What else did you tell Dr. Holly?"

"I love playing Candy Land. Which we was going to play, but you showed up."

"See," said Holly. "Sophie's fine."

Liam tapped the sugar packet on the table and looked up. He trapped Holly with his gaze. "Are you?" he asked, his voice deep and dark.

Her pulse began to race, as it did when she saw him for the first time. It was as if just being near Liam reminded Holly of what it meant to be a woman. God knew it had been a long time since she'd let anything—or anyone—make her feel that way. "I'm fine," she said.

"I know this is forward of me to say, but I don't believe you."

He was right. Holly was agitated. Yet it had as much to do with Liam sitting across from her as it did her business problems.

She was saved from saying something more—something she might regret—by the appearance of the waitress.

"Here ya'll go," she said, setting plates in front of each person. "Chicken nuggets for the princess. A Reuben for Daddy. A burger for Mommy."

"I'm not…" Holly began, ready to tell the server that she wasn't Sophie's mother.

Liam spoke up, his words stopping Holly. "Everything looks great. Thanks."

"Why'd you do that?" she asked. "The server thinks I'm Sophie's mom now."

Liam was cutting Sophie's chicken nuggets in half, blowing on the steam. He shrugged. "It just seemed easier to let her make the assumption than correct her."

Holly picked up a fry and took a bite. It made sense, but all the same, it left her unnerved. Was it because Liam hadn't been bothered by the server's mistake? Or was it that in letting someone else believe that Holly was part of a family, they'd held up a mirror and shown Holly her longest-held dream?

Liam picked up his sandwich and took a bite. It was meaty and salty, with crisply toasted bread—exactly the way a Reuben should be prepared.

Before he could take a second bite, his cell phone began to ring. He glanced at the caller ID.

Marcus Jones.

His stomach roiled. Was this a call about Julia? And if it were, was the news good or bad?

Wiping his mouth with a paper napkin, Liam swiped to pick up the call. "Hello."

Marcus said, "I hope I'm not interrupting. We have some news from the White Wind resort and need to strategize about what to do next."

"Sure," said Liam. "I'll be in first thing tomorrow."

"We actually need you here now."

"I just sat down to dinner with my kid," Liam began.

"This is an imposition, I understand. But the search for a killer doesn't exactly happen during business hours."

Liam smothered the need to curse.

Across the table, Holly held a crayon and wrote on the back of Sophie's coloring sheet. She slid the paper across the table. There were five words written.

She can stay with me.

Liam shook his head, while Marcus continued to talk. The FBI and state police have questioned everyone at the White Wind. Nobody admitted to receiving a call from Darcy Owens.

Then again, Liam wondered, who would?

Holly pointed at the page again.

She can stay with me.

On some level, Liam had understood that his job at RMJ would come with inconsistent and long hours. He also knew that in order to be successful, he was going to have to build a community of trusted caregivers to help with Sophie. It was just that he never imagined needing someone on his first day.

Using another crayon, Liam scribbled a note of his own. *You sure?*

Holly nodded.

Then to Marcus, he said, "I'll be there in five minutes," and ended the call.

While writing down her address, Holly said, "Sophie will be just fine. You don't have to worry about a thing."

"Is that okay with you, Sophie? Would you like to spend some extra time with Dr. Holly?"

Sophie whispered, "Do you think we can play Candy Land?"

It was Holly who whispered back, "I'd love to play Candy Land. I even have the game at my house."

Sophie smiled and ate a nugget. "I can be with Dr. Holly okay."

"Thanks," said Liam. "What do I owe you?"

"Late-night care will run you one burger and fries," she said, teasing.

Liam left enough money on the table to cover the meal and a generous tip.

"I'll have them wrap up your sandwich and bring it home with me," she said.

"You think of everything," said Liam. "What about Sophie's car seat?"

Holly used her key fob and unlocked her car's doors from her seat in the restaurant. "You can set it up in my car."

Standing, he placed a kiss on the top of Sophie's head. "You be good for Dr. Holly. Okay?"

"Okay."

"Holly, you're a lifesaver. Really."

"Hey, what're friends for. Right?"

Was Holly his friend? Honestly, he liked the possibility. Liam strode down the street and used his key fob to unlock his car door. After moving Sophie's car seat, he slipped behind the steering wheel of his own car and glanced back at the restaurant. Holly and Sophie were visible through the window. Holly held up a french fry, offering it to Sophie. With a laugh, the child accepted.

Liam couldn't help but smile. As he drove away, he felt something that he hadn't in many years. Hope.

It took Liam only minutes to drive to the building where RMJ was housed. He was let in by Wyatt, who said, "Martinez stayed at the hospital with Julia. She's out of surgery and in recovery," by way of greeting. "And Katarina is working on some new tech."

"Marcus said there's some news from the White Wind?" Liam asked, bringing up the bit of information that couldn't wait.

Wyatt's face was scanned, and the conference room lock disengaged with a click.

Marcus sat at the head of the table and looked up as Liam crossed the threshold. "We have an ID on the body you found in the glade."

"How'd you get that so quickly? I mean, considering the damage."

"It wasn't easy," said Marcus. "But his dental records were on file, and the CSI team managed to grab prints from surfaces in the bunker. He was William 'Billy' Dawson, wanted for tax evasion by the federal government, Idaho, Wyoming and Montana. The FBI thinks he's been holed up in that bunker for years."

"And he knew Darcy Owens from where?"

"There's absolutely nothing from Darcy's past that connects the two," Wyatt said. "Best guess is that Billy Dawson was out hunting or fishing and found Darcy, who was wounded. He brought her to his bunker and she repaid his kindness by whacking off his head."

Marcus picked up the story where Wyatt left off. "The phone was purchased at a gas station in Bozeman five years ago along with one thousand minutes. Dawson's last known residence was in Bozeman. His prints were also all over the device, along with being on a solar charger found at the scene."

"So, it's Billy's phone. Does that mean he's the one who called the White Wind resort?"

Marcus shook his head. "Couldn't have. The CSI team reckons that Billy died sometime last night. And the Feds were able to determine that the phone was used this morning."

"It means that Darcy called the White Wind," said Liam, filling in the ending to the story. "Who does she know at the resort?"

"That's just it," said Marcus, "the local police questioned everyone—staff and guests both. Several people claim to know Darcy personally—from years ago, though. She was a local girl, after all. That, or they know someone from her family. Or they remember when her father died."

"So, who'd she talk to?"

Wyatt said, "Nobody knows anything about the call, or so they claim."

"And you don't believe that?" asked Liam, already knowing the answer, but not exactly what it meant.

"Not for a minute," said Marcus.

"Which means what?" asked Liam. "That the police didn't do a thorough job?"

"More likely, someone's a good liar. She spoke to someone at that resort for four minutes, but we don't know who—or why."

Liam asked, "Is she at the resort now? Has it been searched?"

"The police did a thorough search—used K-9 units and everything." With a shake of his head, Wyatt continued, "I doubt she's there. It's too public. It's not safe for her."

More than once, Liam had been called upon to find a criminal who tried to escape justice by hiding in the woods or out in the desert. There was always a clue—something in their past that led to their present.

Just like Liam ending up in Wyoming, the place where his family had lived for generations. The path for his life had circled back around.

But would it be true for Darcy Owens?

Liam's pulse raced. Admittedly, he was intrigued by finding a notorious killer. He wanted to be the one to bring Darcy to justice for what she'd done to Julia McCloud. Who, if she survived the surgeries, might never be able to work active duty again.

His mind wandered to Sophie and Holly. He knew that his daughter was safe and happy with her new teacher. Moreover, he wished like hell that he could make up for ruining Holly's meeting with the bank's manager.

But what could he do, really?

He opened his phone's internet browser and entered

Holly's name. There were thousands of hits about her and the book she had written.

Then it was there. The scent on the breeze. The broken branch that led to the trail. It was a clue worth following.

"I think I have something," said Liam.

"What is it?" asked Marcus.

Liam placed his phone on the conference table, a book's cover filling the screen.

"*Childhood Trauma*," said Wyatt, reading the title aloud. He finished with the tagline. "'The moments that define us all, by Dr. Holly Jacobs, PhD.'" He looked around at the group. "I remember when this book came out, but what does it have to do with finding Darcy Owens?"

"Don't we have to know all there is to know about Darcy, including her childhood?" Liam asked. Maybe he should have taken the time to read Holly's book.

"Absolutely," said Wyatt. "But—"

Liam interrupted him. "It'd be good to talk to the author. Maybe let her look over the case file and have her consult." Liam's pulse had started to race. He'd followed trails his entire life and knew when he'd found the right track. "You might have to pay her, but it'd be worth it to get her professional opinion."

"That'd be helpful, sure," said Wyatt. "If we can find her."

"That's what I hoped you'd say," said Liam. "She happens to be Sophie's preschool teacher."

"Really?" asked Marcus. "Where?"

"She owns a day care right here." He inhaled. "In Pleasant Pines."

* * *

Holly sat on her sofa with her legs tucked beneath a blanket. She'd changed from her work attire into a pair of black leggings and a white sweater. The days were sunny and getting warmer, but once the sun set in Pleasant Pines, a chill filled the air.

In Sophie's bag, Holly had found several stuffed animals, along with a fuzzy pink blanket. The child lay on the floor, surrounded by her toys and covered with her favorite blanket. Through half-opened eyes, she gazed at a board book. Holly had set her music app to a lullaby channel and *Für Elise* played softly in the background.

Holly's phone sat on the coffee table. The screen illuminated at the same moment that it began to vibrate. A surge of excitement shot to her toes.

Was it Liam?

Holly checked the caller ID.

It was her literary agent, Franklin. "Hey," she said, swiping the call open. "It's nice to speak to you twice in one day."

"Something interesting happened this afternoon, Holly. I received a job offer for you."

"A job offer?" she repeated, hardly believing what he'd said.

"The University of Findlay is looking for a full-time faculty member to fill in for the rest of the semester. I mentioned your name to the department chairperson, and she was very excited. If hired, you'd be teaching developmental psychology—your specialty."

Back when the book was selling thousands of copies a week, the offers to teach at colleges and universities had been plentiful. But when the sales stopped, so had the offers.

"I'll be honest, I'm a little dubious that a school just so happened to call you on the day you learned I need a new job."

"Can't an agent do a favor for one of his clients?"

"I've never even heard of the University of Findlay. Where is it?" Then again, did it really matter? After Friday, she was out of a job.

"Findlay is in Ohio, about forty miles from Toledo, and it happens to be my alma mater."

"When would they need someone to start?" she asked.

"By the end of the month," he said. That would give her several weeks. "The current professor has a heart condition and needs surgery. At the end of the year, he's going to retire. Can I tell my contact that you're interested in an interview, at least?"

Holly had lived in New York City for several months after getting her doctorate. Yet Wyoming was her home. She owed the town of Pleasant Pines everything and she didn't want to relocate. Then again, did she have a choice?

"Sure, I'll talk to the people at the University of Findlay."

"I'll give Louise—she's the chairperson of the psychology department and my cousin's wife—your number. She said there are other candidates but seemed excited about having the opportunity to talk to you. I'm sure she'll call you tomorrow—day after at the latest."

"Thank you, Franklin. Sincerely."

"You want to thank me? Write another book."

Holly couldn't help but laugh at his urging. The sound of a car pulling into her drive was unmistakable. Sophie's eyes were now wide open.

"Is that Daddy?"

To Franklin, Holly said, "Listen, I have to go. Someone just stopped by. And thanks again."

She ended the call at the same moment that her front doorbell chimed. Holly peeked out the window. There, bathed in the glow of the porch light, stood Liam. A dark shadow of beard covered his cheeks and chin. His shoulders were broad, and his legs were long and muscular. While studying him from a distance, Holly realized that Liam was more than handsome. He was her idea of a perfectly formed male.

Sophie clambered up onto the sofa next to Holly and peered out the window.

"It is Daddy!"

"Should we go let him in?"

The child ran to the entryway. The minute Holly opened the door, Sophie launched herself into her father's arms.

"Baby girl," he said, catching his daughter and lifting her high. "Did you have fun with Dr. Holly?"

"We had the best time. I introduced her to all my animals and then we played Candy Land. And she read me books and let me look at this one myself." Sophie held up a small, square book with a fuzzy rabbit on the cover.

"Wow. You did have the best time. Why don't you go and get your toys? We need to get home and Dr. Holly needs to rest."

Sophie ran into the living room and Holly stepped aside. "Would you like to come in?"

He gave a quick shake of his head and Holly couldn't help it. A pang of disappointment caught her in the chest.

Liam said, "It's been a long day for Sophie, so I'm going to take her home now. But can I ask you a question? Do you ever work with outside agencies? You know, consult on cases?"

"What do you mean by 'outside agencies'?"

"The police, maybe. To help them understand how trauma might turn someone into a criminal."

A flush crept up Holly's cheeks. In all honesty, she was flattered. Then again, most new parents studied her school's website. Liam's curiosity had more to do with her professional life and nothing to do with his interest in her personally. "Have you been checking up on me?"

His lips twitched into a smile. "I might have done an internet search. I found your book."

"To answer your question, sure. I've worked with law enforcement on occasion. But honestly, all of that was years ago. Almost another lifetime."

"I got my stuff," said Sophie. She approached, her arms full of animals and her blanket.

"Then we better get going."

"Tell Dr. Holly good-night."

"G'night, Dr. Holly. I love you."

Holly's heart filled until she thought it might burst. "Good night, Sophie. Be good for your daddy." And then she remembered. "Hold on one sec. Liam, I have your food."

Holly had stowed Liam's uneaten meal in her fridge. She grabbed the container and brought it to the door. He reached out and their hands touched.

Holly's skin warmed. It was more than the brief contact with Liam—who was wholly male and virile. It was that being around him reminded Holly that she was also a woman who had too long neglected many of her needs.

Chapter 8

Marcus Jones stood in the middle of the situation room. Pictures of Darcy Owens were tacked to the wall. He stared at each photo, his vision blurring until he saw only dots. It was early Tuesday morning. He hadn't slept since yesterday, when Darcy Owens was spotted in the woods. With a curse, he rubbed his dry and tired eyes. "Where are you?" he muttered to himself, not for the first time.

The serial killer was out there, somewhere. Rocky Mountain Justice had failed to catch her a second time. Hell, he was the team's leader, so the failure was personal.

Without the help of Billy Dawson, Darcy could have succumbed to her wounds, the elements or both. Had she? Marcus would be foolish to think that it wasn't a possibility. And Marcus was never a fool.

Still, he had a feeling—a tickling at the base of his spine—that the serial killer was out there, somewhere. That meant something even worse. That Rocky Mountain Justice had failed. Hell, he was the team's leader, so the failure was personal.

"Hey, boss?" a voice came from just outside the door.

Marcus turned to see Wyatt standing in the doorway. Holding a tablet computer, the other man said, "I think that Liam is onto something with the local psychologist. I read her book last night. She has some interesting theories."

"Interesting enough that we should talk to her?"

"I have her work address," said Wyatt.

"What are we waiting for?" Marcus asked. "Let's speak to Dr. Jacobs and see what kind of help she can give."

The drive to Dr. Jacobs's place of work took only minutes, and soon they pulled into the parking lot of Saplings. "To be honest," said Marcus as he put the SUV into Park and turned off the ignition, "I didn't expect to find such a noted expert at a small-town preschool."

"From what I gathered from my research, Dr. Jacobs used all the money she made from her book and opened this school. Local girl made her fortune and returned home—you know the story."

After pocketing the keys, Marcus opened the door and stepped into the morning sun. He exhaled, his breath visible in the early chill. "I hope she can bring something to this search. Because if the new guy, Liam, can't deliver, we're out of options."

It took only a moment for Wyatt and Marcus to get an appointment with Holly Jacobs. She met with them in a spare classroom, where all the furniture was too small. Tiny tables. Tiny chairs. Tiny sink. Tiny squares of carpeting. Leaning against the wall, Marcus felt like a giant.

"Thanks for taking time with us," said Wyatt. "We're with Rocky Mountain Justice. It's a private security agency. We're working with the district attorney's office on the Darcy Owens case."

"Darcy Owens?" Holly repeated. "Isn't she that serial killer?"

"Yes," said Marcus, glancing at Wyatt. "She's still at large, but we have intel that she was abused as a child. We know that your expertise is on childhood trauma, and we're hoping that you can give us some insight into our suspect. How she might act or react to being on the run. Anything that might help us in our search."

"To be fair," said Holly, "I don't know much about the case, beyond what I've seen in the media. One thing I found in my research is that those who suffer trauma often return to the place where they were most vulnerable—a way to undo the past."

"That doesn't make sense," said Marcus. "Wouldn't they want to avoid the place where something bad happened to them?"

"Simply put, trauma is an emotional response to a stressful situation. That means we all experience trauma because it's part of being human," said Holly. She sat on a small table and looked up at Marcus. "But what happens if the trauma is severe, prolonged and begins at an early age?"

"It can lead to a schism within the self," said Wyatt.

"Exactly," said Holly. "Basically, a person who is exposed to trauma again and again can lose a piece of themselves and/or their humanity. It's worse with kids, who don't yet have a definite sense of self. It's why abused children end up with abusive partners—that or they become abusers themselves. They're drawn to the familiarity of the situation, despite the fact that—on some level—they know it's unhealthy. But my theory, and the premise of my book, is that people engage in the unhealthy or even dangerous relationships because they're trying to undo the past."

Marcus nodded. It was an interesting theory. It also gave him a notion of his own. "So, she might go to the place that she began killing."

Holly said, "If she has a strong bond to the area, then perhaps." She handed him a business card. "My cell phone number is on the back. Call if you have any more questions."

"What do we owe you for your time?" he asked.

Holly shook her head. "Nothing. I'm not going to charge you for answering a few questions."

"Thanks. Much appreciated." Marcus tucked the card into his back pocket and strode quickly from the building and through the parking lot. "Las Vegas," he said to Wyatt as they walked. "My money is on Darcy trying to get back to Vegas."

"How do you figure that?"

"You heard what Holly said. Our killer will try to regain a part of herself. She committed her first string of murders in Las Vegas. Ergo, that's where she'll head."

Wyatt asked, "What's our next play?"

"As soon as Katarina gets into the office, I'll ask her to hack into the camera system run by LVPD. Every person we get can be run through facial recognition. Who knows, maybe we'll get lucky."

"I have a few problems with your theory about Vegas," said Wyatt.

"Which are?" Marcus asked.

"First, Las Vegas is a long way from Wyoming. She ditched RMJ's vehicle at a truck stop, so to get to Nevada, she's going to need a ride. And she doesn't have any other known accomplices."

"Key word," said Marcus. "*Known*. What about the call to the White Wind? Couldn't that person have picked her up? Given her a ride somewhere or provided her with another car? Besides," Marcus continued, while fishing the SUV keys from his pocket, "you said that Darcy was devious and intelligent. I'd say she could figure out how to get anywhere she wanted to go."

He used the remote to unlock the doors. As he slid behind the steering wheel and started the engine, Marcus's gut burned with the indignation of failure. Putting the car into gear, he dropped his foot on the gas. Tires squealed as the acrid scent of burnt rubber wafted through the air. The big vehicle lunged forward.

"You okay?" Wyatt asked.

"Not really. I still can't believe that we let her get away."

"Come on, Marcus. She's eluded capture for years. The fact that she remains at large isn't a reflection on you or your abilities, or this agency."

Funny, thought Marcus, as he pulled onto the road that led back to the RMJ building. Darcy Owens escaping seemed pretty damn personal to him—as was the need to bring her to justice.

Liam spent the morning doing the one thing he hated most in the world—busywork. Katarina had given him a passcode for all the doors at RMJ. He'd also been given his own office—a repurposed bedroom on the second floor. Now he sat—without moving—while his face was scanned for the facial recognition software. The IT hub, a room full of monitors, was also on the second floor. Along the back wall, a server hummed quietly.

"There isn't a more secure building in the state," Katarina said proudly as she tapped on a keyboard. Liam's face appeared on a large monitor. "Government or privately owned."

"So, what's next on the agenda?" Liam asked. His expertise was in the natural world, not in the world of technology.

"We're waiting for a final verdict on the White Wind resort."

"I thought they decided that Darcy wasn't at the resort and nobody said that they'd spoken to her."

"Both are true," said Katarina. "But she called the main number and, from there, spoke to someone. It means that whoever she called is lying to protect her."

"Or to protect themselves."

"Either way," said Katarina, turning to tap on another keyboard. "She might call them again. By the way, the scan's done. You can move now."

Liam stood and stretched. He'd dropped Sophie off at school that morning, all the while hoping to see Holly Jacobs again. A new teacher had taken over her class and he wondered what both his daughter and Holly were doing.

He also wondered if he'd ever have the chance to see Holly again. There was something about her—an honesty, maybe—that made him feel drawn to her. Never mind that she was beautiful.

A phone sat in the middle of the keyboards and wires. It rang shrilly, drawing Liam back to the here and now.

Katarina looked at the caller ID. "It's the DA, Chloe Ryder." Activating the speaker function as she answered the call, she said, "This is Katarina."

"Katarina, it's Chloe."

"I have our new hire, Liam Alexander, on the line with me."

"Nice to meet you," said the woman named Chloe. "At least on the phone."

Liam leaned toward the phone. "Same," he said.

"I just got a call from the FBI agent in charge of the Darcy Owens case. They've decided that there's no connection between her and the resort. More than that, there's been a credible sighting in Reno."

"And since she used to live in Vegas," said Katarina, "the resources are going to that search."

"Exactly," said Chloe.

"How do they explain the four-minute call?" Liam asked.

"Easy," said Chloe. "The call went to the main number. While it could have been transferred anywhere in the hotel, there's really no way to find that out after the fact."

Chloe continued, "More than that, the phone system is set to allow a customer to be on hold for only three minutes and thirty seconds before being sent back to the front desk."

"Let me get this straight," said Liam. He tried to keep the incredulity from his voice, but he didn't do a good job. "The theory is that Darcy called the resort but then got put on hold?"

"There'd be more interest in the resort if she hadn't been spotted in Nevada, that's for sure," said the DA. "Obviously, Reno is not part of my jurisdiction. The FBI said we were free to keep our investigation open in Wyoming, so long as we share any leads."

"You're the boss, Chloe," said Katarina. "What are your thoughts?"

The line was filled with silence and Liam wondered if the DA had hung up—or maybe the call had been dropped. After a moment, Chloe Ryder said, "Someone at that resort spoke to Darcy Owens. I'd bet my career on it. We need to find out who that person is and what Darcy wanted."

It was late afternoon and Liam had returned to the conference room for yet another meeting.

Marcus sat at the head of the conference table with Wyatt on his right. Liam sat next to Katarina and opposite Wyatt. Luis Martinez was still in Cheyenne, keeping watch over Julia's recovery. The medical reports weren't promising.

Shifting in his seat, Marcus announced the new objectives of this mission. "I spoke to Chloe Ryder after she called the office. The Pleasant Pines DA wants to continue our contract. We need to find out what connection Darcy Owens has to that resort."

"I've examined their computer system," said Katarina.

A flat keyboard lay in front of her. She tapped on the keys. A screen that had been hidden in the ceiling lowered silently. It filled with an image of the resort—probably taken from a promotional shot. A large hotel sat on an expanse of green. The Rocky Mountains, capped with white, were in the distance.

The vision left his pulse racing.

"This is the resort," said Katarina before changing the image on the screen to a blueprint of the facility. A red dot pulsed in a back corner. "And this is where the surveillance equipment, along with an on-site server, is housed. It's lucky for us that they have their own server."

"It's probably because the rural internet is so spotty," said Liam. Sure, he really didn't care for technology. Yet he'd come to appreciate a strong cellular signal.

"You're right," said Katarina. "And what's more, it works to our advantage."

Works to our advantage? "For what?"

It was Marcus who spoke. "We need to tap the phone system and the security cameras. That will give us access to every call that comes into the White Wind. If Darcy calls again, we'll be ready. This time, we'll be listening."

Liam shifted in his seat. True, he didn't see himself as a team player, but at least he followed the rules. "Is this legal?"

Marcus lifted his hand, measuring out a small space between forefinger and thumb. "It's close to legal."

It was then that it hit him. Marcus Jones reminded

Liam of his cousin, Charlie. A tendril of guilt uncoiled in his chest and Liam couldn't breathe.

Hadn't Charlie been overly sure of himself? Arrogant, even?

The memory of the last time he saw his cousin came from so many years ago, it should've been nothing more than a murky shadow. Yet the recollection was sharp and stark.

Liam forced air into his lungs, certain that his chest would burst. He exhaled long and slow, shoving the past aside. "Is this assignment about justice or making sure that RMJ solves the case?"

Marcus paused. "What does it matter if we find Darcy Owens?"

"It matters if judgment is tainted by ego."

"There are no egos involved in this search," said Marcus.

"No offense," said Liam, "but I don't believe you. The way I see it, RMJ has lost the chance of catching Darcy Owens twice. If one of your operatives brings her in, then the other failures will be forgotten. If not, it becomes a defining and negative moment for the agency."

Marcus seemed to mull that over, then said, "You aren't completely wrong, but you aren't completely right, either. Darcy is dangerous, and she needs to be stopped before she kills again. Sure, she's become RMJ's problem, but I always make sure we fix everything we've broken." He hesitated. "And there's the fact that she attacked Julia and left her for dead. If wanting to go after Darcy Owens makes me a vengeful egomaniac to you, tough. But RMJ takes care of their own. Always."

"I assume you have a plan," said Liam.

Wyatt spoke. "We need to get someone inside the resort. It has to be someone that Darcy has never seen—on the off chance that she visits her contact personally." Picking up a cell phone, he held it out to Liam. "This has special facial recognition software. You need to take pictures of as many people as possible."

"*I* need to take the pictures? What are you saying?" he asked, although he already knew. "Am I supposed to be the undercover operative?"

"You might be the only person at RMJ who Darcy's never seen," said Marcus. "It has to be you."

"And how in the hell am I supposed to do this? My situation hasn't changed since yesterday," said Liam. "I still have a child to take care of."

"No offense, but that's not our problem," said Marcus. "You'll have to find a sitter."

"My girlfriend, Everly, might be able to help out," Wyatt offered.

Liam's pulse raced, hammering in the back of his skull. He inhaled. Exhaled. Reminded himself that parents everywhere needed additional childcare. In fact, didn't Saplings offer overnight care? "I think I can manage, but thanks," he said to Wyatt, thankful for the gesture.

"There's more," said Marcus.

"Why am I not surprised to hear you say that?"

"A single man arriving at the resort will look suspicious," said Katarina. "We need to provide you with a fake wife."

"You?" he asked, pointing.

"In your dreams," she said with a wink.

"We haven't found the right candidate," said Marcus. "Yet. But by the time you leave tomorrow morning, you'll have a new, pretend spouse."

"You know," said Liam, as the perfect person came to mind, "I think I know just who to call."

Holly's day could be described in one word. *Horrible*.

It began when she announced to the staff that ownership of the school was changing hands. She tried to tell herself that the sale was just business, even though she knew that wasn't true.

She'd left Tonya in charge of the late-day pickups. And at 5:00 p.m. she turned out of the parking lot and started the short drive toward Pleasant Pines, and from there, her home.

Her cell rang and a number appeared on her in-car phone system. She didn't recognize the caller but answered anyway.

"Hello?"

"Dr. Jacobs, I'm glad that I caught you," said a male voice she recognized but couldn't place. "This is Marcus Jones again. From RMJ. I was wondering if there's a time that you can meet with my team."

Holly drew her eyebrows together in confusion. She had already discussed the Darcy Owens case with Marcus Jones. Without more detailed information on the subject, she really didn't have anything else to add. More than that, she wasn't in the mood for another meeting. Turning a corner, Holly began to drive down Main Street. Streetlights illuminated the town square and the whitewashed gazebo. "I'm sorry," she said. "I'm not sure that I have anything else to add to the discussion we had earlier today."

"Actually, I need to hire someone on a temporary basis. I think that you're the perfect person for this job."

Temporary job? He definitely had Holly's attention. "Actually," she said, "I'm free now."

"Good," Marcus said. "Can you meet me at Sally's on Main?"

Holly glanced in her rearview mirror. The business district was nothing more than a glare of lights. Ahead of her was home, and safety, and a place to collect her thoughts. Then again, there was no reason to go home now. No children. No husband. Shoot, Holly didn't even have a cat.

She turned around in the middle of the deserted street. "I'll be there in five minutes."

Chapter 9

Holly pulled into a parking place next to Sally's on Main and looked up and down the street. It wasn't simply scanning her surroundings, she knew. Rather, she was looking for Liam Alexander or his silver sedan.

It wasn't there.

Holly walked up the street. Using her shoulder, she opened the restaurant door. Marcus Jones and his co-worker Wyatt Thornton sat at a booth in the back of the restaurant. There were no other patrons seated nearby.

Jones spotted her at the same time she saw him. He stood as she approached. "Thanks for meeting us on such short notice."

She slid into the booth, taking a seat next to Wyatt. Even if Holly could never get the money to pay off all her debts and keep the school open, she did need some kind of cash flow in order to survive. "You said you had a temporary job."

"First, what we're about to tell you is for you alone," said Marcus. "Is that clear?"

"I understand about the need for confidentiality," she said. "Trust me."

"We have reason to believe that Darcy Owens has a connection to the White Wind resort," said Wyatt, his voice low despite the fact that nobody was at any of the adjoining tables.

The news hit Holly like a shock of electricity. It was a sharp pain, followed by a racing pulse. "How could you know that?"

"It turns out that Darcy was hiding in the woods not far from here. We found her hiding place and discovered that she made a call to the resort. The call lasted four minutes. Everyone at the resort has been questioned, yet nobody admits to talking to her."

"I'd say someone is lying, but who? And why?"

"That's what we all want to know. And to find that out, we need someone inside the resort. We have to access the phone system and the security cameras, but because we don't know who we can—or can't—trust, our team has to go in undercover."

Holly had to admit she was intrigued by all the cloak-and-dagger business. Still, why was she sitting here? "How do I fit into your investigation? I'm no IT expert."

"You don't have to worry about any of that. Our operative is being trained in what to do right now. The operative is going to register at the resort as a guest and stay there for two nights. What he needs is someone to pose as his wife."

"His what?" Holly practically yelled, drawing glances from the few other patrons. She lowered her voice and leaned in close. "Look, guys, I really want to see Darcy Owens caught and brought to justice, but if you think I'm going to be a fake wife, then both of you are nuts. Trust me, I have the credentials to give that diagnosis." Reaching for her bag, she slid from the booth and stood. Turning, she stopped short. He was right there. Liam Alexander.

"Hey," he said.

Liam was close enough that she could smell the mint of his gum.

"Hey." Her heart pounded against her ribs.

"Sorry I'm late," said Liam. "Katarina was very patient in teaching me everything I'll need to know about the server."

Just then, Holly understood everything. Liam asking if she consulted with police on cases, followed by the arrival of Marcus and Wyatt. Liam's intake form at the school with private security listed as his occupation. The mention of his coworker who'd been injured and airlifted to the hospital. It all made sense now. "Did you suggest that I pose as your wife?"

"I did," he said. "Your background makes you an asset to this case. You might be able to figure out why someone would help a killer."

Suddenly, the plan didn't seem so bad to Holly.

"You'd get paid," said Liam.

Holly looked over her shoulder and met Marcus's gaze. "What's your rate?"

"Consultants get a thousand dollars a day. We'd need you from Wednesday until Friday."

Friday. The same day that her school would be sold to cover all her loans. "I'm not sure this is a good time for me…" she began.

"Twenty-thousand," said Liam.

"Twenty-thousand, what?" asked Marcus.

"Holly needs twenty-thousand dollars to go to the resort with me."

"You've got to be kidding me," said Marcus with a shake of his head. "No way. We'll find someone else."

"With her qualifications? By tomorrow morning?" Liam asked.

Marcus sighed. "I won't give you that kind of money unless you find a clear connection to Darcy Owens."

Liam asked, "If we don't?"

"Holly gets what she earned."

"Understood," said Liam. "Holly, what do you say? Will you help me?"

She paused. "I don't have anything to lose and everything to gain." And then she said, "What about Sophie? You can't bring her with you. Us."

"I already spoke to Tonya. She's going to pick up Sophie for school tomorrow morning. She'll bring her home at the end of the day and stay at the house both nights. That way Sophie's at least in her own home."

Holly smiled. Liam had told her that he was worried about his lack of parenting skills. From what she saw, he was already a really good dad.

"Now that's settled, let's get down to business," Marcus said. "Your reservation is for tomorrow morning. I need you there on time."

"Sure thing," said Liam. "Holly, I'll pick you up tomorrow morning."

"No way," said Holly. "If we're supposed to be prompt, I'll come and get you."

Just before eight on Wednesday morning, Holly pulled her car up to the curb next to Liam's house and turned off the engine. The lawn was tipped with white frost. Spring in Wyoming meant she should expect almost any conditions and today was no exception. According to her weather app, the morning would be cold, the day mild, and then rain showers in the evening.

For a two-night stay, Holly had packed enough for a week-long trip. She wrestled the suitcase, filled with everything from gloves and a winter coat to a bathing suit for the pool and sauna, from the back seat and crossed the lawn. With a sigh, she rang the doorbell and waited as far-off chimes echoed throughout the house.

"One minute…" Liam's voice came from somewhere inside. After a moment, he asked, "Holly? Is that you?"

Pressing her mouth to the door frame, she called back, "Everything okay?"

"Yeah, it's just… Come on in," Liam called. "I'm going to be a few minutes."

Holly pushed the door open and stepped into the house. The small entryway was hazy with smoke. A smoke detector blared somewhere close. A duffel bag sat next to a set of stairs. Holly stowed her bag with the other. "Liam? Sophie? Everything okay? It smells like something's burning."

"Come into the kitchen," he said. "I'm making breakfast."

Holly followed the sound of his voice through a darkened living room, full of moving boxes that had yet to be unpacked. The kitchen sat at the back of the house. Like all of the homes in the neighborhood, it had been built in the early 1900s. Most had been renovated at least once, and Liam's home was no exception. From the color scheme—avocado green and marigold yellow—she guessed that the last set of updates happened in the 1970s.

Sophie, clad in leggings and a sweater, sat at the table in a booster seat. Liam wore only flannel sleep pants and his dog tag necklace. Standing under a smoke detector, he was waving a dish towel. His pecs and abs were well-defined and covered with a dark sprinkling of hair. The hair narrowed to a trail that dove straight down the waist of his low-hanging pajama bottoms. Gesturing to a plate of blackened bread and dry scrambled eggs, Liam said, "Burned the toast and eggs."

For a moment, she was powerless to do anything beyond wonder what it would be like to kiss Liam Alexander. Collecting her thoughts, and her libido, Holly said, "I can see."

"I figured Sophie should have a full breakfast. He snorted. "Clearly I'm not used to day-to-day parenting."

"You'll get the hang of it," said Holly. "How long will Sophie's mom be gone?"

Liam said, "Erin won't be back for a whole year."

"Wow," said Holly. "You've all made a huge sacrifice."

"It is for Erin, of course." Liam tilted his head toward his daughter. "And for Sophie."

"But not for you?" she asked. The smoke detector stopped wailing and her voice was overly loud in the quiet room.

"Erin and I were never a couple. We dated for a little while, but we weren't really right for each other. Then she called me a few weeks after we stopped seeing each other. She was pregnant, and we agreed we wanted to work things out and figure out how to co-parent. Nine months later, Sophie was born." He smiled at his daughter, who was drinking from her PAW Patrol cup. "Don't get me wrong, Erin is an amazing woman. But we weren't meant to be, even if we did create a terrific little girl together."

Holly wasn't sure how to respond. As a teacher, she encountered lots of different families. More than once, she'd seen parents stay together for the sake of the children. In the end, everyone was miserable.

"Sophie is a great kid," she said. "I'm sure you're both fantastic parents."

"To be honest—" Liam reached for the dog tag that hung from a leather cord around his neck "—parenting full-time is a lot harder than I thought. Erin is an incredible mom. I have big shoes to fill."

Holly opened a window over the kitchen sink. The fresh morning air sucked out the stench of smoke. "It looks like you've got lots to take care of. Why don't you let me make some breakfast for you and Sophie?"

"I can't ask you to do that," said Liam, wiping his brow with the dish towel.

"You didn't ask. I offered. Go and get ready." Holly lifted the lid to the garbage can and threw out the burnt toast and dried eggs.

"Thanks," said Liam, sighing. "I guess I really could use the help."

"I'm happy to pitch in, really."

"Are you always this helpful?"

Wasn't that Holly's dilemma? After what happened in high school, she could never really be helpful enough. It was as if the accident were a stain on her soul, and service to others was the only way to cleanse herself. Yet, the car wreck had left an indelible mark, one that she could never wash away.

Seeming not to notice her changed mood, Liam placed a kiss on his daughter's head. "Be good for Holly."

"I will," said Sophie.

Waiting until Liam left the kitchen, Holly turned to the little girl. "Since your daddy made you scrambled eggs, I guess that's how you like them."

Sophie shook her head. "I like sunny eggs, but Daddy only knows how to make them scrambled."

"One egg," said Holly. "Sunny style."

As the egg cooked, Holly dropped a piece of bread into the toaster. Both egg and toast were done at the same time, then Holly put the meal in front of Sophie.

"How's that look?"

"Better than Daddy's," said Sophie.

Holly smothered a laugh. "I think he only needs a little practice and one day soon, he'll be great at everything. Even sunny eggs."

"I wish I had your confidence. I haven't even unpacked any of our stuff," said Liam. He stood in the doorway. His hair was damp and curled at the ends. He wore a pair of tight-fitting jeans and a flannel shirt in olive and black. He almost looked as good as he had in his pajama bottoms—almost, but not quite.

"How long have you been standing there?"

"Long enough to hear you say something nice about me."

"I wouldn't say it if it wasn't true," said Holly.

"What about the other night when you called me a jerk?"

"I never told you that you were a jerk."

"I overheard you on the phone with your friend, remember?"

"Well," she said. Her face and chest warmed. "That was true."

"Was true?" he asked. "Or is true?"

"That depends on how the rest of the day goes," said Holly, with a wink. "How do you like your eggs?"

"You don't have to make me breakfast. I can take care of myself."

Turning back to the stove, she said, "We need to get going, and if I cook, you can clean."

"Fair enough," said Liam. "Scrambled is fine."

Holly set about making the eggs as Liam loaded the dishwasher with dirty dishes and wiped down the counter.

"Here you go," she said. She set the plate at a seat next to Sophie's.

Liam slid into the chair and took a big bite. "Very good," he said.

"You know what my belly says to me, Daddy?" Sophie asked.

"What, baby girl?"

"It says that we should have Dr. Holly over for breakfast every morning."

* * *

Tonya arrived to take Sophie to school just as Liam and Holly were ready to leave. Liam's heart broke just a little as his daughter's bottom lip began to quiver and tears filled her eyes. She'd begged to come on the trip and promised to be good. In the end, Sophie had been mollified by Liam's promise to bring home a new stuffed animal.

For her part, Tonya had been told that Holly was helping Liam for a few days of work while consulting on a case. If she thought anything was amiss, she didn't comment.

Now, Liam drove while Holly sat in the passenger seat and stared out the window. The sun crept higher in the sky and bathed her in a rosy glow. Her lips looked coral pink in the gathering light. Gripping the steering wheel tighter, Liam forced his eyes back to the road.

Typically, Liam would have been fine with silence, allowing his mind to become a blank canvas. Today, his thoughts were a jumble of questions. He wondered what movie Holly liked best. Or how she prepared her coffee. If she'd ever had her heart broken, or broken the heart of another.

Basically, he wanted to know everything about Holly Jacobs.

"We have another thirty minutes to go," he said, glancing at the GPS. "Do you want to start with your life story? Or should I?"

Holly laughed, and Liam's chest grew warm from the sound. His foot dropped on the gas and the car surged forward, hugging the road as it followed the mountainous terrain.

"You go first," she said.

Her gaze flicked to the speedometer. Did he see a look of a concern in her eyes? He tapped on the brake, slowing the car to just below the speed limit.

Holly eased back in her seat and exhaled.

So, she didn't like to go fast. Liam couldn't help but wonder why. Yet he'd sat without speaking for too long and said, "Me? There's nothing interesting about me."

"Your job is to find a hack into a computer so you can find a serial killer's accomplice. That's hardly boring."

She had a point. He shrugged. "My job is pretty intense, I guess."

"How'd you start working for Rocky Mountain Justice?" Holly asked.

"I'm an expert in the field of mountain rescue. RMJ needed someone to find Darcy Owens and, not to brag, but I am the best at what I do. They called and offered. I need a job that keeps me in one place day-to-day, so I can take care of Sophie."

"Rocky Mountain Justice gives that to you?" She sounded somewhat skeptical.

"To be honest, I'm not sure that this is the best place for me. First, the hours aren't exactly constant. Second, they're very big on being a team."

"You aren't?"

His heartbeat took on a cadence. *Charlie. Charlie. Charlie.*

For a moment, he saw his cousin's, face. Liam pushed the memory away. He'd yet to answer Holly's question.

He needed to say something.

"The best part of being a kid and spending summers

in Wyoming was my older cousin, Charlie. We'd leave the house at dawn run around in the forest all day. It was in these woods that I learned to be quiet and listen to what nature had to say."

"And that makes you a bad team player?"

"It's…hard to explain myself, I guess." He was quiet for a moment. "It's just that…having other people around makes it hard to hear."

Liam glanced at Holly, trying a gauge her reaction to his confession. She looked out the window, nodding—as if what he had said made complete sense. It was the first time Liam felt as if someone understood him.

Yet, what would she think of him if she knew about Charlie?

"My family was some of the first settlers to this area. One grandpa back about a bazillion generations was a gunslinger. His son was a preacher."

Holly laughed. "I didn't take you for a Wyoming native."

"Me? I was born in sunny Southern California. But my grandfather's house was near where the White Wind resort was built."

"In taking the job at RMJ, you came back home," Holly said.

It wasn't exactly a question, but Liam answered, anyway. "My dad was in the navy and deployed a lot. My mom brought me and my sister to Wyoming every summer. We'd stay for two months. I guess I kind of grew up in both worlds." Instinctively, Liam reached for the cord around his neck.

"You sound close to your family," she said.

Liam shrugged. "I suppose."

"What about you?"

"My dad was the chemistry teacher at Pleasant Pines High School. My mom was a Realtor. They retired a few years ago and moved to Arizona, where there's no cold to bother my dad's arthritis. No other family."

"But you must've stayed in Pleasant Pines for a reason. I mean, what do you want from life?"

"You mean aside from keeping the school open?"

"Uh, yeah." His face stung as he realized that he had something to do with that. "You seeing anyone?" Liam gripped the steering wheel tighter. He really wanted to know, but hadn't meant to be so blunt in asking.

She smiled. "No. Not right now."

So, she was single. A plan was forming in the back of his mind.

The rest of the ride passed quickly, and soon Liam turned on to the long and winding drive that led to the White Wind. The chassis rumbled as Liam drove over the one-lane bridge that led to the property.

A castle of timber and stone stood on a rise. More than a compound of pricey log-cabin-chic rooms, the resort boasted an eighteen-hole golf course, a day spa and two Michelin-rated restaurants on-site.

This playground for the rich organized trips for big-game hunting in the fall, and backcountry skiing in the winter.

The developer had promised jobs and good money to those who sold their land. His grandparents had been paid well. Yet, without the land to connect them, the family scattered. Liam had lost touch with most everyone.

A bellman, dressed in a dark uniform with gold

braiding on his epaulets, approached the car. Liam lowered the driver's window as the bellman said, "Welcome to the White Wind. Will you be staying at the resort?"

"We have reservations for two nights," said Liam, giving the alias RMJ had used to book the room.

The bellman consulted a tablet. "Welcome. We can get your bags delivered to your suite and you can go inside to the registration desk. A valet will park your car."

"Nice service," said Liam under his breath.

Holly lifted her eyebrows. "And did I hear him say suite?"

"I guess if we have to work, this is the best place to do it."

"Agreed," said Holly as she got out of the car.

Liam slid out of the driver's seat and took a moment to scan his surroundings. Thick woods encircled the complex, which consisted of a stable and paddock, tennis courts and two heated pools—an outdoor one with three waterslides, and an indoor Olympic-size one as well.

Yet, Liam had to remember that he wasn't at the resort for rest or relaxation, but to find a connection to a serial killer. How many people did it take to run a property this large? A hundred? Two-hundred? Possibly more? And then there were all the guests.

The list of those who might've helped Darcy Owens was longer than Liam had imagined.

"Enjoy your stay," said the bellman as he handed Liam tickets for both the valet and their luggage.

"Thanks," said Liam, giving the man a generous tip.

Placing a protective hand on Holly's back, he walked toward the main building—the one with all the guest rooms. The front doors opened with their approach and they stepped into the spacious lobby. A water feature flowed behind the registration desk and a fireplace, large enough to fit a small car, filled the wall opposite. The floor was reclaimed pine and reflected the glow of more than a dozen brass chandeliers.

A security guard passed. Next to him was a man in a lab coat. Their heads were bent in conversation.

"You're sure that the damage to the cabinet is new?" the security guard asked.

"Of course I am," said the man in the lab coat, his tone peevish. Liam guessed he was the on-site physician. "More than the door to the medical cabinet door being bent, some of the instruments had been tampered with."

"There's no way to get into the infirmary without the master key," said the security guard. "Are you sure nothing's missing?"

"Nothing, but obviously someone broke into the infirmary and attempted to steal drugs." The physician was furious. "And I want to know who did it."

"We don't cover that part of the hallway with security cameras, in order to protect patient privacy, but I'll check video collected from other cameras and see if anything turns up."

Liam paused and watched them pass, his mind spinning.

Darcy had been gravely injured. Not just by Billy—she'd spent weeks in the woods with an open gunshot wound. If any of her injuries had gotten infected, it would certainly be tempting to steal some pain medication.

Had Liam been wrong? Was there still a trail to fol-low? All the same, he wasn't in his element. That meant that Liam had to be all the more vigilant as he tracked his prey.

Darcy looked up and down the hall. Just as she had hoped—empty. Armed with the master key issued to all members of the housekeeping staff, she swiped the card over the electronic lock. She waited for the green light to flash and the latch to click while it disengaged. Push-ing open the door, Darcy stepped into the room. Even though her shift had ended hours before, Darcy still wore her housekeeping uniform—black pants, along with a black-and-white smock adorned with maroon piping. A shiny gold name tag with her alias, Claire, completed her disguise.

This was the seventh room she'd entered in the past half hour, looking for medications. Beyond over-the-counter painkillers, she had nothing to show for her troubles. Even after having taken several pills, her shoulder still throbbed and a thin sheen of sweat cov-ered her brow.

The room was empty, just as she knew it would be. The guest, a man named Kevin Carpenter, had booked a full round of golf earlier in the morning. She didn't expect his return until later in the day. Still, nothing was gained by wasting time, so she crossed to the bath-room—the likeliest place to find any useful prescrip-tions.

Flipping on the overhead light, she shut the bathroom door. Her reflection filled the mirror. The changes to her appearance were stark and startling. Now, she had dark, short hair and wore heavy-rimmed glasses. There was also the fact that she'd lost weight and her face was narrow. The angles of her cheeks and chin were sharper.

Darcy almost didn't recognize herself.

Housekeeping had yet to tidy up and several damp towels littered the tile floor. On the back of the vanity sat a brown leather shaving kit. Grabbing the bag, she rifled through the contents. There were two prescription bottles. One for a decongestant. The other was for an antibiotic. To Darcy, the antibiotic was more valuable than gold. With weak fingers, she pried the cap loose and dumped two pills in her hand. After filling a glass with water from the tap, she swallowed both with one gulp.

The outer door opened, and Darcy froze.

"Yeah," said a male voice. "Steve got sick. He had too much to drink last night and then this altitude finished him off. We only played seven holes this morning. We'll go back after he gets cleaned up."

Damn. Kevin had come back early. From the conversation, Darcy guessed he was on the phone. Maybe the call would be enough of a distraction that she could leave his room without arousing any suspicions.

She slipped the lid on the pill bottle and silently placed it in the shaving kit. After putting the kit where she had found it, she retrieved the used towels from the floor. With an armload of laundry, Darcy exited the bathroom.

Keeping her eyes on the ground, she said, "Excuse me. I'll return later. I don't want to disturb you."

"Hey," said the guest. "Hold up there one minute."

Damn. What had he seen? What did he know? "Yes?"

"Let me call you right back," Kevin said to the person on the phone. Then to Darcy, he asked, "Are you with Housekeeping?"

"I am. Do you need something?"

"Not really," he said. "I'm just surprised that you are with Housekeeping."

She had to leave before the man suspected why she was really there. Had she put the shaving kit back in the proper place? If she hadn't, would he notice? "Surprised? Why?"

"It's just that you're really pretty. It seems a shame to hide someone as hot as you in a bunch of messy rooms."

Darcy flicked her gaze to the man's face. He was tall and fair-haired with clear blue eyes. Her stomach filled with a fluttering of excitement and her pulse began to race. He was just like the other ones—the ones who needed to die.

"I should go." Clutching the dirty towels to her chest like a shield, she lunged for the door.

The man stepped in her path. "I'm sorry if I made you uncomfortable."

"No apologies necessary," Darcy said. "I should go and let you get on with your day."

The man didn't move.

She stepped to the side.

He mirrored her movement.

The man held up his hands. "This has gotten awkward," he said. "Let me make it up to you."

"No need," said Darcy.

"When do you get done with your shift, Claire?" he asked, reading the name from her name tag.

Her heart pounded against her chest until her pulse

became a drumbeat in her skull. She was deaf to every sound but the *thump, thump, thump* of blood rushing through her veins. She felt alive. Powerful. Omnipotent.

"I—I should go," she said once more.

"Do it." The voice was a whisper, barely audible above her palpitating heartbeat. It was the Darkness. Even here, with a new identity, the Darkness had still found her.

"One drink," said the man. He held up his index finger. "Just one."

"No," said Darcy, speaking both to the man and the Darkness. "I can't."

"Why not?" Kevin asked.

"I just can't," she said. She silently cursed for not being more vigilant and getting out before he could see her. "It's not a good idea."

"I think it's a great idea," said the man.

"I don't know you," she said. She kept her eyes trained on the towels in her hand as she worked a loosened thread free. "You know nothing about me."

"My name is Kevin," he said, by way of introduction. "Besides, isn't that why we'd have a drink? That way, we can get to know each other?"

"Do it. Do it. Do it," the Darkness urged.

"No," Darcy screamed in the confines of her own mind. "No. I can't. I won't. Not anymore."

"You can," teased the Darkness. *"You will. You cannot change your nature any more than I."*

"I can see that you're tempted," said Kevin. "Besides, my buddy and I came here for golf. He's not feeling well and you'd be doing me a favor by keeping me company."

Shaking her head, Darcy said, "No."

"Come on," said Kevin. He touched her chin and lifted her face. "One drink. We can meet in the bar downstairs. I'll be a perfect gentleman. I promise."

Lifting her gaze, Darcy met the man's eyes.

"You know he's lying," said the Darkness. *"You know he deserves to die. Think about him. Think about all the others. Billy. Your father. They are all the same kind of filth. It is your job to rid the world of this type of trash."*

Darcy's stomach threatened to revolt.

Kevin smiled, his handsome face becoming sharp and lupine. But if he was the wolf, what did that make her? The sacrificial lamb? Or the lioness—queen of her domain? As if she stood on a tightrope, Darcy felt herself teetering on the edge. Beneath her feet was nothing but the Darkness, seductive and safe.

"Eight o'clock," he said. "Meet me in the bar for one drink."

"I really shouldn't," she said, smiling for the first time in weeks. "But just this once, I will."

Chapter 10

At the registration desk, Holly and Liam were given key cards for their room. It was on the third of four floors. Yet to call it a room didn't give justice to their accommodations. It was a suite, complete with two bedrooms, a well-stocked wet bar and minifridge, a fireplace in the living area, which just so happened to be larger than the living room in Holly's home. The furniture was butter-soft leather in dove gray and navy blue. Floor-to-ceiling windows overlooked the Rocky Mountains and the cloudless Wyoming sky.

"Wow," said Holly as she set her purse on the bar. "These are some swanky digs."

"RMJ definitely didn't spare any expenses, that's for sure," said Liam.

Two bedrooms sat at opposite sides of the suite. One,

had a king-size bed, complete with a master bath. There were two twin beds in the other.

"It looks like they delivered the luggage," said Holly. She stood on the threshold of the master bedroom. Her bag sat on the bed, right next to Liam's. A quivering rose from the pit of her stomach at the possibility of sharing a bed with Liam. "What should we do?"

"You can keep the master bedroom. I'll take the spare."

Holly nodded her agreement. His plan made complete sense, yet there was an unexpected twinge of disappointment. Taking the clothes from her bag, Holly placed them in the provided dresser. After setting up her toiletries in the bathroom, she returned to the living room.

Liam stood at the window.

She moved to stand next to him. The Rocky Mountains rose in the distance, the peaks still covered in snow. "Everything about this place is impressive," she said. "Even the view."

"Yes, it is."

What was wrong with his tone? He almost sounded angry. From the corner of her vision, she studied Liam's profile. His nose was straight and his jaw strong. Dark eyebrows covered eyes the color of the forest—green, brown and gold. He almost seemed to be the vestige of a bygone era, and it made Holly mourn for a past that she never knew.

In the distance, she could see the one of the greens of the golf course—the flag for the hole fluttered in the breeze. The paddock, complete with several horses, was just to the left. A roan mare trotted to the fence.

"I think I've discovered something important. I can't tell just yet exactly what it is—I've got to dig a little."

"Tell me," she suggested.

Liam glanced at Holly before turning his gaze back to the window. "I overheard a doctor and security guard discussing a break-in at the resort infirmary."

"Some medications can be sold on the street for a lot of money," said Holly. "You might have found a trail to follow. But I'm not sure what that has to do with anything, especially a serial killer."

"True," he said.

"Talk to me. Tell me everything you know about Darcy," said Holly. She was part of the team because of the book she wrote—albeit, it was many years ago. "Marcus and Wyatt gave me a little background, but if you can flesh her out for me, maybe I can come up with a new angle for the investigation."

"I have a limited case file in my bag," said Liam.

He disappeared into the spare bedroom and returned moments later with a laptop in hand. He set the computer on the table and turned on the power.

While opening a file, Liam asked, "What do you know about Darcy?"

"Other than what I've gotten from the media and Marcus, not much."

"I'll keep it succinct. Darcy has been killing men for years. All of her victims have a similar look—blond hair, blue eyes, handsome. She meets them for drinks, or so we assume. They consume too much alcohol, then she gives them something toxic. After that, she takes them to the middle of nowhere and leaves them for dead."

"Any idea why she kills? The motivations for her murders are going to be the key to what she does next."

Liam spoke while scrolling through the document "The theory is that she was abused by her father." He continued, coming to the final page. "Darcy was shot in the shoulder while trying to escape after killing Carl Haak."

"I knew that," she said. "He's the former sheriff of Pleasant Pines." She didn't add, *and was a friend to my parents*.

"Exactly."

Holly let out a long breath. "I hate to say it, but this case file doesn't help me much."

"I was afraid of that. If you want, I'll ask Wyatt for more information. See what he's willing to share."

"What do we do until then?"

Liam removed a cell phone from his pocket. "I guess we'll have to go through the resort and take pictures of as many people as possible."

"Just pictures?"

"This has facial recognition software," said Liam. "We need to verify identities. See if there are unknown connections to Darcy Owens, or reasons why a person might lie to the police about knowing the killer."

Holly faked a shiver. "Sounds like spy-novel stuff. I'm game, but let me grab a coat," she said while turning from the table. Her fingertips brushed against Liam's arm and yet, she didn't pull away. The muscles of his biceps were unmistakable. She was drawn to the heat of him. The question was, how close could Holly get before she got burned? "Sorry," she whispered, as she stepped from the table...and Liam.

He reached for her, his hand on her elbow stopping her retreat. "Why are you sorry?" he asked.

She looked at Liam. Surely, he wouldn't want a woman like Holly. Wasn't Sophie's mother in the navy? A woman of action, just as he was a man of action? Holly was, well…a planner. An arranger. Not a woman who took charge at all.

If she was, she might not be in this situation.

"I didn't mean to touch you," she said, dropping her gaze. "It was an accident."

"You don't need to apologize about that," he said. His voice was deep, a rumble of thunder coming from a stormy sky. He moved closer, his breath warming her shoulder. "I'm not sorry."

"Shouldn't we be professional?" asked Holly, her pulse racing.

"Why?"

"I think it's for the best. Don't you?"

"No," he said. "I want to talk about us."

"There is no us," said Holly.

"It doesn't have to be that way."

"Yes," she said, jerking her arm from his grasp. "It does."

Liam touched his fingertips to Holly's chin. Tilting her head up, so she met him in the eyes, he said, "Tell me there's no chemistry between us."

Holly's mouth went dry. She licked her lips. Liam moved closer.

"Tell me you don't want to kiss me."

She only saw his lips—they were so enticing. "I don't want to kiss you," she said.

"Liar."

"You don't want the truth."

"Try me," Liam said.

"I have a plan for my life," said Holly. "I want to keep Saplings open. That's the only reason I'm here with you. To me, this is a job."

Liam's hand slid from her chin. "That was harsh," he said.

"You asked for the truth," said Holly. All the same, she wanted him to insist—to push a little harder. If he asked once more for a kiss, she'd never be able to hold back.

Holly turned back to the table. She watched him from the side of her eye.

She wanted to say something. But what?

Without a word, he walked away.

Exhaling, Holly dropped into a chair. She knew that she needed to be honest with Liam. She wasn't interested in a relationship and it was wrong to let him think anything different. Yet, if she'd done the right thing, why did she feel like she'd just made a huge mistake?

Hand in hand, for the sake of the operation, Liam and Holly walked through the lobby. A group of women stood in front of the fireplace.

Holly leaned in close. She wore a polar fleece jacket that turned her cheeks the color of a ripe peach. Her jeans hugged her hips and rear. Her scent, vanilla and roses, wafted over him and Liam's pulse spiked.

"I'll pose near the women and you take my picture," she said, her voice a whisper. "Hopefully, it's enough for facial recognition."

Lifting that phone with the recognition software to

his eye, Liam shifted the aspect to focus on the gathered women. He snapped several pictures. He stopped, figuring he'd gotten enough. Yet, with a wide smile, Holly stared at the camera. There was no reason to capture her image, yet he did.

"Give me a second to run these pictures through the app," he muttered to Holly.

"Sure thing. I'll wander around for a minute."

Liam watched her walk away. She looked as good from the back as she did from the front. Yet, her rebuke from only moments ago was still fresh and echoed in his ears. *I have a plan for my life,* she had said. *I want to keep Saplings open. That's the only reason I'm here with you. For me, it's a job.*

Holly had made it painfully clear that to her, he was nothing more than a means to an end. Yet, what was she to him?

Staring out over the foothills of the Rocky Mountains, Liam realized that the only reason he'd accepted this assignment was Holly. He knew that Marcus Jones was desperate to find any connection to Darcy Owens and he would spare no expense in bringing her to justice. Holly needed money, and Liam could get it for her. If not for that fact, Liam would never have left Sophie at home—even with a competent sitter.

Returning his attention to the camera, he scrolled to the first photograph. Liam entered the woman's visage into the embedded software. A red light flashed—no connection found to Darcy's known history. He repeated the routine for each person. Nada.

Next, he sent electronic copies to his coworkers. Marcus and Wyatt had more powerful equipment at the mobile headquarters, and would be able to confirm identities more thoroughly. Stopping at the final photograph, he stared at Holly's image. Her smile was contagious, and Liam's lips twitched.

"You ready?" she asked.

Liam slipped the phone into his pocket as his face warmed and sweat collected at the base of his neck. He felt as if he'd been caught doing something wrong…and perhaps he had. Holly had been clear. She didn't want a relationship, and especially not with him. Why torture himself by continuing to think about it?

"Come on," he said, taking her hand. "There's something I want to show you."

Together, Liam and Holly walked down a cobbled path. A hill rose to their right.

"I told you that my family used to live around here."

"Sure," she said. "Gunslingers. Pioneers. Settlers from before Wyoming was a state."

"My family isn't just from Wyoming. We're actually from this land." Pointing to a ridge, he said, "There used to be several homes up there, built so close that they were nearly one on top of the next. As an adult, I know that my mother's family was poor. As a kid, I never noticed. During visits, I just played with my cousins and stole melons from my great-aunt's garden." Pointing to an outcropping of rock, he continued, "My sister and I used to jump off those stones. We'd tie towels around our necks and pretend to be superheroes. I was always so sure that one day I would really fly."

He stopped and silently cursed. Liam hadn't meant to step so far into the past, or share such secret memories with Holly. He could almost imagine Charlie running up the ridge, motioning for Liam to follow.

"Where's your family now?"

"They all sold the land to the resort's developer and moved."

"It must be odd to find yourself back here, then."

"I feel like I lost something, and I can never get it back," he said.

"I don't know what to say," she said. She watched him with those aqua-colored eyes of hers.

"It doesn't matter. Words won't change anything." Liam recognized that the wall he'd constructed to keep others out was close to crumbling under the weight of her stare. He shored up his defenses and stepped away from her gaze. "Besides, I've rambled on too long. We've got a killer's accomplice to find."

"What do we do now?"

Liam and Holly were alone, with no one to photograph. Ahead, the cobbled path led through the woods. "I remember this path," he said. "All those years ago, it wasn't covered in stones. Just trampled-down dirt. It used to lead to a boulder field." His voice caught. He cleared his throat. "I'm sure it's gone. I wonder what's there now."

"There's only one way to find out," said Holly, stepping beyond the tree line.

Liam wasn't one to believe in spirits or ghosts. Yet, as he stepped into the woods, he knew for certain that some places were haunted.

His lips twitched with the memory of playing capture the flag. It was replaced with another memory, and he reached for the dog tag.

"You okay?" Holly asked. "You look, I don't know... Pale."

"It's nothing," he said, letting go of the leather cord.

Holly dropped her questioning, and they continued up the path without speaking. Dappled sunlight shone through the overhead branches. With the trees beginning to bloom, the light in the woods turned hazy.

Looking left and right, Liam constantly searched for broken twigs or scuff marks on a trunk. A mountain breeze blew down from the highest peaks. Barely buffeted by the trees, the wind still held a chill.

"Are you cold?" he asked Holly.

She shoved her hands deep into the pockets of her polar fleece. "A little," she said.

"Maybe we should head back," he suggested. Certainly, they wouldn't find anyone to photograph this deep into the woods.

"Sure," she said. Turning, she began to walk down the trail.

Yet, Liam remained.

Images came to him, like pictures caught on film, but faded with time.

Charlie running ahead, laughing.

Liam, his legs aching and chest burning while trying to keep up.

The low rumble of conversation carried down the trail and interrupted his thoughts. As if the temperature had just plummeted, gooseflesh covered his arms. The hair at the nape of his neck stood on end. Liam paused.

"What is it?" Holly asked.

"Did you hear that? Voices?"

She stood without moving. "Yeah. They're that way." She pointed up the path.

The woods gave way to an expanse of the green lawn of the golf course. He almost laughed. The dangerous boulder field—the place he was warned about as a child—was gone. Now, it was a benign fairway, covered in grass.

Two men stood next to the ninth hole with metal putters in hand. One had light brown hair and blue eyes. He was tall, fit and the kind of guy that women found appealing. His companion was shorter, thicker, and had a receding hairline.

With temperatures settled in the low fifties, it seemed too cold to golf. Then again, to Liam golf was boring. Still, he understood that those who loved the game would be out on the links as soon as the snow melted enough that they could find their balls.

Holly's hand in his, Liam moved closer to the golf enthusiasts.

"Yeah," the handsome one said. "She's a tall brunette. A housekeeper. She was in my room when I came back."

"Don't tell me that you…?" The balding guy gyrated his hips.

"No, of course not," said Handsome. "Not yet, at least."

They both laughed at the lewd joke.

Liam didn't have a lot of close male friends—or any, really. At times he wondered if he needed the camaraderie one could only get from a male buddy. Yet, if this is how guys acted, Liam figured that he wasn't missing much. He looked at Holly and she rolled her eyes. Apparently, she shared his opinion.

"How do you always find the willing ladies, Kevin?" the other man asked.

"It's a skill," he said. "Kind of like golf."

Kevin putted the ball. It skipped over the hole. He cursed.

The other man laughed. "I hope you have better skills with your maid than you do with the ball." He putted his own ball. It dropped into the hole.

"You're just jealous that I have game."

"You mean you have lame?"

"Shut up, Steve," said Kevin.

The air around Liam warmed again and he let out a breath that he didn't realize he'd been holding. Melting into the woods, Liam and Holly turned back to the resort. As they walked, he wondered how a maid who was conveniently in Kevin's room fit the profile of a dangerous killer.

Chapter 11

Without saying much, Holly and Liam walked back to the hotel. The quiet gave him time to process everything they'd seen and heard. He didn't know what to make of any of it—not yet.

With Holly at his side, he stepped out of the woods. His cell phone pinged with an incoming text. He glanced at the screen. It was from Marcus Jones.

On-site. In white florist's van. Parked in employee lot. Report ASAP.

Liam typed out his reply: On my way.

Turning to Holly, he said, "I need to meet with Marcus and Wyatt. Why don't you go back to the room? I'll be back in a few minutes."

"Sure," she said. "I'll see you soon."

Liam watched her walk toward the main building. Her tight-fitting pants hugged her curves as she walked, hips swaying. He had to force himself to tear his gaze away. Nothing was more important than catching Darcy Owens and getting back to his daughter.

But he had to admit, more than her obvious allure, Holly was smart and caring. He could do worse than to fall for a woman like her.

Too bad she didn't want him.

Liam turned for the parking lot. The van was parked in one of the spaces farthest from the resort and the rear doors opened as he approached.

"Come on in," said Wyatt.

The van was completely outfitted as a mobile HQ. Monitors and keyboards lined one wall and an arsenal of weapons was on the other. A low table, with four chairs, sat in front of the monitors. Marcus Jones sat in one seat and Liam dropped down into another. Wyatt took the seat at the end, leaving Liam with the sense that he was trapped.

"Do you have anything to report?" Marcus asked, without a greeting or any preamble.

"Someone broke into the infirmary," said Liam. It was weak intel but all he had.

"Once you get into the room with the server, we can access the video," said Wyatt.

"Was anything taken?" Marcus asked.

Liam shook his head. "Nothing."

"Without video we can't really do anything. We might be able to fix that problem, though," said Marcus. He held up a canvas bag emblazoned with the White

Wind logo. From it, he withdrew a plastic disk, thin as a dime and no bigger than a pencil's eraser. Liam's face appeared on one of the monitors. "Install this camera in the hallway outside the infirmary. The feed will come to the van."

"There are a dozen cameras in the bag. It took Katarina all night to get them ready," Wyatt added while handing over a sheet of paper. "This is a schematic of the building. I've marked the spots where cameras should be placed, including in here." He pointed to a building that was well away from the main resort. "That's where the resident staff lives. The cameras are easy to set up. There's adhesive on the backside and they're wireless."

"And here's a copy of the master key, to get you into almost every place in the resort," said Marcus, while holding up a small, white card.

"Gaining access to the security room is our main mission. You have a fifteen-minute window when the room will be empty," said Wyatt. "According to the footage we've collected, there are two guards assigned to the resort from midnight to five o'clock in the morning. They spend most of the time in the security room, except when they do rounds at two thirty-five."

"Will this key get me into the room with the server?" he asked, waving the white card.

Wyatt said, "That has a different code. Katarina's working from her end. Hopefully, you'll be good to go by tonight. If we're lucky, you can leave in the morning."

Leave in the morning? Sure, Liam should be excited to get home to Sophie a day early. And mostly, he was.

It was just that as soon as he left the White Wind, his time with Holly would be over. Hell, within a few days, she might even be leaving town. For good.

Then again, Liam learned long ago that there were some things he couldn't change—like what Holly wanted. And there were things that he could change—like placing all of the cameras around the resort.

After looking over the printout Wyatt had given him, Liam knew that it would take more than an hour to place all the cameras. He quickly formed a plan. He should take Holly with him—for the sake of his undercover persona, at least.

Placing the camera back in the bag, he changed the subject. "I showed Holly the case file. She thought that she might be able to find something useful."

"Did she?" Wyatt asked.

Liam shook his head. "The file's pretty thin, but if you had more information, you could pass it on to her."

"Sure," said Wyatt. "Why not. I'll get something to her soon."

"Anything else?" Liam asked.

"Keep sending us as many images as you can," said Marcus. "With you in the resort and these cameras, we have the technology to find whoever is helping Darcy. I'm sure of it."

Liam said nothing, but he was sure of it, too. In the woods, he'd heard the whisper of a single word: Murder.

Liam returned to the room and told Holly the plan to place remote cameras throughout the property. Her role was simple. She need only accompany him—providing him with cover and serving as a lookout.

As he had done before, Liam slipped his fingertips into Holly's open palm. She liked the feel of his hand in hers. She liked being close to him, the heat of his body, the scent that surrounded him. Perhaps Darcy Owens wasn't the real danger that Holly would face. Pretending to be Liam's wife was forcing Holly to confront a future that she wanted but had been too afraid to hope for.

"Let's start with the staff quarters," he said. "And work our way back to the resort."

"Makes sense," said Holly. "Lead the way."

Liam kept her hand in his, even after they'd wandered away from the resort. The scent of pine filled the air and an undercurrent of warmth was carried on the breeze. Liam seemed fine to walk in silence, which suited Holly, as well. She really didn't know what to say.

It was moments like this that Holly could no longer believe the lies she'd been telling herself for years. She wanted a husband and children of her own. The busyness of her job and the laser focus she used in running the day-care center were just cheap substitutes for her desires.

True, she was at the resort trying to earn the money she needed to keep the school. Yet for the first time Holly wondered if that was really what she wanted after all.

"This is it," said Liam, letting go of her hand to point to a three-story rectangular building that had been painted the color of mint ice cream. He reached into the tote bag he carried and removed three silver disks. "One for each floor."

Holly's pulse began to race. Was she excited? Nervous? Both?

Before she could decide, her phone began to ring. She fished it from the pocket of her polar fleece jacket. Incoming call. University of Findlay.

In all the excitement of working for RMJ, Holly had almost forgotten about the job her agent had mentioned.

"Do you need to take that call?" Liam asked.

"I really should. Do you mind?"

"Just keep an eye out for anyone coming into the building," he said, slipping out a key card and swiping it over a lock. "Text me if it looks like I need to get out."

Holly connected the call and said, "Hello," at the same moment Liam slipped through the door.

"Holly? This is Louise Nelson. I believe your agent, Franklin, told you I'd be calling? I can't tell you how excited we are to hear that you might join our community in Ohio."

Of course. She should have remembered that Franklin had told her to expect a call from the University of Findlay rep. Scrambling to watch the building and sound intrigued, she replied, "Oh, hello! Yes, he did say to expect to hear from you." She leaned against the building—casually, she hoped—and furtively glanced around. "Can you tell me more about the position?"

"Well, sure." Louise certainly sounded friendly enough. "It's a tenured position. You'd receive a full salary. The university contributes to a personal retirement account for all employees. Plus, there's full medical and dental insurance. I know you've only had a short time to think about this, but we'd love to know if you'd be able to start by the end of the month."

Holly felt light-headed. She'd imagined the potential job in Ohio as a safety net, a place to land if her plan to keep Saplings failed. More than that, she had spoken to Franklin before striking a deal with Rocky Mountain Justice, at a time when she felt certain that she had run out of options. She'd never thought an offer with such steady pay and benefits—such security—would come through at all, let alone with such immediacy.

"Holly?" Louise asked. "Are you there?"

In truth, Holly wasn't ready to accept the job offer. She also wasn't prepared to turn it down, either. What she needed was time to think. "Louise, your offer is so very generous, but I know I'll have some questions, and I'd just like to think it over before I give you my final answer. Can I contact you later?"

"Call me anytime," said Louise. "I'd love to have you join my staff. At the same time, if you can't commit, then I need to find someone who will."

"I understand," said Holly. After a pause, she ended the call.

Holly still felt woozy. She turned her face to the sun and inhaled. The air smelled of pine and the new growth of spring. There was no easy answer. In truth, she didn't want to leave Pleasant Pines. Yet she was too practical to become sentimental about a town, even if that town was her home.

Darcy shared a small apartment with two other female staff members. It was provided by the White Wind as a perk to their employees. The space wasn't much—a bedroom with three separate beds, a chest of drawers for each person, a small living room/kitchen combo and a smaller bathroom.

Lying on her bed, Darcy was thankful for a moment

alone. She found her cheerful roommates to be maddening. Their constant chatter was like an ice pick being shoved into her ear.

After she'd taken the antibiotic, Darcy's fever had abated. Rolling to her back, she closed her eyes.

A hot tear snaked down the side of her face and settled in her ear. She turned, letting the tear run onto the pillow. How was it that some people were blessed while others were cursed? What had Darcy done to deserve her fate?

"That man came to you, remember that," the Darkness whispered, its tone seductive and insistent. The Darkness hadn't forgotten about Kevin Carpenter's invitation to meet for a drink.

"No. I can't. I won't," she said inside her mind. "Leave me alone."

Yet she was taken away by the moments when she'd had complete power and life slipped away from her victims.

Moments when she would have it again.

No.

She was strong enough to ignore the urge. Darcy could let this victim go. Kevin was nothing to her and his death was not worth the sacrifice. Besides, once his body was found, she'd be forced to run again.

"Stay tonight," said the Darkness once more. *"Settle the score. There's no reason to deny yourself the power, especially after so much has been taken from you."*

The Darkness was right—in that truth, she found peace. It was like the calm after a storm. Her limbs became heavy as her eyes began to close. Lulled by the sound of her own heart beating, she drifted toward sleep. Slipping down, down, down, the Darkness whispered once more in her ear, "*You are mine. And I will never let you go.*"

From the hallway came the echoes of footfalls on the concrete and she sat up, holding her breath. The steps stopped and she stared at the door, ready for one of her roommates to enter.

They didn't.

Who was outside?

On silent feet, she crossed the room and pressed her eye to the peephole. A man stood in the corridor.

His shoulders tensed and he looked over his shoulder. Darcy gasped and stepped back.

Had he seen her?

Had he known?

She waited a moment and stepped back to the door.

The man was still there. He glanced left and his gaze swept slowly to the right. Thinking he was alone, he reached into his pocket and removed—what? From her vantage point, she couldn't see. He turned to the wall. Reaching above his head, he pressed a finger into the seam between the wall and the thick, rubberized trim.

She stared at the spot. There was a winking of glass reflecting light.

What in the…?

Was it a camera?

Was she being spied on?

No, nobody knew she was here. If they did, she would've been caught by now, for sure.

Maybe it was just a security precaution on behalf of the resort. Something done by the management without the staff's knowledge. The fact that she didn't recognize the guy didn't mean a thing. There were dozens and dozens of employees. In fact, the vastness of the resort suited her. It provided the perfect place for Darcy to hide—in plain sight.

It was Wednesday evening. Liam wore a pressed dress shirt and sat in the bar adjacent to the restaurant. He sipped from a bottle of beer. Several hours remained before his scheduled break-in of the security office.

Shaking his head, he wondered what his grandfather would think of him now. Or, with a pang of guilt, Charlie?

Was Liam a thief, for stealing the privacy that people expected? Or was he a soldier, fighting for good against evil?

In the woods, Liam had only gotten a fleeting glimpse of Darcy. And he was certain of one thing. She was evil. He thought back to the briefing he'd received on the killer his first morning with RMJ. The cramped conference room with photographs on the walls was as clear to him as the room in which he now sat.

In most of the pictures, Darcy had had blond hair. In some, she was a brunette. The slight change in hair color hadn't been much of a disguise, but it was enough to change her look.

Where was she now?

Turning back to his beer, Liam took a long swallow. A large mirror was affixed to the wall behind the bar. His gaze passed over the reflection and he lowered the bottle from his lips.

Swiveling in his chair, he stared.

Holly stood at the door of the restaurant. A light pink

dress skimmed her lithe figure. The neckline dipped low. An image of his mouth on her chest came to mind. He finished the beer in a single swallow. Did Holly really have to look that good if she was just pretending?

It also meant that she hadn't dressed up for him. She was playing a role. For her, this escapade was all work, and if not for the money, she'd be in Pleasant Pines.

A burning began in Liam's middle, filling him with an emotion he couldn't name. Wasn't sure he wanted to name.

He met Holly at the door to the restaurant.

His chest tightened. Just looking at her was an exquisite torture. *Get it together, Alexander. She's not for you.* Still, his heart didn't agree with his head, and he said, "You look amazing."

The compliment hung in the air.

Color rose in Holly's cheeks. "Thank you."

"Table for two?" the hostess asked.

"Please," he said, following the young woman through the restaurant. The tables were covered with pristine white cloths. A large fireplace sat at the back of the room; the flames cast a glow throughout the restaurant. A bank of windows overlooked a valley filled with evergreens. The predicted storm had arrived, and a cold rain fell, darkening the sky.

They were seated at a table near the window. A server filled glasses with water and left a plate of lemon slices.

"If this weather doesn't stop," said Liam as he pulled out Holly's seat, "we could get stuck."

"Oh?"

"It's just that the river will rise quickly with all the rain and the snow runoff from the higher elevations.

Then the bridge will wash out. Or it used to. Maybe the state fixed the bridge now that a resort sits on the land."

Then again, Liam suspected that being trapped with Holly was just what he wanted. Was there any way that he could make his desire a reality?

Chapter 12

Darcy needed an outfit.

She had half an hour left before meeting Kevin in the hotel bar, and she could hardly go in there in her housekeeping uniform. But she had nothing else to wear.

Her eyes were drawn to the three dressers, all standing in a line at the back wall. Darcy's chest of drawers was practically empty. However, the other two were not. Certainly, her roommates owned some clothes Darcy could borrow, even if she never gave them back.

It took only a moment to find a pair of jeans and a tight-fitting black sweater. A pair of loafers, half a size too large, completed the ensemble. She glanced at her reflection in the mirror. For the first time in weeks, Darcy felt like her old self.

In control.

She strode through the corridors and entered the bar with ten minutes to spare, only to find Kevin Carpenter sitting on a bar stool. He held up a champagne flute as she approached. "It's French," he said. "I thought you'd like something special."

Darcy accepted her drink and took a sip. "How thoughtful. Thank you."

"You're welcome," Kevin said. He lifted a brown bottle of beer to his lips and took a swallow.

Beer? Oh no. Kevin needed to drink something stronger than beer. For Darcy, it was a game and now she needed to outmaneuver her opponent.

"This is a celebration," Darcy said, finishing her drink. "Bartender, two shots of vodka."

Kevin laughed as the bartender filled two small glasses. Darcy gulped her drink. It landed in her stomach like a liquid bomb. Kevin drank the vodka in a single swallow.

"Another," said Darcy.

The glasses were quickly refilled. Kevin drank his shot. Darcy left hers untouched.

"One more," she said.

"You're getting me drunk," said Kevin. "Are you trying to take advantage of me?"

"Maybe," she said. She lifted her drink to her lips. "You need another drink."

Kevin took a third shot, as Darcy quickly dumped her drink into the sink just behind the bar. Her victim looked at Darcy, his expression glazed. Now, all she needed was to get Kevin alone.

"I have an idea," she said. "Let's get our own bottle of vodka and go somewhere more—" she paused "—intimate."

"Wow," he said, no doubt marveling at how easy his latest conquest had been. "I mean, what the hell," said Kevin. "You only live once, right?"

Darcy smiled. "It's exactly what I was thinking."

For security reasons, the RMJ team had left the White Wind resort and now sat in the van at the back of the parking lot of a nearby twenty-four-hour big-box store. Four screens were illuminated. A continual reel of faces, picked up from the cameras hidden around the White Wind, filled each monitor. Each was scanned by their facial-recognition software. Within seconds, databases from around the world were searched and a verified match was listed.

So far, they'd captured over 300 unique persons, but no sign of Darcy Owens.

Marcus Jones looked up from the screen as the van's rear door opened. Wyatt Thornton held a bag of fast food and two steaming cups of coffee. The van immediately filled with the rich aroma of coffee and the smell of cooked meat.

"Anything?" Wyatt asked, gesturing to the monitors with the bag.

Marcus pinched the bridge of his nose. "Nothing," he said.

"What if there isn't a connection?" Wyatt pressed. "What if we've wasted a day following a trail that leads nowhere?"

Before Marcus could answer, his phone rang. "It's

Martinez." Marcus answered, putting the call on Speaker so Wyatt could hear.

"Martinez," he said. "How's Julia?"

"She's improving but she's going to need PT if she's going to have any use of that hand. My God, she's lost two fingers."

"Thank goodness she's going to live," whispered Wyatt.

"Is she awake?" Marcus asked. "Has she said anything about what happened to her in the bunker or anything about what the photographs we found on her phone mean?"

"She dozed off and I stepped out of the room," said Martinez. "I'll call back when she wakes up again."

"Keep us posted as you get information from Julia and the doctors," said Marcus. "And Martinez—tell her we're there for her, whatever she needs."

"Will do," said Martinez.

Marcus ended the call. As the smell of greasy fries wafted through the van, his stomach began to rumble. Pulling the bag toward him, he peered inside. A woman's face flashed across the screen and he froze.

A message appeared on the monitor: Owens, Darcy, 79.5% match.

His heartbeat began to race. "See that?"

"I see it. What should we do? Call the FBI?" Wyatt asked. "Even with a seventy-nine percent match?"

Marcus rubbed his chin. "Bring up the photo we caught."

Wyatt tapped on the keyboard. "This was taken at the bar. Time—7:52 p.m. That's ten minutes ago. We only have the woman's profile and it looks like it was caught in the mirror. Hell, I can't even tell what color her sweater is. Is that black or navy?"

Marcus picked up his phone. "I'm texting Liam. He can check this out quicker than we can get back to the resort." He typed out the message and hit Send.

Marcus wouldn't rest until he had an answer.

Liam's phone pinged with an incoming text. Looking at the screen, his blood went cold, and he turned his attention to the bar at the far side of the room. The crowd had grown, and Liam didn't see his quarry. Yet, it didn't mean that Darcy Owens wasn't in this very room.

"What is it?" Holly asked.

He turned to look at her. "I need to check someone out at the bar," he said quietly. "I'll be right back."

"What's going on?" Holly asked.

Liam eyed the room, certain that each and every person was a threat. "Please, don't ask questions. I'll tell you everything as soon as I can."

Holly worked her jaw back and forth. In the end, she didn't argue.

Liam got up from the table and made his way to the crowded bar. He read the description from the text again. Female. Brunette. Dark sweater. He spotted the woman immediately. Positioning himself next to the target, Liam posed. As if taking a selfie, he captured the woman's image more than a dozen times.

He texted them all to his colleagues.

The reply came in less than a minute.

It's not her.

Liam silently cursed before replying.

What next?

It took Marcus several seconds to return with an answer.

According to the resort's calendar, there's an outdoor concert in 20 minutes. Report there and get pictures of the crowd.

Liam cursed to himself before heading back to his table, wondering how the hell he was going to explain this one to Holly.

With Liam at her side, Holly walked down a path that wound past the paddock and toward an amphitheater set in the woods. The earlier rain shower had ended. The forecast promised more showers overnight, but for now, torches lined the path, illuminating the walkway. Beads of water clung to branches and leaves. The foliage sparkled with the fire's glow. Her breath caught in a frozen cloud and Holly was thankful that she'd thought to bring a warm coat. Aside from the concert, the resort had also set up a table with fixings for s'mores—graham crackers, chocolate bars, marshmallows, skewers. It seemed like the perfect place to be around plenty of guests and staff—any of whom might be the link to Darcy Owens.

If not the killer herself.

Shoving her hands deeper into her pockets, Holly glanced over her shoulder, searching the crowd for Liam. He stood near the firepit, watching her. Their gazes met. He walked toward her with a long and powerful stride. A small smile pulled up at the corner of his lips.

"What?" she asked, her heart hammering.

"You," he said.

"What about me?"

"You're beautiful."

"Oh." Holly didn't know how to react or what to say. All she knew was that if she didn't escape, she was dangerously close to giving in to Liam Alexander and the fantasy of happily-ever-after.

Stepping away from the crowded performance, Holly stood next to the firepit. Liam followed. Sparks from the blaze floated into the night sky. The murmur of voices blended with the music from a country-western band's song. Yet to Holly, it seemed as if she and Liam were the only two people on earth.

He stepped closer.

She arched an eyebrow, a definite challenge. Yet, what was she daring him to do?

Holly could hear the whisper of Liam's breath and smell the fresh tang of his clean skin. She felt an urge to step toward him. Fighting the impulse, she remained where she stood.

He moved to her, until only a few inches separated them. Lifting his hand, he placed his fingertips on her cheek. His touch was warm and strong. Tracing her jaw and chin, he stared into her eyes. "Pretty," he said. "So damn pretty."

He placed his mouth on hers and a spark came to life in Holly's middle. She wanted to ignore the fire that smoldered from within. Yet, with Liam, Holly longed to be burned; consumed by the flames.

He pressed his tongue into the seam of her lips. She opened herself to Liam as he tasted and explored. Holly was drunk with the sensation.

Then she remembered who she was. Holly never did anything without planning—or a reason. She firmly pushed him away.

"I can't," she said, scrubbing her mouth with the back of her hand. "I shouldn't."

Liam stepped back, his hands hanging at his sides. "I understand," he said.

"I'm glad you do," she said, with the shake of her head. "Because I don't."

"Holly, I…"

Thunder rumbled, echoing off the mountains. It was only a moment before the skies opened and sheets of rain began to fall. The moment was gone. Yet as the deluge washed over her, Liam stared at Holly and their gazes held. She had the uncanny thought that he saw more than just what was to be seen. It was almost as if his gaze bore straight through her, where he had a glimpse of everything—even her soul. The notion left Holly feeling exposed and at the same time, she wanted Liam to discover her deepest secrets and claim her for his own.

Liam lay on the sofa in the living room and stared at the beamed ceiling. He examined the whorls in the wood. The grain of the rough planks.

Memories of his cousin had become a constant barrage since coming to the resort. Yet Liam shouldn't be surprised—what, with being back at the place where so many of those memories had been made.

Still, he couldn't help but wonder what Charlie would think about Holly. He'd probably like her, Liam decided. Then again, was there anything to not like about Holly Jacobs?

His focus was so intent that he started when his phone pinged with an incoming text.

He looked at the screen. It was a video sent from Marcus Jones, along with a message.

Traffic video of possible Darcy Owens sighting. Reno, Nevada. 1:57 a.m.

Liam sat up and pressed the triangle that was superimposed on the image of a woman sitting in the passenger seat of what appeared to be a black SUV.

The video began to play. The woman was blonde. Caucasian. About the right age, although in the grainy image, it was hard to tell.

The SUV drove past the traffic camera, the woman's image gone as quickly as it came.

Another text from Marcus.

Is it her?

Liam watched the video once more. To him, it didn't feel right. Then again, the video didn't give him a lot to go on. Was it Darcy?

His reply: Could be.

From Marcus: The facial recognition software has it at an 85% match. Contacting Reno PD to stop SUV.

Liam wasn't sure what else to add to the conversation. Yet his phone beeped with a preset alarm. The time had come for the most important part of the mission—getting into the room that housed all of the resort's security equipment, hacking into the system and allowing RMJ to spy. Failure wasn't an option and adrenaline coursed through his veins.

"Ready?" came a sleepy voice from the doorway of the master bedroom. Holly leaned on the jamb, dressed in jeans and a long-sleeved T-shirt. Her hair was simply pulled back into a ponytail, and he couldn't stop thinking about how good she looked.

"No," he said honestly. "*Hacking* and *tracking* may rhyme, but that's about all they have in common."

She smiled. "See, you're a great parent."

Liam drew his brows together. "How'd you figure that?"

Holly said, "You're already making up your own lame dad jokes."

He smiled, as well. "Who says they're lame?" And then, his tone growing serious, "You don't have to come with me."

"Of course I do. I'm being paid to help you. What happens if one of the security guards returns while you're still working? I'll be outside, ready to ask them to show me the nearest soda machine."

"Swanky hotels like this don't have soda machines. Only the cantina in the lobby."

"Then I'll have them show me to the lobby."

He shook his head and laughed. Liam was already dressed—jeans, T-shirt, quarter zip fleece. "Let's go."

The room occupied by the resort's security officers was located in the basement, accessed only by a special elevator. As they descended, Liam's foot tapped restlessly. But it was more than that. It was the video Marcus had sent.

He knew that his boss was eager to find Darcy Owens. Was that eagerness making him see what he wanted? Or was he right?

"They think Darcy Owens was spotted on a traffic camera in Reno," said Liam.

"Reno?" asked Holly. "Why Reno?"

Maybe that was what bothered Liam the most. "In my experience, hunters—true predators—have their own hunting grounds. It's always an area they know well. They don't move unless there's no more prey."

"Las Vegas seems like a pretty target-rich environment," said Holly.

She was right. "Or maybe Darcy views the police as larger prey—and she's moved areas, but only slightly."

"Maybe," said Holly. Her word was punctuated by the ding of the elevator and the door sliding open.

Liam held up a hand to Holly and stepped into the corridor. The bowels of the hotel were completely at odds with the luxurious guest accommodations. Concrete floors. Cinder block walls. Overhead lights that gave off a jaundiced glow.

The hallway was empty. Motioning for Holly to follow, Liam looked at the map he'd been given.

They found the room without incident. Katarina had done her magic and the key card worked on the restricted door. As promised, the room was empty and both guards were on their rounds of the property.

He held the door open and turned back to Holly. "That's two things off my to-do list, with only about a thousand items left."

"You can do this," she said, turning her wrist so he could see her watch. "But you have to hurry if you're going to get it done."

Liam checked his own watch. It was 2:37 a.m. Two minutes were gone, only thirteen remained.

"Wish me luck," he said.

"Good luck," said Holly, her voice a whisper.

She was so close that he could feel her breath on his cheek. He moved toward her, focusing on her lips, her mouth and his desire for a single kiss.

Holly stepped forward, erasing the distance between them. She stood on tiptoe and placed her lips on his.

Liam wanted nothing more than to kiss her back. He wanted to pull her to him and not let go. In fact, he wanted to do almost anything other than step into the room filled with computer monitors, keyboards and the server, which looked like nothing other than a big black metal box. "Thanks," he said, stepping inside.

The door closed and the lock clicked.

Liam scanned the monitors. There were twenty—four rows of five screens. The upper-most monitor on the left was a live feed of the hallway where Holly stood. She'd noticed the camera, set above the door. Pointing to her watch, she mouthed, "Hurry up."

With a chuckle and a sigh, Liam removed his phone and opened the document with Katarina's instructions. It hadn't been a joke when he said he had a thousand more items to complete—just a slight exaggeration.

He followed her directions, keying in a string of letters, numbers and symbols onto the main keyboard. The code appeared on a computer screen. Liam hit Enter.

A message appeared. *Access denied.*

He checked the code again, but, once more, *Access denied*. Damn. He'd transposed two numbers. After clearing the field, he reentered the code and moved his finger to the enter key. He paused, comparing Katarina's code with what he'd entered. Another mistake would force Liam to start over again. He didn't have time for a second mistake.

Positive that his work was perfect, he hit Enter.

Access granted.

Liam removed the thumb drive from his pocket and found the port at the back of the server. With the drive placed and secure, he returned to the keyboard. There were two more lines of code. Liam carefully entered them both.

Access granted.

Time to download: 4 minutes.

The time on his cell phone read 2:45 a.m.

Would he have enough time?

Three minutes.

Liam searched the monitors and found one of the security guards in the lobby. Elbow on the front desk, he was speaking to the night clerk.

Liam opened the door. "I need you, Holly."

She looked up from where she leaned against the wall. "Anything."

"Go to the lobby and make an excuse to talk to the security guard. Anything to keep him busy. I just need another minute or two."

"What about the second guard?"

Liam looked back to the monitors. He searched each screen but couldn't see the other guy. What was worse, the download countdown had slowed, stopping at three minutes. "I'm not sure, but go now. We need all the time we can get."

He watched Holly, screen by screen, moving through the hallway. She entered the lobby just as the security guard moved to the edge of the frame. She spoke. He stopped.

Time to download: 1 minute.

Holly continued to speak to the security guard. Liam had no idea what she was saying, but the man seemed concerned. "Come on," Liam urged the computer. "Don't stop on me now."

There, on the second row, second screen from the left, was the second security guard. He moved through the corridors. Liam knew exactly where he was. In about fifteen seconds, he was going to turn a corner and the doorway to the security office would come into view. Liam would be trapped. He'd be discovered. The mission would be compromised.

A message appeared on the computer monitor: *Download complete.*

The computer screen went blank at the same time Liam opened the door and sprinted around the corner. His heart raced and his back was dampened with sweat. It was only as he slowed to a walk that he realized what he'd done.

Pulling the phone from his pocket, Liam typed out a message to Marcus.

I left the thumb drive in the back of the server.

Kevin Carpenter had died. In that moment, as his life drained from him, Darcy felt alive. As she drove from the resort, she was still shaking with excitement.

With Kevin's body tucked safely in the trunk of his own rental car, which she had stolen, Darcy planned to be gone before his absence was noticed. How long would it take to drive to Montana? There, Darcy would begin anew.

A torrent of rain fell, leaving the pavement slick and the powerful automobile hard to handle. The car crested a rise. The road was filled with strobing lights of blue and red. It was the police. Two black-and-white cruisers blocked her escape. Vomit rose in the back of Darcy's throat.

"They know what I've done," she said aloud.

She eased her foot off the gas. Kevin's body rolled, hitting the rear liftgate with a *thump.* Darcy glanced out the back windshield, maneuvering the gearshift into Reverse. She had to get away—even if she didn't have any place to run.

A police officer approached the car, wrapping on the window with the butt-end of a flashlight. After fumbling with the controls on the armrest, Darcy lowered the window.

Cold rain buffeted her face. "Yes?"

"Hello, miss. What are you doing out?"

"Going home," she said.

"You work at the resort?"

"I do."

"Hate to break it to you, but the water rose over the bridge. It's not safe to cross. You'll have to go back."

"How long until the road's open?"

The police officer wiped a wet hand down his sodden face. "I can't exactly say, but not before early morning. The storm isn't expected to stop before then."

She looked at the dashboard clock—3:07 a.m.

Darcy wanted to argue. She had to get away. She had to place the body somewhere special. All the same, she knew enough that arguing would arouse suspicion and lead to questions that she wasn't going to answer.

"Thank you," she said.

The police officer nodded before walking away.

Putting the car into Reverse, Darcy dropped her foot onto the accelerator. The car shot backward. The body rolled forward in the trunk, hitting the rear seats from behind.

The police officer stopped and turned around. He held up a hand, motioning for Darcy to halt.

Her heartbeat raced. Undoubtedly, the cop had heard the body.

"*Run him over*," said the Darkness.

No. There was another police officer next to the cars that still blocked the flooded road. Like a rat, Darcy was trapped.

"*Run him over or you'll be sorry.*"

The officer mimicked unrolling a window. Darcy hit the correct button on the second try.

"Yes?" she asked. This time she smiled.

"I think your tire's flat," the police officer said. "Give me a second. I'll take a look."

"*Tell him no.*"

"That won't be necessary," she said. "The weather's awful. I don't want you to get wet."

"What? Wetter than I am right now?" he asked with a chuckle. He walked slowly around the car, shining the beam from his flashlight on each tire as he passed.

"It's not your tire," he said. "Pop the trunk. I'm sure I heard something."

Damn. Darcy should have run him down when she had the chance.

"Oh, that? It's the spare. My boyfriend got a new one and he hasn't bolted it down yet."

"But isn't this a rental car? There's a sticker on the rear bumper."

"It was," she said. "He bought it used from the rental company."

The officer nodded, as if considering the information.

"Speaking of my boyfriend," she said, before the man had time to ask any more questions, "I really should get back to the resort and call him. I don't want him to worry."

He hesitated for a moment, then waved her on. "Drive safe."

Easing her foot on to the accelerator, she maneuvered around on the narrow road. Drawing in a shaking breath, she knew that she'd almost been caught. Good thing that *almost* didn't count.

With no choice but to return to the resort, she was trapped. How much time did she have before anyone knew Kevin was missing…much less dead?

A day? Two, if she was lucky?

She shrugged. The nights were cold, and the days were mild. He'd keep in the trunk for another twenty-four hours.

Yet, after she placed his body, she'd have to leave the resort. Once he was found, the police would know that she'd been at the White Wind all along.

Until then, she had things to do—like decide on his final resting place.

It had to be special, just like it had been for all the others.

Then she remembered. Kevin Carpenter had come to the White Wind to golf. Wasn't there a hole hidden away in the woods? It was the perfect place to leave the body. Then, well, all Darcy had to do was wait. Soon, the road would be open. When that happened, she could leave and truly begin a new life.

Chapter 13

Holly awoke on Thursday morning in the king-size bed. The curtains were drawn, leaving the room dark. Yet sunlight shone through the gap between the two panels.

The muzzy warmth of sleep vanished as several thoughts came to her at once. First, the massive mattress was far too big for a single person. Second, maybe she'd been too hasty in turning away from Liam's kisses. After all, every time he was around, she felt a pull deep within her, as if she were magnetically drawn to him.

But she couldn't possibly think about any kind of relationship with Liam, let alone sleeping with him. Not just because he was the father of her student, but if she failed to come up with the money to keep her school, she'd have to face the inevitable reality that she might not even live in Pleasant Pines much longer.

Rolling to her side, she couldn't help but wonder: Was it wrong to want a lover—albeit a temporary one?

Then again, it had been years since Holly had worried about loving anyone. Or letting anyone love her in return. Rising from the bed, she padded softly into the living room. The light on the house phone blinked with a message. RMJ? Tonya?

The door to Liam's room was shut tight and she decided not to wake him.

Picking up the receiver, Holly waited for the hotel's operator to answer.

"Front desk."

"Hi," she said, "Good morning. I think I have a message…"

The operator said, "A package was delivered for you this morning. I'll bring it to your room now."

A package? "Uh…sure."

Holly took a few minutes to prepare a cup of coffee. As she poured cream into the cup, she heard a light knocking on the front door. A bellman in the White Wind uniform stood in the corridor. He held a large cardboard box, taped shut. "Are you Holly?"

"I am."

"Then this is for you."

She accepted the box. It was heavier than she expected, and the weight pulled her forward. Carrying it across the floor, she sat it on the table next to her coffee. Using a disposable knife that was part of a set of plastic utensils, Holly sliced through the tape and opened the box.

A note, written in cramped handwriting, lay atop a pile of books and papers: *This is everything we have in the D.O. case from her childhood. Let me know if you find anything interesting. The yearbooks were taken from her house. Wyatt.*

First was a yearbook from the middle school that Darcy had attended, Slipper Rock Middle School. Holly flipped through the pages, finding Darcy's sixth-grade class picture. She wore her blond hair in twin braids and looked younger than her actual age—eleven or twelve.

There was a smile on her face, but her eyes were already hard. Was this the first glimpse of the change taking place within her? Had the future killer already witnessed too much?

There were no signatures on the pages. No notes in the margins. One of the pages was bent at the corner, as if dog-eared and then flattened.

Coincidence?

Or was there something special about this page?

It was filled with individual pictures of the seventh-grade class.

Nothing.

And yet, maybe…

Holly moved to the window and early morning sunshine shone through the glass. In the bright light, she saw it and gasped.

"Morning," said Liam. He stood across the room and ran a hand through his tousled hair. He wore flannel sleep pants and a tight-fitting T-shirt. Her mouth went dry. Immediately, Holly dropped her gaze to the book. Liam continued, "I called Tonya this morning and she didn't answer the phone. Do you think something's wrong?"

It *was* a little odd that Tonya hadn't answered. After all, she knew how nervous parents could get. Still, Holly would vouch for her no matter what. She trusted Tonya. "I'm sure if there was a problem, she would have called already. Besides, mornings can get busy. She might've just missed your call."

"I guess," said Liam. He gestured to the yearbook she held. "What's that?"

"I think I found something," she said.

"What is it?" he asked, moving to her side.

"Your team sent this up to the room. It's some of Darcy's things—from when she was growing up. See this page?"

"Yeah," said Liam. "What am I looking for?"

Holly tapped her finger under the picture of a dark-haired boy named Bobby Carpenter. "It's faint, but there's an outline of a heart around his face. Like she traced it but didn't want anything to show."

"A teenage crush? Why would that be important? Don't girls get crushes all the time?"

"If we are assuming that Darcy was being abused by her father, then the abuse was so pervasive that it helped to turn her into a killer. But to answer your questions— a teenage crush is completely normal. Considering the abuse, we know one thing for certain, Darcy's childhood was anything but typical."

"So, this guy is important?"

"He could be," she said.

"Can I see the book?" Liam asked, reaching out.

Holly was careful not to let their fingers touch as she passed it over.

Liam stared at the picture. He seemed to hum with pent-up energy.

"What is it?" she asked, moving closer and trying to see what he saw.

"It's him. I'm positive."

"Who's him?"

"This kid, Bobby. He's grown up now, obviously, and he works here. In fact, he checked us in." He looked at her. "Holly, he's the front desk manager."

"Are you sure?"

"There's only one way to find out."

Holly and Liam changed quickly and walked down to the lobby. The desk clerk was a young woman—and certainly not Bobby. "May I help you?" she asked.

"Can we speak to the front desk manager? He checked us in yesterday morning." Liam continued, asking, "What's his name again?"

"Robert Carpenter, you mean? He's not in right now," said the clerk, clearly worried. "Is something the matter?"

Robert Carpenter. Bingo.

"Will he be in later today?"

With a shake of her head, she said, "He called in. His son's sick and he stayed home." She paused and added, "Bobby Junior has the stomach bug."

"What's his normal schedule?" Liam asked. "Nine to five, Monday through Friday?"

Holly knew what he was asking and why. Could Robert Carpenter have answered the phone when Darcy called?

"He usually works during the day, but he's here Tuesday through Saturday. I mean, this week he was here on Monday."

"Really?" said Holly. "All day?"

"No, just when…" The clerk's cheeks reddened with a blush. Holly could well imagine the woman about to admit that on Monday the resort had been crawling with police, who were looking for a connection to a serial killer. That kind of news would be bad for business. "He came in to cover an emergency, I think. But I don't usually work the overnight shift, so I'm gone before he arrives. Is there a problem?"

"Do you have a picture of him?" Liam asked.

The clerk's eyes darted right and left. Unconsciously, she was looking for a way to escape as she slowly realized that Holly and Liam were after something other than a moment with the manager. "I can take a message for him?" she asked.

"No," said Liam. "You've been more than helpful."

Holly couldn't shake the feeling of unease. It was more than the fact that a classmate who Darcy had been attracted to also worked at the White Wind. It was… Well, something they'd missed. Something they had to uncover. Quickly.

Holding on to Holly's elbow, Liam led her to the bank of elevators. "I'm going to speak to the team from RMJ. It looks like Robert Carpenter is someone who should be investigated. You go back to the room and I'll be up shortly."

The elevator doors opened, and Holly stepped into the car. Her cell began to ring, and she took the phone from her pocket. It was Tonya.

"Hey," she said. "What's up? How did Sophie do last night? I'm sure Liam will want to speak to her."

"My husband's sick," said the other woman, sounding worried. "He's got a stomach flu and a fever."

Holly groaned inwardly. "I heard it was going around."

"I don't want to leave him alone and I can't bring Sophie back to my house. She'd get sick, too. I'm on my way to bring her to you. I'll be there in an hour."

The elevator door slid open and Holly stepped into the corridor, wondering what the hell she should do. Should she really let Tonya bring the child to the resort? Although, Liam's job was to gather intel…not to find or catch the killer. And if that were the case, then Holly could take care of Sophie while Liam did, well, whatever else he needed to do. And if Liam didn't want Sophie at the resort, Holly could always take the child back to Pleasant Pines.

What other options did they have?

The sky was bright and clear, yet Liam guessed that the temperature hovered just below freezing. Hands in pockets, he hustled across the parking lot, his breath turning to steam. He was still upset at himself for last night's boneheaded move. He never should have left the thumb drive in the security office. He'd learned from the past that it was the little mistakes that had the biggest consequences.

Instinctively, Charlie's face came to mind. This time, he was a grown man, in his Marine Corps dress uniform. Liam, still in high school, wore a tux and stood at Charlie's elbow. The wedding march began. And Charlie had leaned toward Liam, his voice barely a whisper—*This is it, buddy boy.*

The florist's van seemed to materialize out of nowhere, despite the fact that it had been his destination all along. It was still parked at the far corner of the employee lot.

As he drew close, Wyatt opened the door. Liam climbed in and closed the door behind him, taking in the smell of stale fast food grease and two worried agents stuck in close quarters overnight.

"I messed up," he said, taking a seat in front of a computer monitor. "I could see that the security guard was coming, and as soon as the download was complete, I bolted."

"First, we'll have to get the thumb drive back. Eventually, someone's going to find it and then there's going to be questions asked that we don't want to answer," said Marcus. "You'll have to go back tonight."

Liam ran his thumb across the table. "I figured."

Wyatt added, "But don't beat yourself up too badly. It would've been worse if you'd been seen. So, you were right to leave when you did. And the program works perfectly. We have access to all calls being made to and from the resort. If Darcy makes contact, we'll know."

"I'm glad it worked out. And I have some news of my own," said Liam. He explained what Holly had found in the yearbook and what they had learned at the front desk, adding that Robert Carpenter wasn't in today, either.

"It's something to look into," said Wyatt, scribbling down the information. "I'll run a check on him now."

"What about the video of the woman in the SUV?" Liam asked. "The one from Reno."

"The cops pulled the guy over, but the woman was gone. He said he met her in a casino and she asked for a ride home."

"Let me guess," said Liam. "She hasn't been located."

"Your guess is right," said Marcus. "But at least the police are looking."

"Anything else?" Liam asked.

"Take as many pictures as you can," said Marcus. "As soon as you get the thumb drive tonight, we'll leave."

He nodded and stood, crouching in the tight space. Then again, there was more to be said. "What about Holly?"

"She did good in finding the connection to the front desk manager."

"What about her payment?"

"Like I said before," said Marcus. "The consultant's fee is a thousand dollars a day. She'll be here for almost three full days, so that's what she's getting."

Liam asked, "What about the twenty thousand we discussed?"

"That's only if we find a direct connection to Darcy Owens," said Marcus. He continued, "If the lead on the manager pays off, she'll get the full fee."

Liam wanted to argue. Then again, he knew it wouldn't do any good. With a nod, he opened the door and stepped outside. He paused and turned back. "What about you guys? Do you need anything? Food? Coffee? Deodorant?"

"It's pretty ripe in here, huh?" said Marcus with a

wry laugh. He reached for the door's interior handle. "We picked up breakfast on our way. The shower's going to have to wait until we get back to Pleasant Pines. But thanks."

Then he shut the door and Liam turned back to the resort. He hated that he'd failed Holly again. Really, he hoped he'd be able to help her earn the cash she needed. More than anything, he realized he was hoping to at least have a little more time with her.

Though what good would more time do if she was leaving Pleasant Pines anyway?

With no other options, Darcy had returned to the resort and spent the night in Kevin Carpenter's rental car. She was worried that someone—somehow—would discover the body in the trunk. That they'd find her. She'd be arrested and would go to jail—a fate worse than death. She'd also decided that she hated her roommates, and if she'd gone back to the apartment, she'd have killed them, too. And sleeping so near to a body, to someone whose life she'd just taken, was a delicious secret.

Running her fingers through her short hair, she sat up.

There, at the far edge of the employee lot, was a white florist's van. It meant nothing to her, and she began to look away. But then she spotted the man who was walking away from the van heading toward the resort.

The same man she'd seen the day before in the hallway of the staff's apartment building.

Who was he? And what did he want?

Darcy didn't know, but she knew one thing. She had to leave. Now.

"*Stay,*" whispered the Darkness.

"No," said Darcy, while clambering into the front seat. "Something's going on and I don't want to wait around and find out what it is." She started the engine and put the car into Drive.

"*I'm with you and I make you invincible. Discover the truth. Vanquish your foes.*"

Darcy slowly turned off the ignition. Truly, she didn't know who the guy was or what he wanted.

But she had the Darkness on her side. And so she decided to return to the apartment and play housekeeper for another day. It was the only way. Because Darcy knew there was something wrong with the dark-haired guy. And she was determined to uncover the truth.

The back of Liam's neck itched. He could feel a pair of eyes on him as he walked away from the mobile HQ. But who? And where in the hell were they? He'd scanned the parking lot—barely at quarter capacity—filled only with empty cars. Yet the surrounding woods were vast, and a person could be hidden anywhere.

Keeping his gait slow and steady, he returned to the resort but didn't enter the main building. Instead, he approached the back, heading toward the woods. Keeping to the tree line, he moved silently and circumvented the building. Liam was in his element. It was predator versus prey.

He moved slowly, examining everything. There were no branches broken by a passing shoulder. No undergrowth turned up by scuffling feet. No signs that anyone had been in the woods—much less watching Liam.

Could it be that working an undercover operation had left him paranoid?

He had to admit it was a possibility.

But no. Liam knew what it was to watch and wait.

He scanned the cars again. This time, from the cover of the woods, he had the ability to look at each one in turn. They were all empty, now at least. Had he missed someone earlier?

It was the same feeling he'd had in the hallway of the staff's residential building. The sense that he was being watched, even though there was nobody there.

Liam wanted to tell himself that being back on his family's land was playing with his emotions and imagination. Then again, he knew better.

Someone was out there, somewhere.

Who was it? And what did they want?

Keeping to the trees, he returned to the resort. His stomach grumbled and he realized that he hadn't eaten breakfast. He checked his watch. It had been almost ninety minutes since he and Holly had gone to the lobby, searching for information about the front desk manager.

What had Holly been doing since then?

And how would she react to Marcus Jones not giving her all the money she'd bargained for?

He entered the lobby and took the elevator to the third floor. Using his key card, he opened the door and stepped into the suite. Holly was at the table. A stack of files sat at her elbow. She looked up as he entered. The sun shone at her from behind, turning her hair the color of coppery fire. His heart squeezed in his chest.

"You look busy," he said, letting the door swing shut.

"Hey, there's something we need to talk about," she said.

"Did you find something else in the case file?" Liam felt pulled to her, his body hardening as he gazed at her, taking her in completely. Then again, what good did it do for him to want her if she didn't want him in return? He stayed where he was and rested his shoulder against the door.

"I did," she said. "But it's not that… It's…"

Why the hesitation? Maybe now was the time to tell her about his conversation with Marcus. "Ah, listen. Wyatt and Marcus are going to look into Darcy's connection to the front desk manager. If it turns out that he's the one she called, or if he has information that leads to her arrest, you'll get the entire twenty thousand dollars. If not—" he shrugged "—you'll get the consultant's fee. Three thousand bucks. That's not too bad."

She closed the folder and turned to face him. "I know you feel completely responsible for the bank not working with me on all the debts. But to be honest, the outcome of the meeting would've been the same even if I'd been on time. It wasn't fair of me to blame you. In the moment, I was upset and wanted to lash out at someone. That someone happened to be you. I'm sorry for that. I made the financial mess and it's my job to clean it up. Still, I sincerely appreciate your help."

Liam didn't know that it was possible for him to like Holly Jacobs more than he had before. As it turned out, he could. "You know, you're damn near perfect."

She laughed. "Hardly."

"You're smart. Funny. Kind. More than that, it's hard to admit to a mistake and apologize. You've done both."

She opened the folder and looked down at a page. "Besides, the consultant's fee will be helpful with the move if I take the job."

Take the job? That was news to him. "What job? Where?"

"I've been offered a faculty position at a college in Ohio. If I'm not able to keep the day-care center, I should probably accept."

"Is that what you want? I thought you liked working with young children."

"I do like the younger kids. It's just…" She shook her head. "I have to be honest. I'm not good at running a business and there's nothing else in Pleasant Pines for someone with a PhD in child psychology to do. Maybe if I moved to Cheyenne, or maybe Laramie, but even there, I'd be working at a university."

"What would you want to do…if you could do anything?"

"I guess write another book."

"Why don't you?"

Holly shook her head. "What would my topic be? All the ways you can fail at business without really trying? Besides, my first book was a success and then…"

"And then, what?"

"Then it wasn't. For months, I was invited to parties and I was interviewed on the radio. TV. Different mental health podcasts. You name it. When the book quit selling, I was forgotten. It was awful. When the fawning stopped, I came home and swore that I'd never get caught up in being a celebrity again."

Liam felt her slipping away, like she was almost in Ohio. He knew that he should let her go. But instead he said, "You don't know if the Robert Carpenter lead will work out or not. Maybe you should give it a day or two before taking the university job."

"Maybe," she said, though her tone told Liam that she was far from convinced. She exhaled and lifted a sheet of paper from the pile. "I was thinking about what you said last night—about predators having a hunting ground. I think I found something."

"You did?" he said, moving toward Holly. Liam stopped himself before he reached her side, knowing that he needed to keep his distance. "What is it?"

She held up a sheet of paper with a pencil drawing. There was a decent likeness of a white farmhouse surrounded by woods. Next to the house was…what? He couldn't really make sense of it. Some sort of black scribble. A tornado? A storm cloud? "Darcy drew this when she was a freshman in high school," said Holly. She pointed to the bottom right corner and a penciled-in date.

"I think this is her house," she continued. "But this," said Holly, tapping on the scribble, "is what I find interesting."

"What is it?"

Holly turned to look at Liam. "I think it's a face."

Liam reached out for the drawing. Up close he could see it, narrow eyes and jagged mouth set into a wedge of black. A chill ran up his spine. Again, he had to ask, "What is it?"

"I'm not sure, but if this person were one of my clients, I'd be spending a lot of time working on uncovering what this is to them. And why they felt a need to try to hide it."

Liam handed the picture back to Holly and returned to his post by the door. "You should talk to Wyatt," said Liam. "Next week, or something."

"Sure," said Holly. "If I'm in town."

If I'm in town. Her words hung in the air between them. What else was there for him to say?

Holly tucked the picture into a file folder. "Not to change the subject, but there's really something I need to tell you." She paused. Inhaled. Continued. "I got a call from Tonya this morning."

Terror gripped Liam's throat as he imagined a thousand and one things that could've gone wrong with Sophie. "Is everything okay? What's the matter with Sophie?"

"Sophie's fine. It's Tonya's husband. He's sick and she needs to be home so she can take care of him. But she can't bring Sophie and risk getting her sick, too."

The thought of his little girl sick with the flu left Liam queasy himself. "Which means what, exactly?"

"Well, I shouldn't have made this decision for you, but it seemed like the only thing to do…" Her words trailed off. Before she could pick up her story, there was a knock at the door and Liam could well imagine what Holly was going to say next.

He lifted the handle and pulled the door open.

Before he could say a word, Sophie launched herself into his arms. "Dad-dee." As she wrapped her arms around his neck, she said, "See, I did get to be on the trip with you and Holly."

Chapter 14

Holly offered to return to Pleasant Pines with Sophie, giving up her last day of payment. When Liam refused her offer, she agreed to watch Sophie, while he continued to work.

To her, it seemed like the best plan. After Liam left to capture images. Holly suggested a dip in one or—or both—of the pools at the resort. Thankfully, Holly had thought to pack her swimsuit, although Sophie didn't have anything with her.

It was a problem easily solved by a quick trip to one of the resort's clothing stores. They quickly purchased a shimmering pink swimsuit and a set of mermaid water wings for the little girl.

"One. Two. Three!" Holly sat near the edge, in the shallow end of the pool. Holding Sophie's hands, she lifted the child on the last count. "Up and *whee!*" she said as Sophie jumped into her arms with a splash.

The indoor pool was housed in a room of glass that overlooked the mountain vistas. The warm temperatures Holly had seen on her weather app finally arrived and the sun hung in the sky of robin's egg blue, but it was still a little too chilly to be in an outdoor pool. For almost ninety minutes, Sophie had been playing in the water. As far as Holly was concerned, it was the best time she'd spent in a long while. Still, she found that her gaze traveled to the grounds, where she kept hoping to catch a glimpse of Liam's return.

Sophie giggled and slapped the surface of the water. Holly couldn't help but smile.

"Hey, Dr. Holly?" Sophie asked.

"Yes, sweetie?"

"When's lunch?"

Shoot. They hadn't made any concrete plans—Liam only said that he'd come and find them at the pool when he was done. Holly consulted a large clock affixed to the wall of the clubhouse: 12:30 p.m. Definitely lunchtime.

"Why don't we get dried off? There's a restaurant. What do you want to eat?"

"Yay! Chicken nuggets, my *faaavorite,*" Sophie chanted, splashing in time with her words.

Holly laughed. "I'm sure we can find you some chicken nuggets."

"Yay!" said Sophie. "You're the best, Dr. Holly."

Holly glanced over her shoulder, worried that someone had overheard Sophie's use of the word *doctor.* But there was no one else at the pool.

If Holly were supposed to be Liam's pretend wife,

then it made her Sophie's fake stepmother. She could hardly expect a child to understand the need for secrecy, but all the same, they did have a cover to maintain.

"Since we aren't at school, you don't have to call me Dr. Holly. You can just call me Holly. Okay?"

Sophie gave a thumbs-up. "O-kay!"

At the edge of the pool, a dark-haired woman in a black-and-white housekeeping uniform hurried past.

"Excuse me," Holly called to the woman.

The woman strode on.

"Excuse me," said Holly again, louder this time. "Do you happen to know where we can get towels?"

The woman stopped. "I'm sorry?"

"Hi," said Holly, stepping from the pool. Sophie was perched on her hip. "Can you get us a towel?"

The woman shook her head. "Ah, of course. I'll get a towel for you and your daughter. We ran out, but we have more inside." She disappeared into the clubhouse, returning a moment later with a stack of thick, white towels and held them out. "Here you are."

Sophie wiggled to the ground as Holly read the woman's name tag. "Thank you, Claire."

"It's my pleasure," she said as she placed the rest of the towels on the metal rack.

Holly unfolded a towel and held it open. "You ready for chicken nuggets?" she asked Sophie.

"Yes. Yes. Yes," said the little girl as she skipped to Holly and the open towel.

"All right," said Holly as she wrapped up the child, ruffling her wet hair with a corner of the towel. "Let's get some lunch."

The dark-haired housekeeper smiled. "Your daughter is adorable."

"Oh, she's not my daughter," she said, a little too quickly. "I'm her stepmother." Holly continued to dry Sophie's hair, all the while hoping the towel muffled anything Sophie might hear of the conversation—or any comment the little girl might make.

"Still," said Claire. "She is adorable. You're a very lucky woman."

"Thank you," said Holly as she wrapped the towel around Sophie's shoulders.

The woman narrowed her blue eyes. It was an accusatory glare, for sure. It left Holly feeling uncomfortable and wondering what she'd done wrong.

The other woman said, "Well, you must excuse me. I have work to do."

"Of course," said Holly. "Thanks again for the towels."

Liam approached the pool from the direction of the golf course. He lifted his hand in greeting. "How are my best girls?" he called out.

"Daddy," said Sophie. Dropping the towel, she ran toward her father.

"Use your walking feet, please," said Holly, out of a long-held habit for safety. "The concrete is slippery."

Sophie slowed her gait. Arms swinging, she moved at a fast walk.

Liam scooped his daughter into his arms for a big hug. "How's my baby girl?"

Holly watched the two of them together, unable to hold back her smile. Then she noticed that Claire still stood nearby, watching the duo intently, as well.

A shiver ran down Holly's spine and she grabbed another towel, draping it over her shoulders.

"Yes," said Claire as she turned to face Holly. Her clear blue eyes had inexplicably turned as dark and ominous as a storm cloud. "You are a very lucky woman."

During the course of the day, Liam had taken hundreds of pictures. None of the faces he photographed had helped in the search for Darcy Owens. In fact, all Liam had to show for his time and effort was a happy daughter.

Now, they were back in the suite, and as he sent off the latest batch of images to Wyatt and Marcus he noticed it was well past Sophie's bedtime.

"Good night, baby girl." Liam had set up Sophie to sleep in one of the twin beds. He placed a kiss on his daughter's forehead. "I love you."

"Good night, Daddy," she said, her voice thick with sleep. "I 'ove you, too."

He turned off the bedside lamp.

"Daddy, I need a night-light."

Shoot. He hadn't known that Sophie was going to be at the resort, too. If he had, he would've brought one from home. "What if I turn on the light in the bathroom and leave the door open a little?"

"Okay," said Sophie, nodding emphatically.

"Good night," Liam said again.

"Daddy?"

"Yes, baby girl?"

"Will Holly be here in the morning?"

"She sure will," he said.

"Good," said Sophie as she snuggled deeper into the covers. "I like Holly."

"Me, too," said Liam.

He slipped out the door, stepping into the adjoining living room. Holly sat on the sofa, with her legs tucked beneath her. She'd donned a long sweater in coral, along with a pair of navy leggings. She was casual, comfortable and sexy as hell.

Looking up as he pulled the door closed, she said, "Hey."

"Hey yourself."

"Is Sophie sleeping?" she asked.

He took a seat at the other end of the sofa. "Almost," he said.

"She's a good kid," said Holly. "I like her a lot."

"Funny," said Liam. His heart skipped a beat. "She said the same thing about you."

"I didn't want to ask you during the day, not in a public place or in front of Sophie," Holly began, "but have you found any more links to Darcy Owens?"

"I heard from Marcus," said Liam with a shake of his head. "The front desk manager—the one who might've been Darcy's crush—was questioned. He admits to having attended the same school as Darcy. In fact, their houses aren't too far away from each other—and by that, I mean there's a mile of woods between the two properties. He knew who she was but not much more."

"Was he at the resort Monday morning?"

"According to the cops who talked to him, he had a job interview someplace else. In fact, he had a follow-up interview today. It wasn't a sick kid that kept him from work." Liam exhaled. "Marcus wants to give our coworker the justice she deserves. And listen—I was there. I saw what Darcy did to Julia, and I can't say that I blame him for feeling that way. All the same…" He shook his head.

"All the same, what?" Holly coaxed.

"All the same, this tactic isn't effective."

"Then why are we here?"

"Pride," he said. "RMJ has had Darcy Owens twice and twice she's gotten away. It's given RMJ a black eye that will never go away."

"What are you going to do?"

Holly shifted, letting one of her feet dangle over the sofa's edge. Her toes were painted bright red. It was a sexy little surprise. He couldn't help but imagine how her toes would look curled, as Holly was claimed by passion. Scrubbing a hand over his face, Liam answered her question. "The hell if I know what comes next."

Without thinking, he lifted her foot onto his lap. Her skin was smooth and warm as he rubbed her instep.

"What are you doing?" she asked.

"Giving you a foot rub. Do you mind?"

"I suppose not," she said, sighing. "That feels good."

His hands traveled higher, from Holly's toes to her ankle to her calf. Holly leaned back, not telling him to stop or pulling away. Liam stared at his fingers as he worked her flesh, unable to meet her in the eye. Was her pulse racing, like his? Did she want him as much as he wanted her?

Lifting his gaze, he looked at Holly. She studied him through half-opened lids. "What?" he asked.

"You," she said.

"What about me?"

"I don't know. There's just something…" With a shake of her head, Holly let her words trail off.

"Well? Is it good or bad?"

"You seem, I don't know, like a man out of place. Like you're from a different time or something."

"You got all that from a foot rub?" he asked, almost teasing.

"It's just the way you looked earlier, when you were standing by the window. It was like you were looking into the past."

How had she known? Since arriving, every kid Liam passed was Charlie. He was at an opposite table, the five-year-old playing on a tablet. Or the ten-year-old who ran through the lobby. Never mind that Charlie 's family wouldn't have had the money for a tablet computer, much less cash for a night at a resort like this. For Liam, his cousin, like the past, was everywhere.

"Maybe I was, but what about you?"

"Me? I'm more concerned for the future," she said. "There's nothing in the past but what-if and should've-been."

"Look at us, we're quite the mismatched pair. Still, we make a decent team." Reaching for her hand, Liam stared at their joined fingers. "Plus," he added, "you're pretty easy to talk to and to trust. I don't do either of those things easily, but then I think you've figured that out already. I like that about you, Holly."

She inched closer, her breath caressing his cheek. "You're not so bad yourself."

He smiled a little. "That's better than you turning away from me or turning me down."

She licked her lips. Looking away, Holly stared at

something just beyond Liam's shoulder. "I don't want to complicate things."

"I understand," he said, even though he didn't. He wanted her. She wanted him. It all seemed pretty simple and straightforward. "I'm not going to pressure you into anything here."

"Do you really understand?" she asked. "Because I'm not sure that I know what's going on myself."

"You have your life plan. You need money to keep your school open. A relationship is a complication. Besides, you could be leaving town, which means us getting involved could be difficult for Sophie."

Holly touched her fingertips to his lips, silencing him. "If I can't get the money to keep Saplings, then I'll definitely have to leave Pleasant Pines," she said. "You said it yourself—I might not be around much longer."

"Now I'm really confused. What are you saying?"

"Kiss me," she whispered.

It was all the invitation he needed. Liam placed his lips on Holly's. Lightly, at first. She sighed. Pressing herself forward, Holly's breasts brushed against his arm. Liam pulled her to him before easing her back on the sofa. Holly's golden hair spread around her like a halo—but in this moment, as passion blazed to life between them, there was nothing angelic about her.

She raked her fingers over his chest. Liam hardened with desire. He wanted this woman, more than anything he'd wanted for as long as he could remember.

His hand moved to her waist and he slipped his fingers under the loose hem of her sweater. His palm traveled higher, stroking her stomach, chest, then her breasts. He teased her nipples until they were hard, straining against the fabric of her bra. A little mew of longing escaped her throat.

Holly's bra latched in the front and Liam worked the clasp free. Without being covered, he could explore and claim and conquer. Yet, he wanted more. He wanted to know how she tasted. Or what it would take to turn her mew of delight into a cry of passion. Tugging at her sweater, Liam lifted it over Holly's head.

"Take me to the bedroom," she whispered. Her top slipped through his fingers, pooling on the floor.

Cradling Holly to his chest, Liam lifted her from the sofa and carried her to the bed. A wedge of light cut across the floor—beyond that, the room was shrouded in darkness. Holly lay upon the mattress. The creamy skin of her chest was luminous against the shadows. Her nipples had taken on the color of a sultry red wine—tonight, Liam intended to get drunk.

"I want you," she said, her voice coming to him, as if from a dream.

He didn't need to be told twice.

Holly wrapped her arms around Liam's shoulders and pulled him to her. He nestled his erection between her thighs. She could feel how much he wanted her, and her head swam with the notion. She wasn't used to being thought of as desirable by anyone. She'd kept herself so isolated for so long that she felt almost drunk on the power. But she needed him inside her, too. And she didn't want to wait.

Sleeping with a man after only having known him for a few days went against everything Holly believed about herself and her life. She was thoughtful. She was deliberate. She never did anything without a reason. Yet, where Liam Alexander was concerned, Holly was far from rational. As he ran one palm over her stomach, the other cupping her breast, Holly yearned to give in to her basest longings.

In the end, it wouldn't matter much. Liam had admitted that he was without the resources to find Darcy's accomplice, even if that person were here in the first place. It meant that Holly had no choice but to accept the job in Ohio. Soon, she'd be gone. And Liam? He'd be part of her past, too.

Without worry for the future, Holly found the courage to live in the moment, to love in the moment…even if it was only temporary.

Fumbling with the button on his pants, she said, "I want you, Liam. Now."

He kissed her harder as she pulled down the zipper of his jeans.

"No," he said, his breath mixing with hers. "Not yet. I want to take my time. I want us both to enjoy every minute."

It had been more than a year since Holly had been intimate with anyone. Now, even a few more seconds seemed like an eternity. She reached into Liam's jeans. Gripping his length, she used a bead of his moisture and stroked his shaft.

"What are you doing?" he asked, his voice a growl. "Unless you stop, I won't be able to control myself."

"Good," said Holly. Lifting her rear, she wiggled out of her leggings and panties. Dropping them to the floor, she said, "Now let's get you undressed, too."

His breath caught. Despite the dim light, she knew he saw it—her scar.

He placed his lips on the line that ran across her abdomen. At one time, it had been jagged, red and raised. Now, it was thin and silver, a subtle, yet constant reminder of what she had done—or rather, what she'd failed to do.

"What happened?" he asked.

"A car accident," she said softly. "When I was in high school."

"How bad?" he asked.

Holly screwed her eyes shut. "The driver died."

"I'm sorry," he said. "I've lost people before. It's difficult. The loss changes you."

Holly wanted to share everything with Liam. The fact that it wasn't simply an accident but an outright tragedy—if only she could have prevented the carnage.

Yet, how could she explain how weak she'd been to Liam, a man who was always so brave?

Liam whispered. "Look at me."

Holly opened her eyes and gazed at Liam's face. His eyes, the color of the forest, held concern. Sadness. Sympathy. She didn't want anyone to feel sorry for her. Holly deserved the scar—and so much more.

Pushing against his chest, Holly moved away from Liam. "We shouldn't do anything. Sophie might walk in."

He hauled himself up and looked at her. "If you don't want to do this, Holly, then say so. It's fine. But please don't use my kid as an excuse."

"It's not an excuse," she said. "It's just…" She paused, wondering if she could really share her fears with this man she barely knew. Maybe it was the gloom that allowed her to hide. Or maybe it was Liam's shoulders, strong enough to bear any burden. Maybe even her own? Or maybe it was the fact that she might never see him again after the next day or two, but Holly found herself giving in. "I don't usually like anyone to see my scar."

"Why?"

"It's hideous. It's—"

"Scars make you human," he interrupted. "A strong and fierce woman. A survivor."

Was that what her scar meant? That she was strong, she had survived where others had not? Was she refusing to live her life because she was afraid of making another mistake?

Or was it what she always feared? Had her actions tarnished her soul until she felt she was truly unworthy of the love and trust of any man?

Then again, did it matter? What she had with Liam wasn't love, anyway. It was simply sex, a primal need.

And yet, a part of her knew, deep down, that Liam Alexander was a man she could love.

"Make love to me, Liam. I won't break," she said, her voice so low that Holly wasn't even sure she had spoken out loud.

"Are you sure?"

In answer, she reached for the hem of his shirt and tugged it over his head. His chiseled chest and abs stole her breath. "You're like a sculpture," she said. "A work of art, really."

"Me? Art?" asked Liam. He dipped his head and took one of Holly's nipples in his mouth. His tongue swirled her into a hard peak. Holly let out a low moan. "Although I was just thinking that you're some kind of magical creature." His mouth moved from her breast to her stomach. He placed a leisurely kiss on her navel. "You have to be, Holly. I'm completely captivated by you."

"Make love to me," she said.

"There's something I want to do first."

Liam moved his mouth lower. He parted her folds, his breath hot. Placing his mouth at the top of her sex, Holly bucked with the sensation. Her hips lifted from the mattress.

Holly tried to think, to put words to what she was feeling. Yet it was too intense. At the moment her ecstasy teetered on the edge of pain, she let go. Crying out, Holly's racing heart echoed throughout her body.

Rising to his feet, Liam stripped out of his pants.

Holly could only form one word. "Condom."

"I've got that covered. After what happened with Erin, I always keep one with me," he said, removing a foil packet from his wallet. Within seconds, he was protected for them both.

Liam moved back to Holly. He hovered above her, his hips pressing into hers. His tip barely touched her sex. She gazed between their bodies. Him. Her. Intimate, but not yet one.

The delirium that followed her passion was starting to wane. In its place was an undercurrent of anticipation. Holly groaned as he filled her, somehow making her complete.

"Look at me," he said.

Liam's face was inches from hers. His dark eyes

were filled with desire. His lips were parted, his breath caught with each thrust—like the punctuation at the end of a sentence. She gripped his shoulders as he drove harder. The bliss from before began to claim her. Like a wind carried to the heavens, Holly rose higher and higher.

Liam was with her. Always together. Always one. Throwing back her head, she cried with satisfaction. He placed hot kisses on her exposed throat. His thrusts became harder, faster, more urgent. Sweat dampened his skin. His pulse raced, beating wildly at the base of his throat. A growl broke free from his lips.

Panting, his hips slowed. After placing a languid kiss on Holly's lips, he said, "I'll be right back."

He slid out of her, before disappearing into the adjoining bathroom. Holly turned on the bedside lamp. Clothes were strewn across the floor. She rummaged through the pile, finding her bra and panties. For now, they were enough. She dressed quickly and slipped beneath the covers just as Liam exited the bathroom.

He donned his boxers and got under the covers with her. He smelled musky from their lovemaking and salty from sweat. Holly drew a deep breath, her sluggish pulse beginning to race.

Snuggling next to her, Liam wrapped his arm around Holly. He placed a kiss on her shoulder.

"I was just thinking," he said.

"I'm glad you can. After that, I can't even remember my last name."

"That might not be a problem," he said.

Holly laughed. Turning her back to Liam, she melded

her body to fit with his. He lifted the hair from her shoulder and kissed her neck.

"I'm not joking," he said. His breath branded her skin.

Holly went stiff. "What are you saying?"

"Marry me."

"Are you crazy?" She batted away his hand. Covers, tangled around her middle, tethered her to the bed. Struggling free, she staggered to the floor. Turning to face him, Holly asked, "*Marry* you? What the hell are you talking about? No."

Tucking an arm behind his head, Liam stared at Holly. His muscles were long and lean. She couldn't help but wonder if he tasted the same way he smelled.

"Why not?" he asked.

Holly refused to argue while wearing nothing more than her underwear. She needed to put on something—anything. Bending to the pile of clothes at her feet, she searched for her sweater. Damn. It was in the living room, she remembered now. Without her own top, she settled for the next best thing and slid Liam's shirt over her head. Finally covered, she answered his question with one or two of her own. "Why should I marry you? How can you even think about a lifetime commitment after only knowing each other for a couple of days?"

"Well, we both stand to gain something from the situation, don't we? Sophie likes you. You seem to genuinely care about her." He looked at her. "We could have more kids, if you wanted to."

Holly was quiet for a long moment, wondering if she had stepped into the twilight zone. She couldn't think of what to say, how to respond to the offer he'd just made. *I can never give you the children you obviously want. I made a mistake and will pay for that for the rest of my life. But thanks, anyway, for the offer of a loveless marriage!* Her throat burned. Her eyes watered. Yet still, Holly said nothing.

Liam continued, oblivious to her internal struggle. "You said yourself that you need money to pay off all your loans on the day-care center. I don't have twenty thousand dollars in the bank. But if we were married, I could help you get the money…"

"Whoa, whoa, whoa." Holly held up both hands. "Stop right there. You want to marry me so I can take care of your daughter and then you'll give me the money for the day-care center? I have news for you, buddy, I'm not a prostitute."

Liam shook his head. "That's not how I meant it. I—"

"I don't care how you meant it. Proposing because I'm good with children and you have good credit is a horrible idea."

Liam got up from the bed. The pulse at the base of his neck throbbed. He stepped into his jeans. Pulling them on, he said, "This would be a good choice for both of us."

He searched the floor. Was he looking for the rest of his clothes? Holly assumed so.

"I have your shirt," she said.

Liam ran a hand over his face. "Keep it," he said. "I don't need it back. I better go and check on Sophie."

"Sure," said Holly.

Without another word, Liam left, pulling the door closed behind him.

She swallowed. How had something that felt so right

gone so wrong? In reality, it didn't matter. Holly knew what she needed to do.

Picking up her phone from the bedside table, she typed a few simple words before hitting Send.

The message went to Louise, the psychology department chairperson from the University of Findlay in Ohio.

Thanks for the job offer, Holly texted. I accept.

Chapter 15

Liam's eyes sprang open. His heart hammered against his ribs. His breath was ragged. Sweat dampened his hair. How had he dozed off when he had to return to the security room and retrieve the thumb drive?

And what had he been dreaming about that had left him breathless and covered in sweat? He could recall nothing, other than a darkness so profound that he would never again see the light.

Drawing in a lungful of air, Liam counted. One. Two. Three. No doubt whatever his nightmare, it had been brought on by all his the recent changes in his life. All the memories of his past that had risen to the surface since he'd returned to his home. His new job of searching for a serial killer. And finally, the ill-advised marriage proposal.

No wonder he'd had a terrible dream.

Liam flinched at the way he left things with Holly. Not for the first time, he wondered what advice Charlie would give. His cousin's voice filled his head. "You shouldn't have been an ass. Now, you have to fix your problem."

With a sigh, he threw back the covers and placed his feet to the floor. After getting out of the bed, Liam crept into the living room.

The door to the master bedroom was closed—a sure sign that he wasn't welcome in Holly's bed anymore. Certainly, his impulsive plan had come across as obnoxious. Arrogant. Really, really selfish.

Damn it. Why couldn't he have kept his mouth shut, just once?

"Going back to the security room?" He hadn't heard her open the door. Yet Holly stood on the threshold of the master bedroom, leaning on the doorjamb. She wore flannel pajamas with a floral print. Not erotic, but on her, sexy all the same.

"I didn't mean to wake you," he said.

"That's okay. I wasn't sleeping."

"I can't believe that I left the thumb drive in the server. It was dumb mistake—seems to be my specialty these days," he said and paused. Should he tell her more? Did he owe Holly an explanation? Then again, he wanted her to know. "I'm sorry about before. The proposal was a stupid idea. I just want to help you. I want to take care of my kid. I want to make things right, for everyone…" He shook his head. "I don't know what else to say, other than sorry."

Holly huffed out a breath, frustrated, yet sympathetic. "It's not wrong to want your child to be cared for. And I do appreciate your concern for me. Honestly. It's just…" She sighed. "It's just that you should want more for yourself than a marriage of convenience. Don't you want to marry someone you love?"

It was then that Liam realized he'd come to care for Holly—and that couldn't possibly come to a positive ending for either of them, considering his track record. "I better go," he said. "Otherwise, I'll miss my window to get into the security office again."

"I'll stay here with Sophie. Liam, be careful." She moved to the sofa and sat down.

Liam nodded and left the room. He conducted his mission carefully, an eye on any possible tail, but his mind on everything that had gone down the night before. As he had done the previous night, Liam used the key card to enter the security room. It was empty. He was relieved to see the thumb drive still in place and retrieved it quickly. He exited the resort through a side door. The cold bit into his flesh. He walked toward the employee lot. For a moment, Liam stepped into his past. It was in this exact spot that Charlie had produced a pack of cigarettes purloined from an uncle.

"Wanna try one?"

They had been twelve and fourteen. Liam had no interest in smoking, but he'd rather have died than disappointed Charlie.

"Sure," he'd said, lifting one skinny shoulder in a shrug. "I'll try."

The smoke had burned his nose, his throat, his lungs. Liam had begun to cough and couldn't stop, even after he retched.

In that moment, Charlie had crumpled up the package of smokes and thrown them into the woods. "I'm sorry," he'd said, bending to look Liam in the eye. "I'll always take care of you."

Too bad that Liam couldn't have made the same promise.

His stomach roiling, he found his way to the florist's van, still in its spot at the back of the property.

He slapped his palm on the back door. "It's me," he said.

The door opened and Wyatt leaned out.

"Here you go." Liam held up the slim piece of plastic and metal.

Wyatt gripped the drive in his closed fist. "Thanks. We're leaving now. You?"

Liam shook his head. "I'll get going in the morning. My kid's here and there's no sense in waking her up."

"Your kid?"

"It's a long story. I'll tell you later."

"Speaking of long stories," said the other man, "Julia's back in Pleasant Pines."

"How'd that happen?" Liam asked.

"She needs to start PT and rehab and she wanted to go back to Pleasant Pines."

"Wouldn't Cheyenne be a better place for that kind of care?"

"You'd think, wouldn't you? Martinez offered to stay until Julia went home, and I guess she didn't want him hanging around the hospital for the next several weeks."

"That's good news," said Liam, his spirits lifted for the first time since he left Holly's room.

"You did good," said Wyatt. "Sincerely, man, welcome to the team."

With a nod, Liam pushed the door shut. A moment later, the van's engine rumbled and the lights turned on. Then the mobile HQ slowly pulled out of the parking lot, the taillights nothing but twin dots of red.

Liam stood in the parking lot. The air was cold, and he shoved his hands deep into the pockets of his jeans. He should return to the room. Yet he couldn't face Holly, not until he'd figured out what he wanted—and why.

He turned from the parking lot and back to the one place he'd always feel safe and at home. The woods.

Darcy was soaked with sweat, yet she shivered with cold. Her bones ached. Her right shoulder throbbed with each sluggish beat of her heart. She'd spent the past five hours dragging Kevin's corpse through the woods, before leaving his body on the golf course. Instead of driving away and never looking back, she now drove back to the resort. Her fever and infection had come back worse than before. She needed more antibiotics and knew just where to find them.

There was still a full prescription in Kevin's now empty room. After that, she'd leave this place.

Then again, could she get back into the resort without being questioned? Would the passkey she'd been given still work?

And, truly, was it worth the risk?

The road was dark, narrow and abandoned. She turned the corner, dimming her headlights, before heading into the employee lot. A white van was parked in the corner. Next to the rear door stood two figures, both shrouded in the shadows.

One of them stepped into a pool of light and her blood went cold.

Wyatt Thornton.

The same man who'd shot her. The same one who'd been chasing her for years.

Wyatt jumped into the back of the van and closed the door. A plume of exhaust rolled out the tailpipe as the lights cut through the darkness. She ducked below the dashboard as the van lumbered past.

She waited until she could no longer hear the engine and peered out the windshield. The second man remained—and she knew him, too. He was the man she'd seen in the hallway of the staff apartment. He'd been at the pool, too.

It didn't take a lot of imagination to figure out that the man, whoever he was, worked for Rocky Mountain Justice.

She saw the man standing at the edge of the pavement. Even in the shadows, she knew it was him. His appearance didn't surprise her. Really, it only confirmed what she already knew.

He was one of them. He was part of Rocky Mountain Justice.

The man walked toward a line of trees, disappearing so completely that it was almost like he'd never been there at all. Like a band had been tightened around her chest, Darcy couldn't breathe.

What was she supposed to do now?

It was the Darkness who answered. *"Make the bastards pay."*

* * *

Liam took the same path he had taken with Holly when they'd first arrived at the resort. Past the outcropping of rocks. Beyond where his aunt's house had sat. Back into the woods and onto the trail.

As he walked, he wondered why he'd brought Holly to the place where so many of his memories had been made? Then again, he knew. For him, she'd been different. Somehow, she was a safe harbor in a constantly shifting world.

He continued up the path. Yet, there was something else about the woods. It was an absolute stillness that was almost like…

Liam stopped where he stood and turned his nose to the breeze. It was there, faint but unmistakable. The scent of decay and death.

Liam's pace slowed as the path led to the fairway. In the distance the flag for the hole hung lank in the mist. A bank of fog clung to the ground.

Liam remained at the edge of the forest and stared at the clearing. He saw it, not as it was but as it used to be—when the land was wild and had been touched by no other hand than nature's.

The hill was covered in boulders, some larger than a car. It was the same place where he and Charlie had played as kids, never knowing that one wrong step could be their last.

He remembered the Thanksgiving when he was twenty-two as being bone-cold, with snow so thick that visibility was next to nothing. The day had started out warm with a clear blue sky.

Liam and Charlie, both on a weekend's pass from the Marine Corps, came home for the holiday.

It was well past dark when they'd gotten a call from the sheriff. A hiker had gone missing. Volunteers were needed. Neither Liam nor Charlie hesitated to join in the search.

It took hours for Liam and Charlie, a team of two, to find the hiker. The guy was stuck on an outcropping of rock. They rappelled down to the hiker, where Liam had attached a tandem harness to the guy and gotten him to the top of the cliff.

Charlie had not followed.

After radioing for help, Liam descended again.

One of Charlie's carabiners had frozen shut.

"I've got you, man," said Liam.

But he'd been wrong.

Liam broke the old carabiner as a gust of wind whipped around the mountainside.

Charlie pitched backward.

Liam grabbed Charlie's harness and swore he'd never let it go. The cold was brutal. The wind, unrelenting. A metal anchor snapped in two and Liam fell back.

"Let me go," Charlie shouted above the wind.

"No way." Liam fought to hold on to Charlie and to the mountainside both.

"You can't save me, and I won't let you die."

"No," Liam screamed, his voice swallowed by the frozen gusts.

Then Charlie unfastened his harness and disappeared into oblivion.

It would have been better if everyone had blamed

Liam. Instead, his family had been understanding, consoling, and so damned kind.

Charlie's wife had given Liam Charlies' dog tag, saying, "You were more than a cousin to him—more even than a brother."

All the while, Liam couldn't sleep without having nightmares about the sound of Charlie's body hitting the ground. But no team had even been able to search for him—the winter storms had moved in by then, so no body had ever been found.

Liam stood in the woods, trembling, as sweat streamed down his face. He held the dog tag in his fist, the metal edge biting into his palm.

Some of the fog lifted.

In the distance Liam saw a form and he knew that death had found this place once more.

There, next to the ninth hole, lay a body.

Chapter 16

Darcy Owens hated her housekeeping uniform. Yet, she was thankful that she'd had enough forethought to keep it, even after Kevin Carpenter had died. She'd changed in the back seat of the car, then entered the hotel through the front doors. As she walked across the lobby, a jolt of pain shot through her shoulder with each step.

A young woman stood behind the front desk. Her eyes were glassy with exhaustion.

"I just saw one of the guests outside." Darcy hooked her thumb toward the sliding doors. "Tall guy. Brown hair. Super-handsome."

The clerk craned her neck to see who Darcy meant. "Do you mean Liam Alexander?"

"Yeah, he said he needs more towels in his room."

The desk clerk groaned and rolled her eyes. "In the middle of the damn night. What for?"

Darcy said, "I don't know. I can take them up for you if you want."

"Thanks," she said. "That's sweet of you to offer." She looked below the desk and shook her head. Another groan. Another eye roll. "Hold on a sec. I have to grab some from the back."

"No problem," said Darcy. "Take your time."

The clerk disappeared into an office. On tiptoes, Darcy looked over the counter's lip. There, sitting in cup filled with pens, was a pair of scissors.

Darcy grabbed the scissors and dropped them in her pocket as the clerk returned with half a dozen neatly folded towels. "Here you go," she said, holding out the bundle. "Hopefully, that's enough."

Darcy accepted the towels. "What's his room number?"

The clerk moved to a computer monitor and tapped on a keyboard. "Suite 307."

"Got it," said Darcy. She walked across the lobby, he scissors heavy in her pocket, and took the elevator to the third floor. She still had her passkey and swiped it over the lock.

The light flashed green. Turning the handle, Darcy opened the door and, silently, she stepped inside.

Holly was curled up on the sofa, determined to talk to Liam as soon as he got back from retrieving the thumb drive. True, his impromptu proposal was a rotten idea.

Yet Holly felt that there was more to be said.

She needed to be honest with him about the accident. She needed to tell him that she'd never be able to give him more kids than the one he already had. Finally, she needed to tell him, that because of what happened, she wasn't a good partner in the game of love.

The door opened and Holly sat up. She drew in a breath, ready to speak. Whatever she was about to say was forgotten as a housekeeper stepped into the suite.

"What are you doing?" Holly began. Then she saw towels in the woman's arms. "We don't need those. I think you have the wrong room."

"No," said the housekeeper. "I don't."

Holly recognized the woman now. "You. I saw you at the pool. What are you doing here?"

"You know why I'm here," she said.

"Get out of my room," said Holly, rising to her feet. Her voice was a whisper, but it came out as a hiss.

"That," said the other woman, "I cannot do."

"Who are you?"

"Who am I?" Walking slowly toward Holly, she asked, "You mean you don't know? I'm really disappointed in you."

Then the realization hit Holly and icy terror filled her veins. With a quick intake of breath, she said, "It's… You're the one they're looking for. Darcy Owens. I should've seen the resemblance from your pictures. Your disguise is good, but not great."

Darcy smirked. "It fooled *you*."

Think, Holly. After all, she was a psychologist. She should be able to talk her way out of danger—and if not, at least she should be able to keep Darcy talking until Liam got back.

Holly's gaze flicked to the table and the opened box that was filled with Darcy's childhood belongings. She remembered the picture with the dark cloud.

"Tell me about your house," said Holly. "The place where you lived as a child."

"My what?" She looked startled. And then, "How do you know about that?"

"I have some of your things," said Holly, gesturing to the box. "I found a drawing you did in high school. It's a picture of your house—quite good. But next to it is something…"

"The Darkness," said Darcy, and the tone of her voice made Holly feel sick.

"Is the darkness a place or a person?"

"The Darkness," said Darcy, working her jaw back and forth, "is everything."

"I can help you," said Holly quickly. All the while wondering where in the hell Liam had gone and when he'd be back.

"I don't want your help," Darcy spat.

"What do you want, then?" Holly asked.

Darcy looked at Holly, her stare unblinking. "What I want," she said, "is for you to die."

Rubbing her eyes, Sophie stood on the threshold of her room. "Holly? What's going on? Where's my daddy?"

"Sophie, get back in your room. Lock the door…" Holly didn't have time to think or react. There was a flash of silver. Then pain, hot and white, filled her with fire. She gripped her middle. Her hand was covered with blood. Darcy Owens held tight to Holly's shoulder, a pair of scissors between them. A crimson bead dripped from the sharpened end.

As if Holly was suspended over a chasm, she felt weightless. All she wanted to do was let go and fall into the abyss. For a moment, she returned to that fateful night when she was in high school…

Sitting in the passenger seat, she watched the speedometer climb. Eighty miles. Ninety miles. One hundred miles per hour.

"That's too fast," she chided as the chassis began to shake.

"I can get this thing up to one-ten," the driver said. The road hugged the side of the mountain. Tires squealed with the strain as the car took a hairpin turn. "You want to see?"

Did she? The speed was exhilarating…and reckless. Breathless, her pulse raced, and she turned in her seat, staring at Jeffery, her first love. His blue eyes glowed in the reflection of the dashboard lights. He glanced her way and smiled. There was a dimple in his cheek and the thump, thump, thump *of Holly's heart.*

"Stop being a worrywart," said her friend in the back seat. Sandra Ford. It was a name Holly would never forget. "Live a little, Holly. That's why we're out tonight."

She stared out the window. Her face was superimposed on the world as it rushed by at one hundred miles an hour.

"Come on," said Sandra. "You don't want to die without doing anything fun. Right?"

"One hundred ten miles," Jeffery said again. Holly's skin tingled as if she'd been caressed by his words. A

lock of sandy brown hair fell over Jeffery's eyes, and he raked a hand over his scalp. "Bet you never went that fast before. Think I should go faster? Or are you too scared?"

Holly was terrified. They were going too fast and needed to stop—or at least, slow down. Yet, she wasn't in the mood to follow the rules. She was young and in love with Jeffery, and above all else...immortal.

Wordlessly, she placed a hand on Jeffery's thigh. It was the first hot day of late spring, and he wore shorts. His skin was warm, and the muscles of his long legs were strong. The car shot forward, pressing Holly into her seat. Her hands began to tremble, and she shoved them under her legs.

A scream of laughter erupted from behind her. Holly turned. Another boy was draped over Sandra in the back seat and his lips were pressed to her neck.

Sandra kissed the boy on the lips, then shouted, "Come on."

Holly waved her hands in the air, eager to join in the moment of freedom and rebellion. She let out a cry. Then the pitch of the scream rose an octave. They spun in a tight circle. Holly braced herself on the dash. A wave of smoke rolled over the car as the stink of burning rubber filled her nose.

The front fender slammed into the side of the ravine. The force of the impact carried the car up and over, again and again. Pebbles of glass pelted Holly as the windshield exploded and the roof collapsed.

Metal screeched in a primal wail as boulders gouged the top and undercarriage of the car, tearing it to shreds. Then they stopped. It was silent save for the creak, creak, creak *as the car rocked gently back and forth, settling at the foot of the mountainside. The wail resumed. It was Sandra. Blood covered her face. Her hair was sticky. Her white T-shirt had turned crimson.*

The seat belt squeezed Holly, making it hard to breathe and impossible to speak. She turned to Jeffery. His blue eyes gazed outward, but even then...she knew he no longer saw her. Jeffery's neck was twisted at an unnatural angle. Holly's heart constricted in her chest, becoming a small, hard thing.

Wetness spread over her stomach, climbing to her chest. She stared at her middle. A piece of metal protruded from her abdomen. The chrome flashed with the interior lights. Her vision began to fade at the edges, and Holly knew that being impaled was punishment for not making them stop. Oblivion continued to creep in from all sides until she saw nothing but black.

Still, the crying continued...

This time, it wasn't Sandra in the back seat of the wrecked car. Holly was no longer a reckless teenager. She heard the sob of a child, calling her name.

"Holly, Holly, Holly."

"Sophie," Holly said. Her voice was a hoarse whisper.

Darcy held tight to Sophie's wrist, pulling the child toward the door. If Holly didn't act now, Sophie would be at the mercy of a calculating killer. What was she supposed to do? Yet, the crevasse still yawned wide beneath Holly, and it was so inviting...

Holly pressed her hand hard into her stomach. A flash of red filled her vision and she cried out with the pain. The agony was real. She focused on the anguish and it gave her strength.

With the other hand, Holly pushed off the wall. She staggered forward. "Let go of her, goddamn it!"

Darcy turned to look at Holly. "Who do you think you are to stop me?"

Holly didn't have time to waste. She lunged forward. Darcy anticipated her move and the scissors swung down. The blade glinted in the light as it came toward Holly, missing her face by an inch. Sophie's small overnight bag was still in the living room. Dropping to her knees, Holly dove for the child-size wheeled suitcase. It was a feeble weapon, but Holly was desperate and only had time to improvise.

Holly swung the suitcase, knocking back Darcy's arm, the scissors connecting with nylon and plastic. With a snarl, Darcy thrust the blade forward. Using the suitcase as a shield, Holly lifted it to her chest. The blade sliced the fabric in two.

Holly needed to think, not react. A flash of memory came to her—Liam, saying that Darcy had been injured while trying to escape, shot in the shoulder weeks ago, with no medical care.

Was it the left shoulder or the right? Holly couldn't recall. Still, the bit of information was all Holly had… and she'd use it. Holding tight with both hands, Holly marshaled all the strength she possessed. She drove forward with the suitcase, hitting Darcy in the right shoulder.

The killer screamed as she gripped her arm. Holly brought up the suitcase again. The rigid edging connected with Darcy's chin. Her head snapped back, her skull connecting with the door at her back. Bone hit metal. A stomach-turning crunch filled the room. Darcy's eyes rolled into her skull. Sliding slowly to the floor, her head lolled to the side.

Holly exhaled. She had fought back...and won. Someday soon, Holly would marvel at her lucky hit. Just not now. Now, she had to get Sophie out of the room.

In the midst of the melee, the little girl had scurried under the dining table. Chairs surrounded her hiding place.

Still clutching the wound in her stomach, Holly held her free hand out to Sophie. "Come here, honey. You're safe."

Sophie cowered in a corner as tears streamed down her cheeks. She shook her head. "No."

Holly's vision blurred. She closed her eyes tightly and opened them again. Hot blood from the cut to her side still filled her hand. Spots floated before her eyes. Holly was tired, so tired. She didn't have long until consciousness slipped away, which meant she didn't have any time to cajole a child, regardless of how frightening the circumstances.

"Sophie," said Holly. Her voice held an edge. "I need you to come to me. We have to get out of this room. We have to get help."

"But the bad lady."

Holly reached her arm out farther. Her stomach burned with each breath. "We need to go *now*, Sophie. I don't have much time."

"But the bad lady," Sophie repeated. Lifting a small finger, she pointed behind Holly.

Holly realized her miscalculation a moment too late.

Slowly, she looked over her shoulder. Her insides turned cold.

Darcy stood behind her, a chair in her hand. She smiled, her teeth stained with blood. She brought the chair down on Holly's head. Pain, a bolt of white, exploded and then, her world went black.

Liam examined the body. The gray pallor. The pliable skin. The stench beginning to set in.

In his estimation, the dude had been dead for more than twenty-four hours. It would take a medical examiner to determine the exact time and cause, but Liam knew a couple of things for certain. First, the guy hadn't died of natural causes. That was because of the second thing he knew—the body being on the golf course wasn't an accident.

Which meant what?

Removing the phone from his pocket, he pulled up the contacts. "Marcus," he said as the call was answered. "There's a problem at the resort."

"What is it?" he asked.

"I found a body on the golf course."

"Have you called the authorities?"

"Not yet, but they'll be next."

"Tell me what you see."

"Male. Late twenties or early thirties. Sandy blond hair. Looks like the eyes are blue. I haven't looked for any identification."

Then again, Liam didn't need to find the guy's license. Even in death he recognized the man. It was Kevin. The golfer who had the date with the maid.

For Liam, all the pieces of the puzzle fell into place.

The break-in at the infirmary. The brunette maid. The fact that Liam had felt someone watching him and yet nobody was ever there.

"She's here," said Liam. He turned in a slow circle, realizing that she might be watching him even now.

"Who's here?" asked Marcus.

"Darcy Owens."

"Are you sure? Reno PD has reported another sighting."

"I'm positive," said Liam.

He turned from the corpse and began sprinting down the trail. "You need to call the police, Marcus. Tell them that the body's on the ninth hole."

"Why not you? Where are you going?"

"Back to the resort. There's a killer on the loose, and I left Holly and Sophie alone and unprotected.

Holly was dying. She knew that.

She couldn't breathe. Her hands were bound behind her back. A cord had been tied to a beam in the ceiling. Then a noose had been placed around Holly's neck.

She knew without question that these were her last moments on earth. She was in a living room—a hotel room.

Her vision began to fade, the room blurred and darkened. In her mind's eye, she saw a face. A man stood alone on a bluff. The setting sun turned his skin bronze. Holly's chest ached, for she also knew that she loved this man.

Her thoughts returned, and she remembered every terrifying moment. Darcy. The fight. The knife. The blood. Sophie, hidden under the table. Holly had taken a blow to the head, and now, she was being hanged. Even as the last bit as oxygen flowed through her body, reviving her brain, Holly knew that there was no way to escape.

She slipped. The noose tightened on her neck as her body weight took up the slack. Looking down, she saw that her feet almost touched the ground. With an upward glance, she observed that the knot holding her in place was beginning to unravel. If she could just get the cord to loosen an inch, then she would be able to touch the floor. Thrusting her hips forward, she began to rock back and forth. The rope creaked, tightening with the motion.

Holly's lungs burned. Every part of her body felt aflame. Slowly, her body twisted. Tears streamed down her cheeks, even though she no longer had the ability to cry. In her mind's eye, she saw the man on the bluff again. He held out his hand to Holly. Her heart filled with love, the kind that lasted through eternity...and beyond.

Dressed in a flowing white gown, she placed her hand in his. Together, they walked toward the setting sun.

Chapter 17

Cold sweat covered Liam's skin as he sprinted through the parking lot, up the winding drive and through the front door of the resort. He didn't stop as he raced through the quiet lobby.

A young woman behind the reservation desk called after Liam as he passed. "Sir, can I help you? Sir, is everything all right? Do you need more towels?"

He ignored the woman while sprinting to the end of the hall. He pushed open the metal door that led to the fire exit. His footfalls echoed as he took the metal stairs two at a time. With a racing pulse, he continued upward, sweat streaming down his back.

He refused to consider that anything bad had happened to Sophie…or Holly. Yet he pushed his body harder. Faster.

The third-floor landing came into view. Liam slammed the door open with his shoulder. The carpeted hallway was silent. Wall sconces were set between each door, filling the corridor with a warm glow. To Liam, it looked like hell.

Their suite was the third door on the left. After swiping the key card over the lock, he turned the handle. Pushing the door open, he came up short.

Holly dangled from the rafters. A thin cord bit into her neck. Her body twisted, only inches from the floor. Her skin was pale. Her lips were blue.

He dove for her legs and lifted her body, taking pressure off her neck. Her skin was still warm. The cord unraveled. Holly's torso flopped over Liam's back. After placing her carefully on the floor, he loosened the rope at her throat, then untied her hands. He felt under her chin. There was a fluttering pulse and the whisper of a breath on her lips.

His eyes stung as a deep sense of relief washed over him. He'd arrived just in time to save her and Liam swore that he'd never let her go—not again.

There was a bruise to her cheek and her lip was split. Her knuckles were scraped. Two of her fingernails had been torn away. Blood leaked from a wound at her side. Without question, Holly had put up the fight of her life. Luckily, she'd survived. Now he needed to know what had happened.

And…where was Sophie?

Holly moaned.

"Can you hear me?" he asked, shaking her shoulders lightly.

In answer, her eyes fluttered.

"Holly, it's me, Liam." She gazed at him for a moment before letting her lids close again. "What happened?" he asked. "Where's Sophie?"

Holly swallowed. "She's gone," she replied, her voice hoarse.

"I'm calling 911," he said. "You need medical care."

Holly placed her hand on his arm. "Don't worry about me. You need to find Sophie. It was the woman who I saw by the pool. She said her name…was Claire. It was…her." She fixed her tired stare on him. "Liam, it was Darcy."

Of course.

"We have to save Sophie," said Holly.

"Save her? I don't even know where Darcy's taken her."

"We," said Holly. She sat up, grimacing with the effort. "I'm coming with you."

Up until that moment, Liam had felt alone—as if he was treading water in the middle of the ocean. To hear that Holly wanted to help his daughter was akin to being given a life raft. "I can't ask you to put yourself at risk, not again."

"This is as personal for me as it is for you," Holly said. "Sophie may very well be your daughter, but I love her, too. Don't put me on the sidelines."

Liam didn't want to waste any more time while his daughter was in the hands of a killer. He needed to know what Holly knew and arguing wasn't going to help him gather any information. After getting to his feet, he held out a hand to Holly. "Come with me. I can patch you up while you talk."

She wound her fingers through his, and he pulled her

to standing. The color drained from her cheeks, leaving her creamy skin gray. She listed to the side. Liam wrapped an arm around her waist to hold her steady.

"Just breathe," said Liam.

Holly drew in a deep breath. "Darcy took Sophie to the place where it all started," she said. "I think she went home."

"Las Vegas? Pleasant Pines?" With his arm still around Holly's waist, he led her to the second bedroom. Gently, he helped her sit on the bed, stepping away to get a first-aid kit. Returning with the kit, he sat it on the bed next to Holly. "Lift your top," he instructed.

She dutifully exposed her wound but returned to his previous comment. "She didn't go back to either place, at least I don't think so."

Using an alcohol swab, he cleaned the cut to her side. "Holly, this is going to hurt. I'm sorry." Using a pre-threaded needle from the first-aid kit, Liam placed two stitches in Holly's side. She sucked in a breath but otherwise didn't make a sound as he finished and then dressed the wound with a large bandage. With his ministrations done, he continued, "I thought you said Darcy went home. She used to live in Pleasant Pines and, before that, Las Vegas."

"Las Vegas might be where she developed as a serial killer. Pleasant Pines is where her identity was discovered, but it's not where her need to kill started. In fact, Darcy's need to kill started in her childhood. It was like what you were saying about predators sticking to familiar ground. Then there was the drawing that I found of her home. The one with the black cloud or the storm."

"Sure," said Liam, starting to understand Holly's thinking.

"She's given that force a name—the Darkness. I think she killed someone while living in that house." She stood. Wobbled. Straightened. "I'd bet money that's where she's taken Sophie. The address has to be in that box somewhere. Let's find it."

Liam had to admit, Holly had a point. It also meant that he needed to ask for help from everyone at RMJ. He couldn't get his daughter back alone. "I'm calling my boss. They can get an Amber Alert out for Sophie."

"Then what are we going to do?"

"You need to see a doctor. In fact, there's one on-site. If I hadn't arrived when I did, you'd be dead."

"Yet you saved me, so forget about leaving me at the resort. I'm going to help you find Sophie."

"I need you to be safe, Holly," said Liam. "I also need to save my daughter. What can I say to convince you to stay at the resort and see the doctor?"

"Nothing," said Holly.

Liam expected as much. "Get changed into clean clothes. Then we're going to track Darcy down and get my daughter back."

Holly sat in the back of what had appeared to be a florist's van, complete with logo and phone number on the side panel. Instead of being surrounded by bouquets and vases, she was surrounded by the best surveillance technology Rocky Mountain Justice could assemble. Several computer monitors were affixed to one wall. A bench with a hard drive, keyboard and three laptops sat beneath. A closed-circuit camera fed images from

inside the resort to a split-screen monitor. The opposite wall held an arsenal of weapons—handguns, rifles,
shotguns, several sets of body armor. The amount of
equipment left her dizzy. Then again, Holly reasoned,
she might be light-headed from the wounds to her neck
and stomach.

Aside from all the gear, Holly, Marcus, Wyatt and
Liam sat in front of the bench, working on a plan to
catch a killer.

"We can assume that Darcy's stolen the victim's car,"
said Liam. "It means that she's off the premises but
couldn't have gotten much of a head start."

"How do you figure that?" Wyatt asked.

"Holly was unconscious when I found her. But she
must've only been out for a little bit, because I was able
to rouse her pretty quickly. I'd guess less than three
minutes."

Marcus glanced at his watch, an old-school timepiece with a leather band and a gold-plated face. "We
can assume that Darcy's been gone for fifteen minutes, no more."

"Let's call in the FBI, the state police. Hell, call
the army," said Liam. "If she's stolen a rental car, then
there's a GPS. She'll be easy to find. We'll have my
daughter back ASAP."

Wyatt held up his hand. "I want to urge discretion
in all of this," he said.

Liam slapped his palm on the worktable.

Holly flinched. There was too much testosterone
contained in the tiny compartment. It left Holly wondering what—if anything—she could add.

"This is my daughter's life," Liam said, his voice a

feral growl. "I don't give a damn about Rocky Mountain Justice or its reputation."

Wyatt didn't blink. "I want to save your daughter as much as you do. But trust me on this. I've been where you are, and I know Darcy. I know her patterns. If she feels trapped or threatened, she's going to lash out, which means…" He let his words trail off.

Liam finished the thought for him. "Which means that she might get spooked and do something to hurt my kid." Slamming his fist on the table, he gritted his teeth. "Not in this lifetime."

Liam worked his jaw back and forth. He let out a long sigh, seeming to make up his mind about something. What that something was, Holly could only guess.

"When we first met," Liam said to Wyatt, "you said that you'd studied Darcy Owens for years. You have to know something. How can we save Sophie?"

Holly's chest ached with the pain that Liam was feeling. Placing a hand on his arm, she said, "I'm in this with the rest of you. I'll do anything to help find that little girl."

"Are you sure?" asked Marcus. "You look like you're a little worse for wear."

Holly's side ached. Her neck was sore, her throat raw. But nothing would stop her from saving Sophie. "Am I sure?" she asked, repeating his question. "I'm positive."

"I'm glad to hear you say that," said Wyatt. "Because I have a theory."

Leaning forward, Liam said, "Go ahead."

"Darcy has two kinds of victims. I think they represent—to her, at least—the two kinds of people she sees as responsible for her formation into a serial killer."

"Formation?" Liam echoed.

Wyatt continued, "We've seen information in her file, provided by the assistant DA, that Darcy was believed to have been severely abused as a child."

"Who does she see as responsible for her abuse?" Holly asked.

"Her parents," said Wyatt. "Her father died in the woods from exposure and alcohol poisoning. Her mother committed suicide by hanging."

Finally, she had something to add. Placing her hand on her throat, she traced her fingers lightly over the welt on her skin. "Those deaths weren't accidental. I have every reason to believe that Darcy killed her parents."

"I do, too," said Wyatt. "I think she's been repeating the same crimes again and again. Men who see her in a sexual way, or whom she sees as a threat, are killed in the same manner she killed her father. Those with whom she has a closer bond get hanged."

"She tried to hang me," said Holly. "Should I be flattered?"

"Yes," said Wyatt. "In a weird, twisted way, at least." He paused a moment, rubbing the thumb of one hand across the palm of the other. "Look, we can call in the FBI. Hell, we might even get them to bring in the army. But a shock-and-awe scenario won't make Darcy cower. She'll fight, or at least try to get in one last bit of revenge before getting taken down. We need to move with caution."

Liam blanched. "You mean that she'll kill Sophie."

Wyatt rubbed the palm of his hand again. "That's my fear."

"So how would we approach her with—" Holly paused "—caution?"

"That's where you come in," said Marcus. "Holly, I want you to make contact."

"No way," said Liam. "I won't let her go. I won't let her risk her life again."

"Let me, Liam? Really?" Holly asked. Even she could hear the incredulity in her tone. "I can make up my mind about which risks I'm willing to take and which ones I'm not."

Wyatt said, "Holly is the best person to confront Darcy—at least, at first. For starters, Darcy assumes she's dead. Seeing Holly might throw her off her game long enough for someone to find Sophie."

"But where would she have taken my kid?" Liam asked.

"Where did Darcy grow up? I know that she's gone someplace connected to her childhood," Holly said.

Wyatt began typing on a keyboard. "I have electronic copies of everything I gave you, Holly," he said. "This is her father's obit. Ten years ago, Frank Owens died of exposure. He was survived by his wife, Shelby, and daughter, Darcy. They lived off Fool's Gold Road."

Wyatt's finger danced over the keyboard, pulling up a map of forest, rivers and roads. A red dot indicated the Owens home. "It's off the main road by at least half a mile," said Liam.

"Seems like that would be the perfect place to disappear," said Holly. "Who lives there now?"

Wyatt tapped on the keyboard some more and the map was replaced with an electronic copy of an official document. "Tax records show that it's been abandoned for the past decade. And…" He typed some more. "Here's a satellite image, taken two weeks ago."

There was a clear picture of a dilapidated two-story white farmhouse. Wyatt manipulated the image, bringing up the rear of the property.

"What's that?" Marcus asked, pointing to the screen.

Wyatt focused the aspect on a set of metal doors. They were set into the house on the ground level at an angle and hidden by an overgrown lawn. "Is that a basement entry?" asked Liam. "It'd be the perfect way to get inside."

"As long as we can keep Darcy focused on something else," said Marcus.

"Like the front door and me," said Holly.

Liam stood. His large frame seemed to fill the small space. "You can't do this, Holly. Please. Stay at the resort and see the doctor, I'm begging you." He touched the cut on her cheek. "I don't want to see you hurt again."

"No way," she said, getting to her feet, as well. The cut on her side filled with fiery pain. She sucked in a ragged breath. "Face it, you need me. Otherwise, it'll be impossible to take her by surprise."

Marcus said, "It's a solid plan, Liam. Admit it."

"I hate it." Liam exhaled and stared at the floor.

Marcus turned his attention to Holly. "We'll get a mic on you first. That way we can hear everything you say—and everything Darcy says, as well. You can drop us off along the driveway, and we can use the woods as cover. While you're distracting Darcy, Holly, the rest of us can sneak around to the back and find Sophie."

"There is no *we*. Or *us*," said Liam. "I already told you that I work alone."

"I used to work better alone, too," said Wyatt. "Now I'm part of a team. Face it, brother. You are, too."

A small microphone was taped to Holly's chest. Aside from having her conversations picked up by the device, every word she said would be transmitted to the men from RMJ and also sent back to the van and recorded.

"It's ready," said Marcus as he reached for a laptop. "I'll turn it on now."

Liam held up his hand. "Can you give me a minute? I want to talk to Holly. Alone."

"Sure thing," said Marcus.

Liam and Holly walked back to the resort and back to where Liam's car had been left in the valet lot. She understood that they needed his vehicle to get Sophie back, but she hated every second that the little girl was forced to spend with the killer.

Because there was something else she knew but could never say. Darcy Owens might not have simply kidnapped Sophie. The serial killer could very well be planning to take the little girl's life—if she hadn't already.

After they got into the car, he turned to Holly, pinning her in place with his stare. "Darcy almost killed you once already."

"I know," she said.

"I can't have you risk your life again."

"You can't stop me, Liam. Besides, you need me."

"I don't need anyone," he said, staring out the windshield as he drove. "Not anymore."

"That's not true, and deep down you know it."

Liam shook his head but said nothing. Holly could feel him rebuilding the wall that he lived behind. This time, she refused to let him hide.

"What happened?" she asked.

Liam continued to drive, his gaze like flint and his jaw tight. She thought he would ignore her, but he spoke, his voice a whisper.

"Thanksgiving about a dozen years ago, my cousin, Charlie, died. We were helping to find a missing hiker. Charlie had an issue with his equipment. It shouldn't have been fatal, but the weather conditions made it impossible for me to save him." He gripped the dog tag around his neck. "It's why I work alone—I don't want to take on the responsibility for anyone. I especially don't want to be responsible for someone who means a lot to me."

"I'm so sorry. I had no idea," Holly said, reaching for his arm. She knew what it was like to lose someone that she loved. To hold herself responsible for their death. She knew how that guilt had the power to define a life.

Was now the time to share her past with Liam?

Holly opened her mouth, ready to confess. Liam spoke first and she remained silent.

"At least now you know why you can't go." He met her eyes. In his gaze, she saw that the wall Liam built to protect his heart had started to crumble.

"I'm going with you," she said. "I survived. I'm ready for her now. I understand her. This time, Darcy won't get a second chance to make me a victim."

Chapter 18

Darcy planned to kill the kid all along. In fact, the Darkness had urged her to act. Yet Darcy knew what it was to be a frightened little girl, and instead she took Sophie to the one place they could be safe. Home.

The house from Darcy's childhood hadn't changed much since she'd abandoned it a decade before. The same furniture sat in the same places. A moth-eaten jacket of her mother's dangled limply from a wire hanger in the coat closet by the front door.

Sure, the home had fallen into disrepair. Faded paint peeled from the walls and chunks of plaster had fallen from the ceiling. Still, it was home—the place of her origins.

The shabbiness notwithstanding, there were more differences, subtle but unmistakable, from the last time

Darcy had lived in this house. Her mother was no longer in the kitchen, humming while preparing a meal and happily ignorant of the horrors her daughter faced every single night. Her father's heavy footsteps had gone silent. The stink of alcohol fumes no longer wafted through the hallways. Her cries of anguish were no longer smothered with his soft hand and a hard grip.

Through her own actions, Darcy's parents had faded to nothing more than shadows and dust. Gone now, they were part of a nightmare that had been chased away with the dawn.

Billy. Her parents. All of the men. She'd outlived them all. Casting a glance at Sophie, Darcy smiled. Tears had dried on her small face, but at least the child had stopped wailing, thrashing and whining for her father. It was a good sign. She was already compliant and coming to accept Darcy as her savior. From this day forward, life would be different. This time, Darcy would be the loving and protective mother. She'd keep her child safely hidden away from the cruel world.

The crunch of tires on gravel startled her. Standing behind the drapes, she looked out at the drive. The sun had not yet risen. Mist hung in the air, and droplets of water clung to the grime-covered windows. There was nothing.

Then a light cut through the gloom. Headlights. A car. It was gray—just like the predawn. Darcy's pulse slowed as she watched the approaching automobile. It lurched to a stop. From her vantage point, she could see the indistinct outline of a lone driver.

Sure, there was the possibility that someone had lost

their way, but Darcy wasn't an idiot. Someone was coming for her. Yet, who?

She'd abandoned the car, stolen from Kevin Carpenter, miles back. Then taken a pickup truck that was too old to have GPS tracking.

The car's engine still idled, and the lights shone directly into the front window. Darcy stepped back, hiding in the shadows.

Sophie, her eyes rimmed in red, sat on the floor. She clutched an old doll to her chest and rocked back and forth. She saw the headlights, too, and sucked in a noisy breath.

"Is that Daddy?" she asked.

It was the same question Darcy was asking herself.

"I don't know," she said honestly. A sliver of fear ran through her body.

With the lights still on and the engine running, the car door opened. Darcy's breath caught in her chest. Her throat tightened, and she gave a strangled cry. The form was shrouded in mist. It was moving up the path slowly, and as it came into view, the fear that had stabbed Darcy grew. She felt as if she was seeing a ghost come back from the dead to drag her to hell.

But there were no ghosts. This was a woman. A single raised welt stood out on her pale neck. Her face and hands were marked with cuts and bruises. She moved slowly, no doubt because the knife wound to her side still caused her pain.

"Who is it?" asked Sophie. She moved next to Darcy. Standing on tiptoes, the child looked over the sill. "It's Holly!"

Darcy gripped the child's arm, pulling her away from the window. "We can't be seen."

It was too late. Holly stared at the house, and her eyes were filled with fury.

Again, a shiver ran down Darcy's spine. She was unaccustomed to fear, and in that instant, she realized a single important truth. Just as the vile actions of her parents had created the Darkness, so had Darcy's deeds brought about a change in Holly. What once had been a mild-mannered woman had morphed into a fierce and fiery adversary.

Still, Darcy refused to give in to the unfamiliar emotion threatening to take over her mind and body.

Grabbing Sophie by both arms, she shook the child hard. "Do *not* make a sound. Remember what I told you. Holly wants to steal you away from your family."

Silent tears slid down the child's cheeks. Her bottom lip quivered.

"If Holly sees you, she'll take you away," Darcy continued before opening the closet door. Shoving the child into the dark space, Darcy ordered, "Don't make a sound. Don't show yourself. Do you hear me?"

"Y-yes," Sophie stuttered.

Satisfied that the child was suitably frightened, Darcy slammed the closet door closed and strode to the front door. Inhaling deeply, she pulled it open and stepped onto the porch. The morning air was cold and Darcy folded her arms across her chest to keep from shivering.

The cord around Holly's neck had come loose, she told herself. Or maybe a hotel worker had heard Holly's struggles and entered the room at the last minute. Obviously, something had gone wrong, and in truth, what that was didn't matter.

She shivered as Holly slowly climbed the steps. "I guess I'm harder to kill than you thought," the other woman said. "You look pretty scared to see me."

"Don't worry," said Darcy. "I'm a fast learner. I won't make the same mistake a second time." She paused. "How'd you find me?"

"Easy," said Holly. "I understand you now. I studied you. This is where it all started. This is where your need to kill was formed."

"I bet you think you're clever." Darcy's pulse spiked, sending her heart into a frenzy. "You've outsmarted me and now what? What do you want? Why are you here?"

Holly remained calm and her gaze impassive. "Give me Sophie. If you do, I'll leave and never come back."

Darcy laughed. The lie was flimsy and obviously part of a trap. "You couldn't have thought it would be that easy."

Holly's eyes slipped from Darcy's face. She looked into the room beyond. The back of Darcy's neck tickled, as if someone were watching her from the shadows. Instinctively, she turned. There was nothing.

"You want easy, give me the child."

"Why would I do that? You claim you came here by yourself, that you haven't told anyone what happened. What's stopping me from killing you a second time?"

Gun in hand, Liam crept through the woods. He also wore an earpiece and heard every word that passed between the two women.

Marcus and Wyatt, both armed as well, followed in

his steps. The FBI had been alerted. Even now, they were parked at the end of the drive, waiting for word that Sophie was safe so they could storm the house.

The place came into view. It was just as he had seen from the satellite image. The old farmhouse had been painted white years ago and now was a dusty beige. The black trim was faded and chipped. The porch sagged, and the bottom step had split in two.

Since the schematics appeared correct, it meant that there was a basement entrance at the rear of the house. All Liam needed was another minute or two and then he would save his daughter. Then he'd make Darcy pay for what she'd done. His steps faltered.

Liam knew that his personal mission was about more than justice. It was also about more than finding his daughter. What Liam wanted was cold-blooded revenge.

Walking again, he used the woods as cover and stopped once he was even with the front porch. His car, which Holly had driven, was parked nearby. The door was still open, and the engine was running. It was a brilliant move on her part—perfect for a quick getaway.

From behind a copse of trees, Liam watched Holly. She still stood on the porch. Shoulders squared and jaw tight, she faced down the killer with only feet between them. Holly was doing her job and keeping Darcy distracted.

For a moment, a deep pang of guilt gripped his middle. He shouldn't have allowed Holly to put herself in such a dangerous situation. Then again, she had insisted. More than that, she'd been right. Liam couldn't get Sophie back without help.

Without thought, he lifted his gun. Lining up the

sights with the middle of Darcy's forehead, he exhaled. All he needed to do was pull the trigger and the gun would fire. Traveling at twenty-five hundred feet per second, the killer would be dead before ever hearing the gun's report.

Sure, this hadn't been the initial plan. Yet Liam knew that sometimes plans changed. Often, you got only one shot—and you took it.

In a blur, his view changed. Holly shifted to the left, placing her head in the line of fire. Lifting the gun to the sky, he drew a shaking breath. How close had he been to pulling the trigger? How close had he been to accidentally shooting Holly? Liam knew the answer to both questions—he'd been too damn close for comfort.

Wyatt put his hand on Liam's shoulder. He whispered, "Remember, Darcy's the only person who knows Sophie's whereabouts. Until we have your daughter back, we have no choice but to let her live."

Dammit. Wyatt was right. Liam had to get his head back into the mission.

Pointing to Marcus, Liam whispered, "You stay here and cover the front of the house." Then to Wyatt, "And you, go around the property and come up to the front door from the opposite side. I'll take the back."

Both men nodded their agreement.

Crouching low, Liam soundlessly crept through the trees. He crossed the overgrown lawn, coming up to the back of the house. There were three windows along the upper floor. On the lower level, four. Set into the side of the house at an angle, the double doors to the basement were metal and painted black.

There was a single important detail that the satellite image had failed to capture.

A chain had been looped through both handles. The ends were connected by a padlock, which was rusted shut. Stealth and speed were his best weapons, so taking time to pick the lock or cut the chain was unacceptable. It left him with the windows as the only possible way of entry. After holstering his gun, he pushed on one. It didn't budge—the frame had swollen shut, making it impossible to open. He tried the next one and the one after that. No luck.

As if his heartbeat were a clock ticking down the seconds, Liam wondered how much time he had before Darcy made her next move.

Minutes? Or was it less?

Either way, he didn't have time to waste. What Liam needed was to think of another plan…and quick. Because if he didn't, Holly was as good as dead.

Wiping his palms on his pants, Liam pushed on the final windowpane. The glass was covered in dirt, and his hands slipped. Or had the old wooden frame moved? He pushed again. The window slid upward, opening completely. Liam hefted himself onto the sill. He paused, half in, half out, and removed the gun from its holster.

Soundlessly, Liam dropped to the floor, landing on a threadbare carpet. A cloud of dust rose out of the rug, surrounding Liam in a decade's worth of dirt. He smothered a cough as he surveyed his surroundings. He was in a dining room, complete with a chandelier of tarnished brass hanging from the ceiling. A china cabinet had tipped forward and was held up by the table. Chipped plates and broken glasses littered the floor.

Yet where were Holly and Sophie? Standing still, he listened.

The sound of voices carried from the front of the house. From the cadence and pitch, he recognized one as belonging to Holly. Redoubling his vigilance, he moved toward the conversation.

He heard Holly speak first. "Give me Sophie. If you do, I'll leave and never come back. I won't say anything about you or where you've gone."

Holly's delivery had been convincing. Yet her explanation was implausible. All the same, he needed only a few more seconds. Liam crept down a darkened hallway. The air was stale and stank of mold and decayed wood.

The other woman laughed; the sound was louder. Liam knew that he was close. "You couldn't have thought it would be that easy."

Liam stopped at the end of a dim corridor. He pressed his back to the wall, peering around the corner. Darcy Owens on the porch, her back to the room. Just beyond, Holly stood on the stoop. Her eyes darted toward Liam. Their gazes met for a split second before she returned her attention to Darcy.

Liam slipped back into the shadows, his heartbeat hammering in his ears.

Holly said, "You want easy, give me the child."

"Why would I do that? You came here by yourself. You haven't told anyone what happened."

Darcy continued, "What's stopping me from killing you a second time?"

Liam didn't need to hear any more. Launching himself from the hallway, he came up behind her.

"Me," he said, fury in his voice. "I'm the one who's going to stop you." He pressed the barrel of his gun hard into the base of Darcy Owens's skull.

Chapter 19

Liam wanted nothing more than to pull the trigger.

"Where's Sophie?" he demanded.

"She's not here," said the killer, with a smile. "And I'll never tell you where she is."

"It's a lie," said Liam. "You didn't have enough time to take Sophie anyplace else."

"Are you sure?" Darcy asked.

Gripping Darcy's shoulder, Liam turned her to face him. "Where's my daughter?"

"Wouldn't you like to know?"

He pressed the gun into the middle of her forehead. His trigger finger itched. "Tell me or I'll splatter your brains against this wall."

"Go ahead," said Darcy. "Kill me. Then you'll never know what happened to your kid."

Liam's heartbeat raced. The thumping echoed in his skull. Or did it? Holding a hand for quiet, he asked, "What's that?"

It came again—a soft thud—as if the house had a heartbeat.

"It's her—it's Sophie," said Holly. "Stay with Darcy. I'll find her. I promise!" She shushed him as he started to protest. "We're not leaving without her."

Holly pushed past Darcy and entered the house. "Sophie!" she called out. "It's me, Holly. Where are you?"

Thump, thump.

Liam turned to the sound but kept his eyes on the killer. "It's coming from the closet!" he shouted.

Holly opened the closet door. There, in the back corner, with her knees pulled under her chin, his daughter trembled with fear. That same bone-deep need to protect his child was met with a desire for one thing: revenge.

"Sophie," said Holly again, opening her arms. "I'm so glad we found you."

Wide-eyed, Sophie scooted back, disappearing from Liam's view.

"Sophie, it's me, Holly. I'm here with your father. We've come to take you home."

"But she said you would lie to me about Daddy."

"Who said I would lie? Darcy?"

Holly, her jaw clenched, met Liam's gaze. "Your dad's here with me now."

"Daddy?" the child called out.

"I'm here, honey," Liam answered. "I'm here and Holly's with me. You can come out now, baby girl. You're safe."

* * *

Sophie ran straight to Holly and wrapped her small arms around Holly's neck. Relief washed over Holly and she sagged against the wall. In the distance, the sun crept over the horizon, starting a new day. Friday. Had it been only five days since Liam and Sophie walked into her school? Into her life? To Holly, it felt like years had passed. Or maybe, because of them, she was a different person.

Tucking her head onto Holly's shoulder, Sophie said, "I knew that you weren't bad. I was just so scared."

Holly hugged the child tight. "You are a very brave girl," said Holly. "I've got you now and I'll never let you go."

"Promise that you'll never leave."

"I swear."

Stepping away from the closet, Holly carried Sophie back to the living room. The scene hadn't changed. Liam still held the gun to the middle of Darcy's forehead. The killer still presented her palms. Was it a gesture of supplication and surrender? Or was it only a ploy?

Liam's finger rested on the trigger. A bead of sweat trailed down from his hairline. "Take Sophie out to the car," he said. "I'll be there in a minute."

Holly rushed out the front door just as Marcus Jones and Wyatt Thornton raced onto the sagging porch with their guns drawn.

She ran toward Liam's waiting car, anything to leave the nightmare behind. The whole time, she reassured Sophie, "It's okay. You're okay. It'll be okay."

Heat signatures rose in the distance a moment

before four black SUV's came into view. The promised backup had finally arrived.

The vehicles pulled onto the overgrown lawn, and FBI agents armed with guns and clad in bulletproof vests jumped out of the vehicles. They swarmed around Darcy, pushing the killer to the ground, securing her hands with metal cuffs.

Despite the distance that separated Holly from the house, she could still see through the open door. Her eyes were drawn to Liam. His chin sagged to his chest. With a shake of his head, he lowered his gun.

"You should have let him do it," said Darcy. Two men in navy blue windbreakers ushered the killer toward a waiting car. "You should have let him kill me."

Liam came to stand next to Holly. He placed his hand on her shoulder. He was strong and warm and solid. He was everything she needed.

"It looks like our hunch about the White Wind paid off," said Marcus as he approached.

"How's that?" asked Liam. "Did they find her accomplice?"

"No," Marcus continued. "But it proves that she had one at the resort. Soon, we'll all know who."

"By the way, Liam," said Wyatt, "you did a good job."

"You know I didn't do any of this alone." Liam gave Holly's shoulder a squeeze. "Holly's the best partner I've ever worked with."

"That's saying a lot that she worked with you at all. I thought you were a loner," Wyatt teased.

"Sometimes things change," said Liam.

"Speaking of change," said Marcus. "I need your

bank account information, Holly. Then I can arrange a transfer of funds."

"Oh, yeah," she said. "The consultant's fee."

"No," said Marcus. "I'm a man of my word. You earned the entire sum discussed for helping apprehend Darcy Owens," he continued. "Twenty thousand large."

Liam took Sophie from Holly's arms.

"The money," she said, her voice a whisper. Funds to pay off the bank loan and save her school had been the only reason she had gotten involved in this case. Yet the reasons she had remained were so much more important. "I had forgotten all about the money."

"You don't have to take the cash if you don't want it," said Marcus. He winked at Holly, a sure sign he was joking.

"No way," said Liam. "Holly has very important plans with that cash."

"I need the money to pay off debts. If I don't have the money today, the bank is going to sell my school to another buyer."

Marcus said, "I can take care of the transfer now. The money will be waiting for you when you get back to Pleasant Pines."

Holly gave Marcus the routing number for her account.

"I'll drive you back," said Liam.

She turned to Liam. "Won't the FBI need to interview us about what happened?"

"Yes," said Marcus. "But go now. We can talk to you later."

"Come on," said Liam. He shifted Sophie to his

hip. Holding out his free hand to Holly, he continued, "Let's go."

"Yeah, Holly, let's go," Sophie said, echoing her father.

Holly reached for Liam. He took her palm in his own. She laced her fingers through his. With a deep breath, Holly said, "I'm ready."

Liam sat behind the steering wheel of his car and pressed his foot down on the accelerator. The powerful engine revved as the speedometer climbed. Holly sat in the passenger seat with her cell phone cradled to her chest. In the back seat, Sophie napped.

"It amazes me that Sophie can take a nap after all she's been through," said Liam. "But even as a baby, she was a good sleeper."

Holly gave him a wan smile. "Rest might help her make sense of everything that happened with Darcy."

Liam gripped the steering wheel, his knuckles white. "Do you think it'll stay with her? All the terror and confusion? Will Sophie always bear emotional scars of what happened today?"

"All scars heal with time and care. But, Liam…you need to understand that she was terrified. She was afraid of losing you."

"I *do* understand, damn it. I felt the same way. But what—"

"What does that mean? A lot. She could react any number of ways. She might have nightmares—bad ones, Liam—for a long time. I remember she asked for a night-light at the resort, but that might not be enough, not at first. She might have severe separation anxiety for a while. Eventually she might not remember much of what actually happened, but as a teenager or adult, it's possible that she could develop other symptoms," Holly said. "Like claustrophobia. But if you take your time with her, care for her, give her the love and space she needs to recover…maybe she'll grow up to be as strong as you."

"Is that your professional opinion?"

"It's my sincere hope," said Holly. She smiled at him once more and looked out the window.

Liam turned his eyes back to the road. "I wanted to kill Darcy," he said. "It's not enough for her to go to jail. I wanted her dead."

"You were caught up in your anger," she said. She reached for him, placing her hand on his arm. Her touch was soft and warm. She was a good person. Could she ever care for a bad man? Holly continued, "You wanted to make sure your daughter was safe—not just now, but always. But, Liam…"

He glanced at her.

"I would have done whatever I could to stop you. Because whatever happened to Sophie when she was with Darcy, it would have been worse to see you take that step. You could have lost each other forever."

He felt shame spike through him. She was right. In that moment, he felt an intense relief that the FBI had shown up when they did. Most of all, that both she and Sophie were safe.

"She'll spend the rest of her life in jail," she said. "You know that, right?"

"It wasn't enough, not for me at least. I needed to…"

"But you didn't," she said, cutting him off.

"No."

"Why not?" she asked.

He dared to look at her again. "I've been asking myself the same question," he said.

"What's your answer?"

He took a deep breath. "You." There, he'd said it.

"Me?"

"Holly, for you, I've broken every rule I created that keeps order in my life. It's made me a different—a better—person."

Her eyes glistened with unshed tears. "Liam, I don't know what to say."

"Say that you'll stay in Pleasant Pines."

"I've accepted the job in Ohio."

That was news to Liam. It struck him in the gut like a sucker punch, leaving him breathless and in pain. "When did that happen?"

"Last night," she said. She paused and added, "Afterward."

After they'd made love. After he'd proposed. After they'd fought and he'd left the bedroom, hurt and petulant. Was there any way he could undo the mess that he'd made?

"Fair enough," said Liam.

He checked the clock: 7:29 a.m.

The bank would open at 8:00 a.m. They had more than thirty minutes of driving to reach Pleasant Pines.

"What if I get you back to the bank as it opens? What then?"

She paused. "Really, I don't know. These past few days have given me time to think—and ask myself what I really want."

"And what's your answer?"

"Something different. Something more."

With his chin, he gestured to the phone that Holly still held. "Try calling the bank," he said. "We've got to be close to a cell tower, even out here."

Holly looked at the phone. "I've got a couple bars of coverage." Touching the phone's screen, she added, "I'll put the call on Speaker."

The car filled with a trilling sound. One ring. Two. Three. Liam continued to count. Four. Five rings. "You've reached Thomas Irwin," said a recorded voice. "Leave a message and I'll get back to you."

Holly cast a glance at Liam. Her cheeks were flushed. Was she excited? Nervous? Worried?

The message ended and was followed by a long beep. "Thomas, this is Holly. I'm on my way back to Pleasant Pines. I have the whole payment. I'll be there soon. Don't do anything until we talk. Please." She ended the call.

Liam pushed the car to drive faster, watching as the speedometer crept upward. The tires squealed as they hugged the mountainside road.

"What are you doing?"

"Getting you to the bank."

"You can slow down," she said. "Nothing is that important."

He remembered the scar on her abdomen—along with the confession that it had come from a car accident. Letting his foot off the accelerator, the engine slowed, and the speedometer dropped.

"Besides," she said, "you need to take Sophie to see a doctor and make sure she's okay."

"And you, too," he said.

She sighed. "You're probably right. Then I'll go to the bank."

Still, Liam was resolute. He would get Holly back to Pleasant Pines and to the meeting that would determine her future…and his.

Chapter 20

Liam drove them all to the hospital. Sophie was examined first by the town physician and given a clean bill of health. Then it was Holly's turn. She encouraged Liam to take Sophie home, but he wouldn't relent, promising to wait while she was examined by the doctor.

Doc Lambert had been Holly's doctor for as long as she could remember. More than that, he'd always looked the same—close-cropped gray hair with a matching silver mustache and goatee.

"It looks like you've gotten yourself into quite a tussle," he said while he cleaned the wounds to her face.

"I guess you could say that," she said.

"I heard a rumor that you were tangled up with that killer Darcy Owens."

"You shouldn't believe everything you hear," said Holly. "But this time, it's true."

"Then you are one blessed woman. More than one of her victims has been brought through the hospital's morgue. Then again, you seem to always have luck on your side."

"I guess I did what I had to do." Holly's words were dismissive, but her hands began to shudder. Delayed shock, she realized. "Do you remember when I was in high school? The car accident?"

"You and three other kids," said Doc Lambert. "Sure, I remember. A real tragedy."

"There's more than that," she said. "I knew we were going too fast. I should've…" Holly choked on her words.

"Everyone in that car knew you were going too fast, and maybe you're right. Maybe if you'd said something or done something, then everything would've been different. But it's not. You need to let go of that past, or at least make peace with it. That's the only way you can have a future."

Despite the hard knot in her throat, Holly nodded. "Maybe you're right."

"There's no maybe about it. Why you lived and that boy didn't might never make sense. But you've been given the gift of life twice. What you need to do is make sure that your life is worth living."

Doc Lambert's words settled on the room like a dusting of snow. He continued, returning to her current physical state. "None of your injuries are life-threatening, but I want to keep you overnight for observation."

"I can't stay," she said. Was Doc Lambert right? Did Holly deserve happiness? "I have too much to do."

"You're always busy with one thing or another, aren't you? Well, now you have something new to write about in a book."

Sure, Holly had sworn off writing another book more than once. Yet the first lines of her newest work came to her unbidden. Could she really go back into the world of publishing? Or maybe the question Holly should be asking was whether she could really leave the story of Darcy Owens untold.

Doc Lambert prodded the bruising on her neck. His touch was light, yet Holly winced. "Let me see your stomach. I should stitch that abdominal wound properly."

She lifted her shirt. "Whoever tended to this cut at the beginning did a decent job," said Doc Lambert. "Who'd you say provided first aid?"

"Liam," said Holly. Her voice caught. "Liam Alexander."

"You were lucky he came along when he did."

"I couldn't agree more," she said. She truly was lucky to have met Liam. Yet now that the case had ended, was their time together over, as well? Was now the time for her to say goodbye?

Liam had stopped by the small hospital café and gotten Sophie a yogurt—strawberry, her favorite flavor—while waiting for Holly to finish her exam. Yet there was one person he needed to see.

The hospital was small—less than two dozen rooms

for patients and a separate suite of rooms for those in rehab.

Julia's room looked more like a dorm with wooden furniture and a desk than a hospital room with an adjustable bed and various monitors. Julia, dressed in sweats, lay on the bed with her eyes closed. A thick bandage covered her right hand. Martinez sat in a chair next to the bed, staring at an e-reader. Liam wasn't surprised to see the former cop staying close to his friend.

Standing next to the door, Liam coughed quietly. Martinez looked up.

Sophie leaned her head on Liam's shoulder. "Mind if we come in?"

"Come in," said Martinez, rising to his feet. "Who is this cutie?"

"Sophie, can you say hi to Agent Martinez?"

She opened and closed her hand, shyly hiding her face in Liam's shoulder. "Hi."

"I just wanted to see how Julia was doing."

Liam recalled the moment he looked into the bunker and saw Julia's bloodied body sprawled across the floor.

Martinez said, "Julia got lucky."

"Did I hear someone mention my name?" Julia asked, opening her eyes.

"You have visitors," said Martinez. "Liam and his daughter, Sophie, came to see you."

"Hey," said Julia. "It's my hero."

"Daddy's a hero?"

"He sure is," said Julia.

Liam shuffled, uncomfortable with the title. "I don't know about that."

"I also heard from Marcus that you brought in Darcy Owens," said Martinez.

"I guess I helped a little," said Liam.

"Thank goodness she's locked up," said Julia, while smothering a yawn. "I'm not sure if I'd be able to rest if she was still out there."

"I should let you get some more sleep," Liam said.

"Thanks for stopping by," said Martinez. "I'm glad to have you on the team."

With a nod, Liam took Sophie and walked down the corridor. The scent of disinfectant was thick in the air. One word stuck with him. *Team.*

Liam had to admit, even if only to himself, that he had finally discovered a group of people he respected. More than that, he'd found a place where he belonged.

Holly left the examination and made her way to the hospital's front entrance. There, in a seat by the doors, sat Liam Alexander. Sophie was curled in her father's lap and asleep once again.

"Hey, what are you doing here?" she asked.

"I thought you could use a ride to the bank." He looked at his watch. "It's a quarter past nine. They should be open by now."

"I can walk," she said. "It's only a few blocks…"

"You've been through a lot. Let me help you this one last time."

The drive took only minutes and soon they pulled into the parking lot of the Pleasant Pines Savings and Loan. There were several cars in the lot, including a late-model luxury sedan that Holly knew belonged to Thomas. Thank goodness he was already at work.

"Does that car belong to the bank's manager, the one you called?"

Holly nodded. "It does."

"Maybe he got your message and hasn't processed the sale."

"I hope you're right," she said. She glanced at Liam. If she stayed in Pleasant Pines, would they have a future together? Yet before she worried about romance, she had a business to save and money to transfer. She continued, "Thank you, for everything. Without you, I wouldn't be able to pay off the loan."

"It was you who earned that money," he said. "What are you waiting for? Go and talk to the manager."

She opened the car door. The air was warm and the sky was blue. Spring, with all its new beginnings, had finally come. Was this the time for Holly's new beginning, as well?

"Wish me luck," she said.

"Good luck."

She walked toward the bank and watched as cars drove up and down Main Street. True, Holly had seen the town of Pleasant Pines most every day of her life. Now it seemed like a different place. What had changed? Yet she knew.

It was Liam.

Now she couldn't remember what her life was like before they'd met. In a short time, he'd become a part of her world—her partner.

She needed him with her now. Turning, she sprinted back to the car.

Liam unrolled the window as she approached. "What's wrong? Do you need something?"

"Nothing's wrong," said Holly. "What I need is you. We are a team. You helped me get the money. It's only right that you help me pay off the loan."

Sophie sat in her car seat, blinking. "Are we home?"

"No," said Liam. "We're at the bank. Want to go to a meeting with me?"

"Then can we go home?" she asked. "And have chicken nuggets?"

"Absolutely," said Liam. He unbuckled his daughter from the back seat and jogged over to Holly. Hand in hand, they opened the bank's door. Several tellers stood at the counter. A single office sat in the far corner. The name Thomas Irwin was stenciled on the door.

Holly's pulse raced as her steps slowed.

"Ready?" Liam asked. He squeezed her hand.

His touch filled her with strength. "I was born ready," she said.

Pushing open the office door, Holly said, "Good news, Thomas. I have the money…"

Whatever else she planned to say died on her lips. Thomas, along with two men in dark suits, sat around a glass-and-metal table. She immediately knew that the men were from Texas. They were the ones who'd be taking over her school. They didn't look at all like teachers—but rather accountants. Businessmen. Which she assumed that they were. Still, could they run the school? Or just turn a profit?

Thomas Irwin stood. "Holly, what are you doing here? When we spoke on Monday, you seemed ready to sell."

"I'm here now and I called earlier," Holly said. Her

voice was filled with flint. "You gave me until today to pay off the loan."

Thomas's high forehead reddened. At least he had the decency to look embarrassed. "The paperwork has already been signed. The school has been sold."

"You can't do this," said Holly.

The other two men stood. To her, they looked exactly the same. One of them said, "We'll be in touch about any personal belongings in the building."

They left the office.

Holly went numb. Her ears buzzed and her vision blurred. She couldn't let them go, not without putting up a fight.

"Wait," she called after the men, following them into the bank's lobby.

The duo stopped and faced her, yet said nothing.

Holly said, "Even if I lose my business, you can't let my staff go. They're good teachers who've bonded with the students. More than that, they need their jobs."

One of the dark-suited men nodded at the other. "We aren't laying off any of the staff. You can rest assured that your former teachers will still have jobs."

"That's all I can ask, then," she said.

With that, they were gone and all of Holly's dreams were taken with them. Light streamed in through the bank's front window. The town park was across the street. The gazebo was brilliant in the morning light.

"What now?" Liam asked.

"Take me back to my car." Holly felt as if she'd been hollowed out of every thought and feeling. It left her as a shell—not even a whole person.

"We could hire a lawyer," he said. "You had an

agreement with the bank. They pushed the meeting up without notifying you—"

"No," she interrupted. "I'm tired of fighting and I can't, not today."

"I wish I could help," he said.

Turning from him, she looked out the window. "You can't," she said simply. "What's done is done. It's just…" She shook her head, letting her words fade away.

"It's just what?"

"Never mind."

"I can't drop it," he said. "I care about you. I want to help."

For Holly, it all came down to the accident. It happened more than a lifetime ago, yet it was with her every day. Certainly, losing the school was all about being punished for having the audacity to hope.

It was why Liam, if he ever knew the truth, wouldn't want her. It was why Holly maybe should leave Pleasant Pines—and this time, not come back.

It was Sunday afternoon. Holly had spent the last two days packing up what she could of her home. Dishes. Clothes. Books. All the boxes had been loaded into her car. A moving company had been hired to deliver her furniture to the apartment she had rented, sight unseen, in Ohio. It would all arrive later in the week and Tonya had agreed to oversee the packing.

For the job, Holly had donned a set of black leggings and a gray University of Wyoming sweatshirt that was two sizes too big. She hadn't bothered doing either her hair or makeup. A purple bruise had bloomed on her cheek. Her stomach still hurt, despite Doc Lambert having prescribed a painkiller.

Yet there was more that hurt Holly than her injuries.

Liam's face flashed in her mind, and Holly's eyes began to burn. She had no choice but to leave town.

Closing the door to her little house for the last time, she twisted the knob to make sure the lock was engaged. The late-afternoon sun hung low in a cloudless sky of cornflower blue.

She'd thought a lot about leaving without saying goodbye but decided she couldn't do it to Sophie. So she drove to Liam's house and once again parked on the street. Without many thoughts and even fewer expectations, Holly crossed the lawn and stood on Liam's stoop. With a deep breath, she lifted her hand, ready to knock.

The door opened. Dressed in a plaid flannel shirt of rust and red, along with a pair of jeans, Liam stood on the other side of the threshold.

Her cheeks warmed at the sight of him. "Hey," she said simply.

"Hey, yourself." He added quickly, "I saw you pull up. Are you leaving for Ohio?"

She nodded. "I wanted to say goodbye."

"Thanks. For everything," he said.

"Same to you. The money I made with RMJ will be helpful while I relocate."

He looked down, nodding.

Holly knew this was the perfect moment to put Liam Alexander and all their adventures in the past. All she had to do was walk away. Yet she remained. "How's Sophie?"

Eyes still downcast, he said, "She seems fine. I've taken off the next week just to be with her."

"That's smart," said Holly. "Has she said anything?"

"She asked a couple of questions about Darcy and where she was taken." He looked up, his gaze meeting Holly's. "She's asked about you."

As if an iron band had wrapped around her chest, Holly found it difficult to breathe. "Give her a hug for me, will you?"

Before Liam could say anything, a whir of pink flew past him.

"Holly." Sophie hugged Holly around the legs. "You came to see us. Are you going to stay for dinner? We can have chicken nuggets."

Holly glanced at Liam, who rolled his eyes. "I swear, I do feed her other things."

Holly laughed but couldn't hold his gaze. Especially not as she heard Sophie's plaintive voice.

"Will you stay, Holly? Will you?"

Holly bent down, putting herself at the child's level. "I can't, sweetie," she said. "I'm sorry."

"Tomorrow?"

Holly brushed a soft strand of hair from Sophie's cheek. "I can't come over tomorrow, either."

"Why not?"

"Actually, I came to say goodbye. I'm moving."

The little girl's lip trembled. "But...you promised you wouldn't ever let me go."

Holly had indeed made that promise. Yet, in the moment, she had meant only to reassure the child that she was safe. "I need a new job, sweetie. Without a job, I can't stay in Pleasant Pines."

"I don't want you to go."

"Neither do I."

Sophie ran away, leaving Holly with whatever excuse she was about to give. Standing tall, she faced Liam. "I'm sorry about that."

Waving away her apology, he said, "Right now, she doesn't understand. I hope someday she will." He looked tired. "Like you said."

"Well…" She turned and looked at her car. "I better go. I want to be on the road before it gets dark."

"Sure," said Liam.

What should she do? Shake his hand? Hug him? Kiss him and never let him go?

She gave a little wave. "Well…goodbye, Liam," she said, turning to go.

"Holly, wait."

She stopped and faced him.

Liam had his hands at the back of his neck. After untying the leather cord, he held out the dog tag. "Here," he said. "These belonged to my cousin, Charlie. He'd want you to have them."

"I—I…" Holly stammered. "I don't know what to say."

"Don't say anything. Just take the necklace. Think of me every now and again."

Holly's eyes burned with unshed tears. Turning, she held up her hair. "Can you help me get it on?"

Liam looped the cord around her neck before tying the thong in the back. The leather was still warm from the heat of his body. She placed her hand on the metal tag. "Thank you," she said, facing him once more.

He was already back inside his house. Lifting his hand once more, Liam shut the door.

After Liam closed the door, he leaned against the wall. Holly was gone, and she'd never come back. It was best if he got used to the idea. Sophie sat on the stairs, her chin in her hands.

Kneeling next to his daughter, he asked, "You okay?"

"No," she said.

"What's the matter?"

"I want Holly to stay."

Liam sighed. "We don't always get what we want, baby girl. Besides, Holly needs a job."

"She has a job at Saplings."

"Not anymore. The bank sold her school."

"She can buy another school here," said Sophie.

"For that," said Liam, "Holly needs a lot of money."

He paused. The answer was crystal clear. Why hadn't he thought of it before?

Yet Holly was gone. Or was she? It had been only a minute—no more. He pulled open the front door and stepped onto the lawn. Her car was no longer parked at the corner. He muttered a curse as his heart sank to his shoes. He peered up the street. Her taillights blazed as she slowed for a stop sign.

Could he catch her? Where were his keys?

Sophie stood at the front door.

"What are you looking for, Daddy? Is it Holly?"

Who said he needed a car to chase after love?

He dropped to a knee. "Hold on to my neck, baby girl," he said.

"Where are we going?"

"To catch Holly and bring her back."

With that, Liam took off at a sprint. His legs pumped as they carried him down the street. Holly let off the brake. Her car rolled forward.

"Hey," he yelled. Waving his arm, he yelled again, "Hey, Holly!"

The car accelerated, moving faster than he could ever hope to run. That meant only one thing. If Holly had seen Liam, she'd decided not to stop.

Holly drove, yet she was tempted to look back, just once. Why? So, she could feel another pain from her heartbreak? Pressing her foot gently on the accelerator, the car rolled forward. As her auto picked up speed, she glanced in her sideview mirror. Inhaling sharply, she slammed on the brake. Holly turned in her seat and stared out the rear windshield. With Sophie clinging to his neck, Liam Alexander ran up the street. Holly put the car into Park and flung open the door.

She jogged toward him. "Liam, what are you doing?"

"Stay," he said, breathless.

"What?" she asked. "I can't."

"Why not?"

"You know why." But really, he didn't. Practically speaking, she needed a job. But in reality, would Liam want a woman who couldn't have children? He already had Sophie—certainly he wanted more.

"Stay." Liam reached for Holly's hand and placed it on the middle of his chest. "Please."

She leaned into his strong and solid chest. "I want to, but I can't." She paused. Maybe now was the time to be honest with Liam.

"You can," he said. "Hear me out…"

She placed her fingertips on his lips. "I can't have children, Liam." She looked away for a moment, then turned back to face him. "It's because of the car accident in high school. I was injured, and now it's impossible."

"I have Sophie." He gripped his daughter's hand. "*We* would have Sophie. We would be together. I don't need any more than that."

"There's more," she said. "The night of the accident, the driver was speeding. He was trying to impress me with how fast his car would go. I never told him to slow down. I should have—and I didn't." She paused. "He died in that wreck."

"That's not your fault," said Liam.

"You're wrong. It was."

"You aren't responsible for what happened. It was an accident. You can't fix everything—even though I imagine that you try. I'm the opposite. After Charlie's accident, I shut myself away from the world. With you, I couldn't hide."

Liam placed his lips on top of Holly's head. "I'm sure you studied trauma because of the car accident in high school. But is that why you came back to Pleasant Pines and opened a school? Because you felt like you had to make amends with your community? Are you looking for absolution?"

She knew that Liam was right. Still, she wasn't ready to relent—not yet. She continued, "But it's too late. I've already accepted the new job and canceled the lease on my house."

"Quit the job and call your landlord. You can re-rent your house. It's only been a few hours."

"Holly," said Sophie, speaking for the first time. "Stay here, with me and my daddy."

Liam said, "For the first time in a long time, I've found someone worth keeping. It's you, Holly. But if you need to leave to be complete, then I have no choice but to let you go."

"If I stay," she said, "what would I do? I don't have a job. I can't open another day-care center. I was a good teacher, a decent administrator, but a lousy business owner."

"What do you want to do?"

A few more words for her next book came to mind. Certainly, the windfall from RMJ would help her survive for a few months—plenty of time to get a proposal to her agent.

"Please, Holly," said Sophie, filling the silence. "Stay. Then we can have breakfast together every morning."

"I don't know what to say."

Liam looked at her. "Say that you'll stay. Say that you'll help me make a family. Say that you love me as much as I love you."

"Oh, Liam." She wrapped her arms around his neck. She also collected Sophie in her embrace. "It's crazy to have fallen so fast, but I love you—both of you."

"Then don't leave."

Holly looked at her car, packed full of her belongings. The engine idled, and a wave of exhaust rolled across the street. Then she looked at Liam. There were two paths for her life. This was the moment where the trails completely diverged. In the end, the choice wasn't hard. "Yes," she said. "I'll stay." For the first time, she was filled with confidence for the future. "Do you think it'll work?" she asked.

Liam wrapped his arms around Holly's waist, pulling her close. He placed his lips on hers, claiming her with his kiss. "Do I think it will work?" he asked, repeating her question. "I do. Now, how about we pull that car around and head for home?"

Epilogue

Darcy Owens sat in the small conference room at the regional jail. Her wrists were shackled and chained to the metal table. The cinder block walls were yellow. At one time the color had been sunny, but it now looked of weak urine. After being arrested, Darcy had received medical treatment for her wounded shoulder. Then she had been given two orange jumpsuits, industrial under-wear and a set of shower shoes, before being thrown into a cell.

Since that time, she hadn't had any visitors other than her lawyer. Until today, that is. The district attorney had come by, looking for a confession. The other woman had provided Darcy with a pad of paper, a pencil and all the time she needed to recount her long list of crimes.

Darcy glanced at the empty sheet before her.

"I can't help you if you don't help me," said Chloe Ryder, the district attorney. "Wyoming has capital punishment. I've heard that the governor's going to ask that you be executed."

Darcy looked up at the dark-haired woman, who sat on the other side of the table. "I want to help," said Darcy, pushing aside the paper. "I know what you said. If I confess to everything, you won't seek the death penalty. It's just that I don't remember much."

"Let's start with what you do recall," said Chloe.

"What do you want to know?"

"Do you know a woman named Everly Baker?"

"Sure," said Darcy. "She was a guest at the Pleasant Pines Inn. I used to work at the inn as a desk clerk. I met Everly a few times."

"Do you recall anything after trying to hang her at the old schoolhouse?"

Darcy shook her head. "I don't remember anything until I woke up in that bunker in the woods."

"Do you know a man named William 'Billy' Dawson?"

Picking up the pen, Darcy moved the pad of paper close. "Do you want me to confess to killing Billy? I will, happily. He locked me in the bunker. He kept me a prisoner there. He forced himself on me."

Chloe asked, "What else do you remember? How'd you end up working at the White Wind resort?"

"I remember you," said Darcy. "I remember that you used to work at my high school. You were a social work intern. You always asked a lot of questions about what happened at home."

Chloe sucked in a breath and sat back. "What about high school?" she asked after a moment.

"You knew what happened at my house," said Darcy. She began to draw a spiral. The rotations grew until the doodle looked like a vortex. "I'm convinced that you knew what my father did. Even though it was your job, you did nothing to help me."

"I talked to you," said Chloe. "I tried to get you to trust me."

"Talk? Trust?" Darcy echoed. "Did you call the police? Or even tell the principal?"

"I talked to some of the other teachers and the administration," said Chloe. "They came to you. You adamantly denied that anything was wrong."

"Anything wrong? Isn't that a polite way to refer to the hell that I lived through?"

"This interview isn't about me," said Chloe. "It's about you and the people you murdered."

"Like I said," Darcy repeated, "I don't remember killing anyone—except Billy. I'll stand before a judge and swear that he had it coming."

"I want you to talk to a psychologist. They might be able to help you with your repressed memories."

Scooting the pad of paper across the table, Darcy eased back in the chair. "You can bring in whoever you want. For now, I'm tired. I don't want to talk to anyone else. Especially *you*."

"I understand," said Chloe.

Her heels clicked on the tile floor as she walked away.

I understand. Chloe's final words echoed in Darcy's head. With a smile, Darcy stared at the ceiling. Darcy doubted that Chloe understood much at all. There were still people in the community willing to help her. And there was more than that. Soon, oh, so soon, Chloe would *understand* a single but important fact. Darcy Owens was much more dangerous in a cage than she had ever been while free.

* * * * *

Look for Luis and Julia's story,
the next installment of Wyoming Nights,
Jennifer D. Bokal's miniseries for
Harlequin Romantic Suspense.
Coming soon!

"Do you remember that summer we turned my mom's
minivan into a fort?" Mark asked.

"We? That was all you and Luke." Charlotte closed
her eyes, recalling those sweet days.

"You were there," Mark said. "Guilt by association."

"Maybe so." She opened her eyes. "This place could
do with some pilfered couch cushions and a hanging
sheet or two."

Mark chuckled. "And gummy bears."

"Yes." She rolled her wrists, trying to get some relief
from the handcuffs. "What made you think of Fort Van…
whatever it was?"

"Fort Van Dodge," he supplied. "You slept in there. I remember your eyelashes."

She sat up and blinked said lashes, wishing for better light to read his expression. "What are you talking about?"

He rested his head against the panel. "Your eyelashes turned into little gold fans on your cheeks when you slept. Still happens, I bet."

Weary and uncertain, she drew his words straight into her heart. She should probably find something witty to say or a memory to share, but her adrenaline spikes were giving way to pure exhaustion. Better to stay quiet than say something that made him feel obligated to take on more of her stress.

"Sleep if you can," Mark said, as if he'd read her mind. "I won't let anything happen."

He clearly wanted to spare her, and she appreciated his efforts, but she had a feeling it would take both of them working together to escape this mess.

*Don't miss
Escape with the Navy SEAL by Regan Black,
available December 2020 wherever
Harlequin Romantic Suspense
books and ebooks are sold.*

Harlequin.com

Get 4 FREE REWARDS!

We'll send you 2 FREE Books plus 2 FREE Mystery Gifts.

Harlequin Romantic Suspense books are heart-racing page-turners with unexpected plot twists and irresistible chemistry that will keep you guessing to the very end.

FREE Value Over **$20**

YES! Please send me 2 FREE Harlequin Romantic Suspense novels and my 2 FREE gifts (gifts are worth about $10 retail). After receiving them, if I don't wish to receive any more books, I can return the shipping statement marked "cancel." If I don't cancel, I will receive 4 brand-new novels every month and be billed just $4.99 per book in the U.S. or $5.74 per book in Canada. That's a savings of at least 13% off the cover price! It's quite a bargain! Shipping and handling is just 50¢ per book in the U.S. and $1.25 per book in Canada.* I understand that accepting the 2 free books and gifts places me under no obligation to buy anything. I can always return a shipment and cancel at any time. The free books and gifts are mine to keep no matter what I decide.

240/340 HDN GNMZ

Name (please print)

Address   Apt. #

City   State/Province   Zip/Postal Code

Email: Please check this box ☐ if you would like to receive newsletters and promotional emails from Harlequin Enterprises ULC and its affiliates. You can unsubscribe anytime.

Mail to the **Reader Service:**
IN U.S.A.: P.O. Box 1341, Buffalo, NY 14240-8531
IN CANADA: P.O. Box 603, Fort Erie, Ontario L2A 5X3

Want to try 2 free books from another series? Call 1-800-873-8635 or visit www.ReaderService.com.

---

*Terms and prices subject to change without notice. Prices do not include sales taxes, which will be charged (if applicable) based on your state or country of residence. Canadian residents will be charged applicable taxes. Offer not valid in Quebec. This offer is limited to one order per household. Books received may not be as shown. Not valid for current subscribers to Harlequin Romantic Suspense books. All orders subject to approval. Credit or debit balances in a customer's account(s) may be offset by any other outstanding balance owed by or to the customer. Please allow 4 to 6 weeks for delivery. Offer available while quantities last.

Your Privacy—Your information is being collected by Harlequin Enterprises ULC, operating as Reader Service. For a complete summary of the information we collect, how we use this information and to whom it is disclosed, please visit our privacy notice located at corporate.harlequin.com/privacy-notice. From time to time we may also exchange your personal information with reputable third parties. If you wish to opt out of this sharing of your personal information, please visit readerservice.com/consumerschoice or call 1-800-873-8635. **Notice to California Residents**—Under California law, you have specific rights to control and access your data. For more information on these rights and how to exercise them, visit corporate.harlequin.com/california-privacy.

HRS20R2

Love Harlequin romance?

DISCOVER.

Be the first to find out about promotions,
news and exclusive content!

f Facebook.com/HarlequinBooks

𝕏 Twitter.com/HarlequinBooks

◉ Instagram.com/HarlequinBooks

ⓟ Pinterest.com/HarlequinBooks

ReaderService.com

EXPLORE.

Sign up for the Harlequin e-newsletter and
download a free book from any series at
TryHarlequin.com

CONNECT.

Join our Harlequin community to
share your thoughts and connect
with other romance readers!
Facebook.com/groups/HarlequinConnection

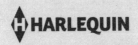

HARLEQUIN

Uplifting or passionate, heartfelt or thrilling—
Harlequin has your happily-ever-after.
With a wide range of romance series that each offer
new books every month, you are sure to find the
satisfying escape you deserve.

PASSION
Harlequin DARE
Harlequin Desire
Harlequin Presents

HOPE & INSPIRATION
Love Inspired
Harlequin Heartwarming

SUSPENSE
Harlequin Intrigue
Harlequin Romantic Suspense
Love Inspired Suspense

LIFE & LOVE
Harlequin Special Edition
Harlequin Medical Romance
Harlequin Romance

HISTORICAL
Harlequin Historical

**FIND YOUR FAVORITE SERIES IN STORE OR ONLINE,
OR SUBSCRIBE TO THE READER SERVICE!**

SERIESIBC2020

HE DIDN'T WANT HER HELP
BUT SHE'S THE ONE HE DESPERATELY NEEDS...

Operative Liam Alexander is a tracker, used to working solo, even in treacherous mountain terrain. He only agrees to partner with child psychologist Holly Jacobs to stop a deadly serial killer. When Liam's daughter is abducted by the twisted murderer, what begins as a working relationship turns into so much more. But can Liam rescue his baby girl without sacrificing the family he's grown to love?

A WYOMING NIGHTS NOVEL

CATEGORY: SUSPENSE

$5.75 U.S./$6.75 CAN.

ISBN-13: 978-1-335-62679-0

50575

9 781335 626790

EAN

*Danger. Passion.
Drama.*

ROMANTIC
SUSPENSE

harlequin.com